OTHER

The Antholo

Boa

Ender's World

Farscape Forever

Finding Serenit

Five Seasons of An

Fringe Science

Getting Lost

Revisiting Narni

Through the Wardrobe

The Science of Dune

The Science of Michael Crichton

Serenity Found

Seven Seasons of Buffy

So Say We All

Star Wars on Trial

Stepping Through the Stargate

Taking the Red Pill

A Taste of True Blood

War of the Worlds

WITHDRAWN

DRAGONWRITER

A TRIBUTE TO **ANNE McCAFFREY** AND PERN

EDITED BY TODD McCAFFREY

WITH LEAH WILSON

AN IMPRINT OF BENBELLA BOOKS, INC. | DALLAS, TEXAS

THE DRAGONRIDERS OF PERN is a trademark of Anne McCaffrey
Reg. U.S. Pat. & Tm. Off.

BenBella Books, Inc.
10300 N. Central Expressway, Suite 530
Dallas, TX 75231
www.smartpopbooks.com
www.benbellabooks.com
Send feedback to feedback@benbellabooks.com

Printed in the United States of America
10 9 8 7 6 5 4 3 2 1

Dragonwriter : a tribute to Anne McCaffrey and Pern / edited by Todd McCaffrey, with Leah Wilson.
       pages cm
    Summary: "Science fiction Grand Master Anne McCaffrey and her work, particularly her Dragonriders of Pern series, are beloved by generations of readers. She was one of the first science fiction writers to appear on the New York Times bestseller list, the first woman to win the Hugo and Nebula Awards, and an inductee to the Science Fiction Hall of Fame. Her death in November 2011 was met with an outpouring of grief and memories from those whose lives her stories had touched. Edited by her son Todd, Dragonwriter collects McCaffrey's friends, fans, and professional admirers to remember and pay tribute to the pioneering science fiction author, from the way her love of music and horses influenced her work to her redefinition of the SF genre"—Provided by publisher.
    ISBN 978-1-937856-83-0 (pbk.)—ISBN 978-1-937856-84-7 (electronic) 1. McCaffrey, Anne—Appreciation. 2. McCaffrey, Anne—Influence. 3. Science fiction, American—20th century—History and criticism. 4. Women and literature—United States—History—20th century. I. McCaffrey, Todd, 1956– editor of compilation. II. Wilson, Leah, editor of compilation. III. McCaffrey, Anne, honouree.
    PS3563.A255Z75 2013
    813'.54—dc23w   2013018670

Copyediting by Brittany Dowdle, Word Cat Editorial Services • Proofreading by Chris Koch and Amy Zarkos • Cover illustration © 2013 by Michael Whelan • Cover design by Heather Butterfield • Text design and composition by E. Strongin, Neuwirth & Associates, Inc. • Printed by Bang Printing

Distributed by Perseus Distribution
(www.perseusdistribution.com)
To place orders through Perseus Distribution:
Tel: 800-343-4499
Fax: 800-351-5073
E-mail: orderentry@perseusbooks.com

Significant discounts for bulk sales are available. Please contact Glenn Yeffeth at glenn@benbellabooks.com or 214-750-3628.

Contents

To all those who have found solace
in the Worlds of Anne McCaffrey and Pern

Introduction

TODD MCCAFFREY

ALL TOO OFTEN we try to measure a person by cold, hard facts: when they were born, when they died, their marriages, their children, their schooling.

Is that really enough to illuminate a soul? What about when they cried in despair, wept for joy, screamed in exultation— aren't those all memorable moments? When they sang, when they played, when they loved?

What is it, truly, that marks a life and gives it shape?

Those of you who are reading this probably have already met some aspect of Anne McCaffrey. Most likely you know of her as the science fiction author of the famous Dragonriders of Pern® series. Perhaps you first found her with *The Ship Who Sang* or with *To Ride Pegasus* or any of some hundreds of other novels, novellas, novelettes, and short stories.

So you know a part of Anne McCaffrey, and you're reading this because you'd like to know more—perhaps to see her through different eyes: ones that knew her in a different light or from another perspective.

Dragonwriter presents essays by people who knew Anne McCaffrey from various stages of her career and various points in her life that we hope will illustrate the life and passion of this marvelous person in ways previously not explored.

You'll get a chance to hear recollections from all three of her children—Alec, her eldest; middle child, Todd (me); and the youngest, daughter Georgeanne Kennedy—as well as from people who knew her most of her adult life, people who only met her through her writing, and people who knew her entirely outside of her writing.

It is not really possible to present Anne McCaffrey to you in a clear, concise way. It is simply not possible to show but snippets of the rainbow of her personality, of the array of ages in her life.

By way of background, from a high-level, distant view, it is possible to say that Anne McCaffrey was born on April Fools' Day in 1926 to a stern disciplinarian by the name of George Herbert McCaffrey and his wife, Anne Dorothy (McElroy) McCaffrey. She was the second of what were to be three children and the only daughter. Her father had served as a lieutenant in the First World War, was a reservist between the wars, would go back into service in the Second World War, and would finally die of tuberculosis contracted while working for the UN in Korea.

While growing up, Anne was called "LeAnn" or "LeeAnn" to differentiate her from her mother. In college, she majored in Slavonic languages and literature (including minor excursions into Celtic literature) with a minor in geology. She wanted to be an opera singer and wound up, after graduation, working in a music store where she met Horace Wright Johnson. He wooed her with recordings of *The Beggar's Opera*.

Her husband, who preferred to be called by his middle name, Wright, got work with DuPont in their public relations department, and Wright and Anne started their family first in Montclair, New Jersey, and later, when the job moved, in Wilmington, Delaware.

Anne had always liked reading, and science fiction had appealed to her as a teenager. She devoured Edgar Rice Burroughs' *Tarzan* and his Barsoom series (*John Carter of Mars* and *A Princess of Mars*). She took up writing as soon as her youngest, Georgeanne (nicknamed "Gigi" for "Gorgeous George"), was old enough to leave under the eye of a babysitter, using her free time to regain her sanity (which had been much put upon by the antics of her second born).

Anne still loved singing; she and Wright were active in the church choir. She had been born Catholic but lost faith during the Second World War and was untroubled by Wright's association with the Presbyterian Church.

It was in Wilmington that she also worked with a local theatre company, scaring me (middle son, Todd) silly when she played Queen Aggravain in a production of *Once Upon a Mattress*.

Life took a major turn when Wright's work demanded that he decamp to Germany for six months. Instead of splitting the family, it was decided to take them all, and so the boys were enrolled in the local German *schule*, and little Gigi stayed home. Anne learned *gekauft Deutsch* ("shopping German") and was surprised to discover that two-year-old Gigi had absorbed enough of the language that when separated on a shopping trip, she approached the nearest motherly person and announced, *"Ich habe meine Mutti verloren"*—I've lost my mother.

In Germany, not only did the family develop a passion for the marvelous fresh-baked breads, but Anne found herself a vocal coach who offered to fulfill her dream of becoming an opera singer. Instead, he destroyed her voice by forcing her to overwork it in a vain attempt to remove a burr she had on one note.

Germany was a milestone in the family's life, and while they toured France, Belgium, and even England, it also opened strains that were ultimately to destroy it.

The family moved again, this time to Long Island, New York, when Wright's job again moved. In order to afford expensive New York, the family agreed to share a rambling eighty-year-old three-story Victorian with another DuPont family, using the pretext that they were "third cousins."

Wright commuted to New York and dealt with such people as the Princess Galaxine while Anne stayed home and wrote. The fissures grew greater, and Wright found himself extolling the virtues of martini lunches and evenings on the veranda. Wright was not a pleasant drunk and took to being violent with the children, something Anne would not tolerate.

The family broke in 1969, and in 1970, Anne moved with her two youngest children to Ireland. At the time she touted the marvelous tax-exempt status Ireland offered artists and writers, but later she confessed that it was to get "3,000 miles away" from her ex-husband.

The move to Ireland was not the complete leap in the dark it seemed; Anne had been there one summer with her favorite aunt, Gladdie, and also knew Harry Harrison, another science fiction writer who had moved there the previous year. Anne's mother, called "Bami," followed not long afterward to add support.

In Ireland, Anne found a nice semi-detached house and sent the children to a private school. Costs were low at the time, prices being roughly half what they were in New York. Anne's marvelous editor, Betty Ballantine, at Ballantine Books, loaded her with contracts, including one to edit *Cooking Out of This World*.

Ireland itself was another world, and Anne learned to love it. Irish pubs were a place where a single, divorced mother could go and not be molested or frowned upon. She met many "characters" who formed the basis of many characters in her later writing. She loved the lilt and weave of the Irish accent, and the turns of phrase soon stole into her writing.

Life in Ireland for the first four years was difficult, very much hand-to-mouth and contract to contract. It became a family joke to talk about the Rolls being in the repair shop and how "wouldn't it be nice to eat pancakes for dinner because we *wanted* them?"

Anne was an excellent cook and learned to stretch food out the whole week.

Her eldest son, Alec, arrived at one of the worst times, adding his bit to the family pot—later on shipping aboard a trawler and bringing back monkfish and other "delicacies" that graced the family table—and keeping the wolf from the door.

In the strange way of life, the upward turning point came simultaneously with several downward turning points in 1974. Her son, Todd (me again), was accepted into Lehigh University in Bethlehem, Pennsylvania; her daughter, Georgeanne, was diagnosed with Crohn's disease after years of debilitating illness; and Anne's mother suffered a massive stroke that paralyzed her left side—fortunately, she did not recover. As Anne said after, "She would have *hated* living like that."

The good news was that Anne had been invited to attend the New England Science Fiction Association's annual spring convention, Boskone—and that they commissioned her at a healthy price to write a special novella to be sold at the convention. In all this turmoil, Anne had trouble finding a time when she *could* write and so got the title for the story, "A Time When." This also became the first part of her third Pern novel, *The White Dragon*.

Boskone was a triumph, the novella sold magnificently, and her two earlier books, *Dragonflight* and *Dragonquest* were given new covers to match the marvelous Michael Whelan cover of

The White Dragon. Anne later said that "those beautiful covers *sold* the books," and she was forever grateful to Michael Whelan for them.

Here, now, you have in your hands yet another brilliant Michael Whelan cover, surely the last for the Dragonwriter of Pern.

And inside that brilliant Michael Whelan cover you have these words from people who knew or were influenced by Anne McCaffrey—words that will give you a greater feel for the amazing woman: Anne McCaffrey, Dragonlady and Dragonwriter of Pern.

To the popular press, David Brin is perhaps best known as the author of *The Postman*, which became a movie starring Kevin Costner. However, for Anne McCaffrey, David Brin was the amazing person who penned *Sundiver* and followed it up with the Hugo and Nebula Award–winning *Startide Rising* and the also Hugo and Nebula Award–winning *The Uplift War*.

David constantly referred to Anne McCaffrey as "Annie," being one of those admitted to such intimacies. Although separated by one continent, an ocean, and thousands of miles, David and Anne kept a long and cheerful correspondence, and he was always a welcome guest at the original Dragonhold and, later, Dragonhold-Underhill.

Anne McCaffrey, Believer in Us

DAVID BRIN

LET ME TELL you about a colleague and friend, a wonderfully vivid writer who entertained millions, who also helped distill for me the essence of my profession.

It happened one day when we were both being interviewed by a reporter who referred to the famous McCaffrey Dragonriders of Pern books as *fantasy novels*.

Oh, how Anne bristled! With clenched restraint, she corrected the reporter:

"I don't write fantasy. I am a *science fiction author*."

Now, a great many people have tried to define the difference between fantasy and SF, two cousin genres that share the same section in most bookstores and the same professional organizations, yet always appear to be in a state of tension. Some try to explain the distinction as a matter of past versus future; or settings that shift from medieval, mystical realms to far, far interstellar space; or the various gimmicks and tools (e.g., swords versus spaceships) that empower characters to make epic journeys or take on impossible odds. One can argue that there is a vast *moral* distinction between magic and science—for example, in the way that mages almost invariably deal in secret knowledge that they share only grudgingly with normal folk. That happens in science too, but those scientists are called villainous or "mad."

And sure, one can easily see how some folks make simple, lazy assumptions about the central epic tale created by Anne McCaffrey. Hey, if it's got dragons, well then, it must belong in the same category as Tolkien, right?

Anne dealt with that part of it swiftly. "My dragons were genetically engineered. Scientists designed them to help colonists save themselves from a terrible environmental threat."

Hmm, well, okay. Only you've got to sympathize, at first, with folks who make the fantasy assumption by glancing at her covers or skimming some random scenes. It's not *just* the dragons, you see. Most of Anne's tales are filled with colorful characters who don't just face challenges and danger; they also have skills, jobs, and crafts that are linked to a feudal-like setting. They farm and weave and make things like candles and ink and tapestries and epic oral poems. There are great stone castle holds, with much talk of herbal lore and fathom-deep traditions. Her pages are rich with duels and nobles and bards and songs and brave knights of the sort that are standard fare in your typical fantasy novel. If you're going to judge by superficialities, like the furniture, then it's easy to see why some people make assumptions.

But Anne was insistent. There is a deeper difference, and it goes to the heart of what makes her tales science fiction, after all. The characters in her Pern epic start out dwelling in a feudal setting, all right. But unlike the endlessly repeated trope protagonists in all those Tolkien-clone universes, *most of them don't want to!*

Moreover, they don't intend to—not for any longer than they must.

In the course of Anne McCaffrey's fictional universe—as the

stories unfold—people discover relics of an older time and learn that things weren't always this way—with peasant-serfs tied to the rocky land, wracked by filth, pestilence, and arbitrary rule by hereditary lords, with gender and class roles stiffly predefined and strictly enforced, with people staring in occasional wonder at the great dragonriders who protect them from raining death.

Sure, their condition is eased by a myriad of lovely traditions and crafts, reflecting the makeshift creativity of brave folk, by improvising—making the best of things across centuries of darkness. As a fallback position, feudalism can be a preferable stopgap to keep from tumbling all the way down to caveman or tribal existence . . . or extinction. Despite all of its wretched aspects, including deep and inherent injustice, feudalism has another side; its horrors can be moderated and softened, even livened by the ingenuity and pride of clever, brave folk. And McCaffrey's Pernese characters—in one deeply moving tale after another—brilliantly illustrate both sides.

Only, during the span of many novels, they come to discover a core truth: that things could be better.

That once upon a time they *were* better.

That their civilization fell, long ago, from a height so great that people once voyaged between stars, cured disease, led unconstrained lives, pondered secrets of the universe . . . and even *made dragons.*

Moreover—and here is what distinguishes the characters of an Anne McCaffrey novel from those who live in similar situations penned by other authors—*as soon as they realize how much they've lost, they start wanting to get all of those things back.*

By the third Dragonriders novel, where they find cryptic remnants from the interstellar times—and as more relics and clues are uncovered in later books—Anne's characters know that there's a different way. People don't have to live in grimy ignorance and violence, even lightened by clever medieval arts.

It will be a long climb back, but they itch to get their hands on flush toilets, movable type, computers, and democracy. And one thing is certain—they are going to quit being feudal, just as soon as they can.

Perhaps when they become starfarers once again, they will remember fondly the lore that stitched them together during the long Dark Age. They may keep singing the songs, and even doff their hats to the scion of a lordly family or the current dragonmaster . . . so long as they have helped bring the renaissance and truly merit honor. Oh, but if those high and mighty ones get in the way? Try to obstruct?

I pity the fools.

Oh, sure. Feudalism tugs at something deep within us. Those images of lords and secretive mages and so on resonate in our hearts because we're all descended from the harems of guys who managed to pull off that trick of grabbing for themselves a pinnacle of inherited power. Why else would we, the heirs of enlightenment heroes, like Franklin and Lincoln and Edison, who finally ended the 6,000-year feudal hell, run off to fantasy flicks filled with bickering kings and elves and wizards and masters of arcane arts? We all have magic crystals on our tables that let us peer at distant lands, sift through all the world's knowledge, and converse with folk all around the globe. But how much more romantic to imagine that only a dozen demigods and mages had *palantírs*, instead of five billion peasant citizens!

No, there is clearly something deeply appealing about those old ways, the symbols and terrors and pastoral pleasures and songs. Anne McCaffrey certainly made good use of those resonating themes, and more power to her!

But Anne's notion of the *time flow of wisdom* was always aimed forward, rooted in a love and gratitude and belief in progress, in our ability to raise better generations, in a hope that more wondrous days will come.

She was a *science fiction author*—one of the best. And I'm proud to say she was my friend.

DAVID BRIN is a scientist, tech speaker/consultant, and author. His new novel about our survival in the near future is *Existence*. A film by Kevin Costner was based on *The Postman*. His sixteen novels, including *New York Times* bestsellers and Hugo Award winners, have been translated into more than twenty languages. *Earth* foreshadowed global warming, cyberwarfare, and the World Wide Web. David appears frequently on shows such as *Nova*, *The Universe*, and *Life After People*, speaking about science and future trends. His non-fiction book *The Transparent Society: Will Technology Make Us Choose Between Freedom and Privacy?* won the Freedom of Speech Award of the American Library Association.

R ead this," Mum said, thrusting *Carpe Diem* into my hands. Son or not, when Anne McCaffrey thrusts a book into your hands, you read it. Later that night, she was roused by the sound of me rustling through her bookshelves looking for more!

Mum totally loved the Liaden universe. Sharon Lee and Steve Miller are an amazing writing team and, as you'll see, very important to Anne McCaffrey.

Why Are You Reading This Stupid Shirt?
Remembering AnnieMac

SHARON LEE and STEVE MILLER

WE TREASURE TWO photographs of Anne McCaffrey, here in the Lee and Miller household. Both of them show Anne enjoying herself immensely, posing with authority and just a little bit of 'tude.

The first photo was taken by Steve, in 1978, when Anne was Guest of Honor at BaltiCon 12. She has one arm casually slung around the domed head of a familiar 'bot, cigarette in one hand, drink in the other. Her head is up, her expression mischievous, and she's wearing a very fannish sweatshirt, or a long-sleeved T-shirt, that puts forth these cosmic questions:

> *Why is man on this planet?*
> *Why is space infinite?*
> *Why are we doomed?*
> *Why are you reading this stupid shirt?*

In 1978, Sharon Lee and Steve Miller were not yet a team, though it happened that they both did, in very different capacities, attend BaltiCon 12.

Steve was a member of the concom (a fannish word for "convention committee") and as such had contributed to the decision to bring Anne to BaltiCon as the Guest of Honor. He was also a full-time freelancer, writing fiction, music, and book reviews while stringing for a couple of local Baltimore-area newspapers. He was on the premises at the Hunt Valley Inn early, and as the only member of the press to ask for the honor, Anne granted him an interview and a photo op.

It was during the interview that Steve snapped the photo described previously; it was used in the *Unicorn Times*, the local Baltimore arts paper, as the lead photo for his story about BaltiCon.

After the interview, Steve and Anne toured the convention venue before it filled up, and before the rest of the concom arrived, since she had arrived the night before from Ireland.

The two hit it off, the way lubricated by the large number of "remember me to Annie!" exhortations Steve delivered from mutual fannish and professional acquaintances. They also found themselves at one regarding the benefits of workshops in writer development, Steve being a Clarion West survivor.

Since Steve's first and second pro stories for *Amazing* had just been published, Anne dispensed advice on good markets and avoidable markets and urged him to join SFWA—the Science Fiction and Fantasy Writers of America—instantly. She also went on at length about how important art was to writers, something she greatly appreciated since Michael Whelan's cover art for *The White Dragon* was making waves and bringing increased attention to the book's upcoming release.

Now, science fiction conventions don't just happen, appearing at a hotel some Friday afternoon and evaporating at Sunday midnight. They are the effort of a particular science fiction community, such as the Baltimore Science Fiction Society, and they are run from opening ceremonies to the dead dog party (and for many months of planning before) by volunteers from the community.

As with all large undertakings, there are sometimes . . . glitches. When a glitch is discovered, members of the community step up to fix whatever's gone wrong.

And so, on the morning of the Friday afternoon on which BaltiCon 12 was to begin, it was discovered that a whole file box full of name tags for the preregistered attendees had not yet been typed. (In 1978, we still did these things by typewriter and by hand.) Friday morning is always a frantic precon time, with a lot of last-minute tasks and setup to attend to—and the badges shouldn't have been one of those "last-minute" things.

There was, on discovery of this lapse, a rather . . . energetic discussion in Ops (a fannish word for "operations office") regarding how the name tags were to be made ready in time to open the registration table at four. The discussion was so energetic, in fact, that no one noticed that the Guest of Honor had entered the room and had heard the whole kerfuffle.

"I can," she said, using all the lung power of a trained singer, "type, you know."

There was a period of silence while people caught their breaths and waited for their ears to stop ringing. Then came a gentle objection from the con chair: Surely, they couldn't ask their Guest of Honor to do gofer work.

"I'm bored," was Anne's answer. "Give me something to do."

And so it was, when Sharon arrived at the convention that Friday evening, Anne McCaffrey was sitting behind the registration desk, happily typing the name tags for the on-site registrants, to many of those across the table just another energetic fan making them welcome at the con.

As Guest of Honor, Anne was, of course, the first and most honored member of the convention, a role she took to with serious playfulness, enjoying the panels and serious side of things, and taking an obvious and more than somewhat fannish delight in the art show and the hucksters room, and later at the numerous evening parties as well. She did this the entire weekend, tirelessly dealing as both pro and fan, with sharp interest in all aspects of her community.

BaltiCon 12 was Sharon's second science fiction convention—ever. In addition to being a newbie, she was desperately shy and scarcely spoke to anyone during the entire weekend, least of all to the Guest of Honor. It was a lost opportunity but not a tragedy because Sharon had been introduced to Anne a decade earlier. At the tender age of fifteen, she had purchased *Dragonflight*—the first, but not the last, book on which she spent the grocery money. In her opinion, it was well worth the price; her mother . . . did not agree.

As it did to so many readers, *Dragonflight* spoke to Sharon— dragons! A strong, stubborn, driven female lead! Partnership between male and female!—so, okay, the guy had to be convinced, but, he had been convinced. A hero who could, and did, think!

It was more than an exciting story with great characters and wonderful world-building, though. It was an affirmation, a promise: Girls could get published, too.

In 1968? That was huge.

And it's not a stretch to say that *Dragonflight* was directly responsible for Sharon's attendance at her first-ever science fiction convention, BaltiCon 10 . . . as the winner of the con's short story contest.

We're going to fast-forward thirty years, now.

It's 1997. Lee and Miller have been a team since mid-1979 and began writing together a few years later. They've seen published a handful of collaborative short stories and three novels set in a fictional space that's come to be called the Liaden Universe®. Their publisher, Del Rey Books—coincidentally, the publisher of the Pern novels—had cut them loose in 1989 due to low sales. They haven't sold a novel since 1988, though they've written rather a number, and—well, not to put too fine a point on it, they are washed-up writers. Their career is, in a word, dead.

In August, 1997, Sharon accepted employment as the first full-time executive director of the Science Fiction and Fantasy Writers of America, Inc.—SFWA—the professional writers organization that Anne had been trying to get Steve to join, way back in 1978.

SFWA had been used to running on volunteer power, sort of like science fiction convention fandom. As news of her hiring spread throughout the organization, Sharon received many letters from past SFWA volunteers and officers, offering congratulations, condolences, and advice.

And one day, very soon after she took up her new duties, she received a paper letter from Ireland.

The return address was Dragonhold-Underhill, County Wicklow.

Of course, Sharon knew that Anne McCaffrey was a member of SFWA, but it was still kind of . . . cool to receive a letter from that particular address. She opened the envelope, expecting a membership question or perhaps a donation to one of SFWA's philanthropic funds.

The letter began:

> Dear Sharon Lee,
> If I say that I am a fan of yours, will you stop reading?

Sharon blinked, flipped to the second page, and checked the signature:

> Anne McCaffrey

She flipped back to the first page.

The letter went on to talk knowledgeably of the first three Liaden books, praising them in the highest possible terms. It was both stunning and warming—who were washed-up writers Lee and Miller to get fan mail from Anne McCaffrey?—and she closed, Anne-like, by mentioning that she had once been SFWA's secretary-treasurer, responsible for much of the work Sharon now had on her plate as executive director, and offering carte blanche any help she could give—Sharon had only to ask.

From this start, a correspondence grew up, migrating eventually to email.

In one of those back-and-forths, Anne wondered why there hadn't been any more Liaden novels after *Carpe Diem*. The answer to that was that the publisher had declined to continue the series, citing lack of numbers. "Numbers" is publisher-speak for "units sold."

Anne's opinion was that sometimes it took a book, or a series, "a while" to reach full potential in terms of numbers. This was something that hadn't occurred to us in quite those terms, but it was borne out by emails we'd started to get from other readers of our first three novels who wondered, as Anne had done, What Happened Next?

There are a lot of writers who'll tell you how hard it is to write—and they're not wrong. But the hardest part of the writer's job isn't the writing—it's sending the finished manuscript out into the world. The assumption must be that it will be rejected—as the overwhelming majority of manuscripts are—so the effort seems not only futile, but masochistic. And it saps the heart right out of you.

But, now, near the end of 1997, the combination of Anne's insight and the emails from other readers gave us the courage to consider what, exactly, we might do in order to come back from the dead. After all, we had all of those books written, and readers who wanted to read them.

The result of those considerations was that, by early 1998, Lee and Miller had a publisher who was enthusiastic and willing to publish their backlist and their front list.

So it was that we had just finished polishing and submitting the fourth book in the Liaden Universe® series to our new publisher when Anne sent an email, asking what we'd been doing.

The completion of the novel was reported, and Anne immediately asked to see it, adding, "I take paperclips."*

So, the manuscript for *Plan B* was duly shipped off to Ireland as an email attachment.

Now *Plan B* was supposed to have been an action-adventure novel, but there was a scene that was specifically character-building right in the middle of a very intense fight-and-flight situation. Long story short, in the final draft, that character-building section was removed and the edges of the excision smoothed out.

Remember this.

The next morning, there was an email from Anne in the inbox. She was full of praise for the novel, the characters, the world-building, but, she thought she would just mention that . . .

There was a scene missing.

And she pinpointed the spot in the narrative from which the slow character-building section had been excised.

Lee and Miller explained that, yes, there had been something there, but that it had been cut to make weight.

From Anne came the direction, "Send it to me."

---

* Paperclip is, as far as Lee and Miller know, a designation unique to Anne McCaffrey. It gave us pause on first reading, but we quickly figured out that what she meant was "email attachment" and that the "paperclip" came from the Microsoft icon of a paperclip, which indicates that a particular piece of email has an attachment.

The cut scene was therefore emailed, and when the next batch of mail was downloaded, there was a return note from Anne. It was brief:

"Put it back."

It's never wise to argue with a force of nature, or with a writer who knows story so well that she could see the place where a scene wasn't and call it out.

Anne wasn't done with us, though.

No sooner had the cut material been restored and the newly compiled manuscript emailed, with excuses, to our publisher, than another email arrived from Anne, with our former editor at Del Rey, who happened to be Anne's current and longtime editor, copied on the note.

Anne waxed effusive about *Plan B*—it was a wonderful book; she predicted that we'd have no problem selling it (though she knew it had already been placed), and she looked forward with great anticipation to the continuation of both the long-interrupted story and our careers as writers.

Lee looked at Miller; or perhaps Miller looked at Lee; and one of them said to the other, "She's going to get us killed."

In fact, there was no reply—that Lee and Miller ever heard about—to that note; life went on; in due time *Plan B* was published, and, of course, the authors sent a signed book to Anne McCaffrey, to thank her for all her many kindnesses.

A few weeks after that, the Lee and Miller household received the second of those treasured photographs, this taken about twenty-one years after the first and on the very premises of Dragonhold-Underhill.

Del Rey Books had asked, as publishers sometimes will ask their writers, to send an updated publicity photo for use in promoting her new book. Anne had her picture taken with Pumpkin, the resident Dragonhold-Underhill Maine Coon cat, sitting in front of Anne's work computer. To one side of the computer is a large stack of books, and near the top of the stack, in line with Anne's cheekbone and Pumpkin's frown, is *Plan B*, the title on the spine admirably readable.

This time, Lee and Miller were resigned, amused, and well-delighted to receive the picture, which was promptly framed and hung.

Over the next few years, Anne's involvement in Lee and Miller's return from the dead and continuing career was active. She demanded the right to write the introduction to the omnibus volume that reissued the first three Liaden books. She bullied Lee and Miller's publisher into sending her unbound signatures of each of the then-seven books—but she refused to say why.

We soon found out.

Now, during this time, there had been a free exchange of packages between Ireland and Maine. Pine cones, puzzles, and moose may have been involved.

So, it wasn't completely unusual for Lee and Miller to return home from a convention to find a box from Ireland sitting on the porch. It was rather larger than previous boxes, and it weighed a ton.

There was a reason for that.

Inside the box were two complete sets of our books, bound in red leather, stamped in gold.

Lee looked at Miller and said, "I'm afraid to touch them."

Miller looked at Lee and said, "Why would she do this?"

Anne's answer to that—the tone of the email a sort of half-surprised *doesn't everyone?*—was that she always had her favorite books bound in leather.

When life, health, and work get complicated, correspondence tends to fall off. So it was with Lee and Miller and Anne

McCaffrey. We'd get a note when a new book came out—often before we'd gotten our authors' copies. Sharon once told her that she shouldn't ever have to buy a copy of one of our books, that we'd be pleased to send her as many as she could read.

Anne's answer was, "Writers don't make money by giving books away."

In early 2005, though, an email arrived from Ireland.

The message was simple: "I'll be at Dragon*Con this year. So will you."

Still too wise to argue with a force of nature, Lee and Miller packed and drove from Waterville, Maine, to Atlanta, Georgia, in all the heat of August, to see Anne McCaffrey.

It turned out that Anne was still as much a fan as a pro about conventions; she took huge delight in reading T-shirts and in admiring costumes. If she now traveled by scooter, it was a well-directed scooter moving brusquely where she wanted it to go, and woe to those who remained slaves of bipedal motion.

Anne's Dragon*Con schedule at that point was pretty hectic for a woman born almost eighty years before, but in the midst of it all, we managed to meet for dinner. The topics of conversation ranged from book plans to computers and search engines to characters to upcoming Worldcons and potential TV or movie deals. She maintained the same lively interest in new writers becoming part of SFWA and taking advantage of workshopping opportunities as she had when she'd met Steve in 1978.

Eventually the restaurant where we'd met for dinner needed our table for a reservation—and like any number of fans at any number of conventions, we parted with plans to see each other the following year.

Then the Dragonlady pulled into pedestrian traffic at a spanking pace, leaving us to find our way back on our own.

Anne died in November 2011.

Since then, Lee and Miller have been to several science fiction conventions, as guests of honor and as panelists. An Anne McCaffrey appreciation panel has been part of each of those conventions. The panelists are a testimony to the wide swath Anne cut through the science fiction community—writers, editors, artists, filkers*, con runners—all of us have stories.

That's warming, but not particularly extraordinary. Panelists are, after all, asked to speak about subjects of which they're knowledgeable.

No, what's been . . . notable . . . is the number of people in the packed-to-the-walls audiences who knew Anne as well or better than the panelists and whose stories and memories are no less precious, personal, and extraordinary.

In the end, we're all memories and the stories that people tell.

Anne left us some damned fine stories and memories like stars on a cloudless night.

Ciao for now, Annie.

Maine-based writers SHARON LEE and STEVE MILLER teamed up in the late 1980s to bring the world the story of Kinzel, an inept wizard with a love of cats, a thirst for justice, and a staff of true power. Since then, the husband-and-wife team have written dozens of short stories and twenty novels, most set in their star-spanning Liaden Universe®.

Before settling down to the serene and stable life of a science fiction

---

* Filker—someone who sings filk—the "folk songs" of the science fiction and fantasy community. Attributed to a typo in a program book that went viral many decades ago.

and fantasy writer, Steve was a traveling poet, a rock-band reviewer, reporter, and editor of a string of community newspapers.

Sharon, less adventurous, has been an advertising copywriter, copy editor on night-side news at a small city newspaper, reporter, photographer, and book reviewer. Both credit their newspaper experiences with teaching them the finer points of collaboration.

In 2012, Lee and Miller were jointly presented with the Skylark Award for lifetime achievement, given by the New England Science Fiction Association. Among previous Skylark recipients are Sir Terry Pratchett, George R. R. Martin—and Anne McCaffrey.

Way back in 1984, Author Services Inc. established the L. Ron Hubbard Writers of the Future Award. They approached the best science fiction and fantasy writers of the time and asked them to be judges. Isaac Asimov, Robert Silverberg, Algis Budrys, and many other luminaries agreed—which was a resounding endorsement of the award. Shortly after that, Anne McCaffrey was asked if she would be a judge, and she agreed. If there was one constant in Anne's life, it was her adherence to the creed "never simply return a favor, pass it on," and this was very clearly a case of being able to do so.

John Goodwin was there from the beginning. He and Anne developed a great relationship, and they were always thrilled at any chance to get together.

Anne loved being able to greet new writers and encourage them in continuing in the craft, and she loved the chance to sparkle and show off her best self—she even managed to get me in a suit!

Star Power

JOHN GOODWIN

I GOT TO know Anne McCaffrey through the Writers of the Future, a program initiated by L. Ron Hubbard to help discover and promote budding writers.

In 1985, Anne became the first female judge for the Writers of the Future contest—which is a funny story in itself. She was speaking with Algis Budrys—a renowned writer, editor, and critic—at a West Coast convention. He had just purchased one of Anne's first stories, "The Ship Who Sang," and he told her about his new job working with the Writers of the Future. He said that with the writing contest they'd have several celebrity judges who would read the stories. To which she replied, "Gee, that's a great idea," and passed it off. But the next time she saw Algis, she asked why all of his judges were male. She proceeded to list names of stellar women writers like Kate Wilhelm, Ursula K. Le Guin, and Andre Norton, emphasizing the potential candidates for a female judge. In Anne's own words, from a video interview with me, "I could get rather stuffy about lack of females when there should be some, and there was no reason why there weren't some on that." Algis agreed with a simple "Yes." A short while later, the contest sent a letter asking Anne to be one of the judges. "So," as

Anne put it in that same video interview, "I ended up putting my feet where my mouth was."

Anne served with distinction as a judge. Dave Wolverton, coordinating judge, describes Anne as one of his "go-to" judges.

"She was always eager to judge," he says of her, "even when she was sick, or busy, or tired. She was one of those special people who made time to help. She loved new writers, and when she took an interest in one, Anne would follow the writer's career for years. She would ask me about them, and sometimes even called a new author to express her appreciation, offer encouragement, or give advice."

In fact, several years after Dave himself won the contest back in 1987, he began getting mysterious faxes in the middle of the night—faxes that showed how his books were doing on bestseller lists in England. Curious to discover who was behind this, he called the number that the faxes had come from, and Anne answered the phone. He asked, "So, did our agent ask you to do this?" (They both had the same agent.) Anne replied, "Why, no, I'm just a fan and thought that you should know how well you're doing." Others could report similar tales of her kindness.

But while I felt that I got to know Anne from the very first book I read of hers—*The Crystal Singer*—it wasn't until I was able to spend time with her at a series of Writers of the Future workshops that I discovered her passion for the performing arts. She had initially studied to be a Broadway singer. She had persisted in trying to make a career of it, and it wasn't until her coach told her that a burr in her voice would prevent her from ever truly making it as a singer that she finally agreed that it was not for her. At that point she decided to give writing a try— something she had not done before. She submitted her first story to *Science-Fiction Plus*, a short-lived magazine. It wasn't the home run that every new writer hopes for; again in her own words, "I got $1 thousand for it, which was a cent a word. But it was printed with my name on it and that was just after my son Alec was born and that was great stuff."

After she told me about her change in career direction, I asked if she would be interested in performing in one of our theatrical productions of a Hubbard short story at Dragon*Con, the annual science fiction and fantasy convention in Atlanta, Georgia, that featured a full track of programming dedicated to her Pern series. At that time, the Writers of the Future awards event took place annually just before Dragon*Con. I suggested that I could get together with Pat Henry, the show's director, and we would work together to bring Anne to the States to attend our respective events.

It was as if I had opened a long-shut part of her, which geysered forth. Her eyes became very bright and excited at the thought of being in a performance, and in her countenance you could see that young girl who so many years earlier had wanted to perform. As it turns out, David Carradine (*Kung Fu*, *Kill Bill 1* and *2*) was already attending Dragon*Con and had made himself available to perform on any show we could arrange. Hubbard was one of his favorite authors, and he had performed in several other radio theater shows of Hubbard's works back at our Golden Age Theater in Hollywood. So, Anne and David teamed up, along with other local actors, in what was to be Anne's first theatrical production in decades—as one of the key characters in Hubbard's *Ole Doc Methuselah*.

It wasn't until 2006 that Anne performed in her next show for us. By this time, she was in her electric scooter, on which she rapidly developed a reputation of being, shall we say, an "aggressive" driver—meaning you had best move out of the way when she came careening down an aisle on her way to one of her many signings or panels. We held our Writers of the Future awards event in San Diego at the Air & Space Museum that year, which was followed just a few days later by the Sixty-Fourth

World Science Fiction Convention in Los Angeles (L.A.con IV). Galaxy Press, as an exhibitor at the convention, was able to sponsor a show. This time Anne costarred in the performance of *The Dangerous Dimension* with actress Karen Black (*Five Easy Pieces, Airport 1975*). Among this audience, Anne was every bit on par with Karen in her "star power."

These were the only two shows that Anne performed for us, although she continued to attend our Writers of the Future workshops and awards ceremonies, where she always seemed to enjoy speaking with each year's winners and presenting them with their awards, and where, in 2004, she was the recipient of the L. Ron Hubbard Lifetime Achievement Award. I continued writing to Anne via email after she stopped doing any long-distance travel and found her continuously promoting the Writers of the Future contest and doing what she could to help each year's new crew of winners. Anne was a friend, not just to me, but to all who aspired to the arts. She proved to be a woman of many talents—with wisdom and compassion to match.

JOHN GOODWIN, president of Galaxy Press—publisher of the fiction works of L. Ron Hubbard and the annual Writers of the Future anthology—has been involved with book publishing since 1986. He is a board member of the Audio Publishers Association, a national organization of the audio publishing industry. He has become very active in the Hollywood community the past several years, serving as a board member of the Hollywood Chamber of Commerce and a board member of the Friends of Hollywood Central Park (an organization creating a forty-four-acre park over the Hollywood Freeway). He is also one of the main organizers of the Hollywood Christmas Parade. He is a member of the Explorers Club, Science Fiction Writers of America, Mystery Writers of America, and Western Writers of America, as well as the Dubai Press Club, as part of an international effort to introduce Galaxy Press' publishing program into the Middle East.

In 1969, as Anne McCaffrey's marriage was falling apart, David Gerrold's life turned topsy-turvy, and they found themselves talking long-distance: each consoling and counseling the other. Shortly after Anne arrived in Ireland in 1970, she invited David to come over, extolling the joys of tax exemption for writers and artists.

David came and found digs of his own not long after. And, in a case of reality being sometimes weirder than science fiction, he called Anne one day with the startling news, "Annie, Lessa is my landlady."

Jan Regan, at five foot *mumble* and ninety pounds soaking wet, with dark brown eyes and long hair, was the embodiment of Lessa in looks and, it turns out, in character, too. Unable to find dragons to ride, Jan was an exercise rider for racehorses.

David has remained a friend of the family ever since.

How the Dragonlady Saved My Life

DAVID GERROLD

ANNE MCCAFFREY REDEFINED the term "Dragonlady." She made it a good thing—so much so that Terry Pratchett based a major character on her in his Discworld series. But before Anne McCaffrey was the Dragonlady of Dublin, she was also a pretty damn good science fiction author in her own write. And she had a singing voice that could crack mahogany.

I'll begin at the beginning. As I have noted elsewhere, 1969 was a particularly horrible year for me. It was the worst year of my life. I won't go into the details here; I'll put it in a book and let you pay for the privilege of sharing the horror. Two people saved my life. One was Harlan Ellison; the other was Anne McCaffrey.

I had met both of them in 1968. I met Harlan at a small Los Angeles convention in July. I met Anne two months later at Baycon, the 1968 World Science Fiction Convention, held at the Hotel of Usher in Berkeley. I rode up there on my motorcycle. Despite having sold a script to *that* TV show (the one with the guy who had bangs and pointy ears), I was still a skinny, awkward kid who had not yet outgrown various adolescent self-esteem issues.

I met Anne McCaffrey in the bar. In those days, the *real* convention always happened in the bar. I also met Frederik Pohl, Harry Harrison, Robert Silverberg, Terry Carr, Randall Garrett, Frank Herbert, Fritz Leiber, Poul Anderson, Gordon R. Dickson, Philip Jose Farmer, Lester del Rey, Betty and Ian Ballantine, John W. Campbell, Damon Knight, Kate Wilhelm, Leigh Brackett, A. E. van Vogt, and almost every other author who had informed my childhood and teenage years with hours of wonder. It was better than Disneyland.

Anne McCaffrey was the secretary-treasurer of the Science Fiction Writers of America.

The SFWA had been founded in 1965 by Damon Knight. For several years, SF writers had been muttering that they needed some kind of organization. One day, Damon Knight sent out letters saying, "Send me five dollars for your dues." And that was how the SFWA was started. By 1968, Anne McCaffrey had taken on the unrewarding duties of collecting dues, managing the membership roles, and publishing the newsletter. In effect, she was the organization. This made her the reigning queen of science fiction.

In those days, the only qualification for membership in the organization was that you had to have published a science fiction story. I asked Anne if writing a script for *that* TV show would count. She made an immediate executive decision that it did and collected my five dollars. Since then, membership qualifications have been made much stricter, but I do not believe that this was my fault.

Anne and I hit it off immediately. I can't say what the magic was—because it was magic. Magic doesn't work if you analyze it. But there were sparks struck at that convention that triggered a lifelong friendship. Anne was nominated for a Hugo Award; so was I. I sat next to her at the awards banquet. I held her hand when she won; she held my hand when I didn't.

I celebrated with her; she commiserated with me. That cemented the bond.

In July and August of 1969, I experienced several of the life lessons that fuel much of the world's greatest literature. It is one thing to use words like *ecstasy* and *joy* and *horror* and *anguish*— it is quite another to experience those emotions and discover that words alone are simply insufficient. I'll say this much—testifying at a murder trial was never on my list of things I wanted to do. It's not a fun experience. I've had fun; that wasn't it.

But it was a turning point. Writers are people who process emotions into words, attempting to capture, evoke, and recreate those feelings. So if I had to pick a moment at which I began to shift from someone who just typed to someone who was actually writing something worth reading, I would pick the aftercrash of 1969.

The 1969 Worldcon was held at another Hotel of Usher, this one in St. Louis. Seeing Anne again reminded me of how much fun was still available in the world. Anne seemed to move in a cloud of white light. She glowed. She sparkled with fun and generosity. She made everyone around her feel loved.

After the convention, we kept in touch by letter, by phone call (very expensive long-distance phone calls), and finally, she invited me to visit her in New York for Thanksgiving with the McCaffrey-Johnson clan. It was an old-fashioned holiday, and the emotional nourishment was far more lasting than the physical.

In 1970, just as Anne was realizing she had to get out of New York, I was beginning to realize that I had to get out of Los Angeles. I was talking with Anne almost every week now. I don't know if she knew it because there was a lot I wasn't saying, but it was those long conversations that provided the emotional lifeline back toward sanity. Anne was going through her own stuff too, having recently divorced her husband, and was now

working her way through her own emotional upheavals of relo-
cating to Ireland with two of her three children in tow. So for a
while, we may have been two of the walking wounded, holding
each other up. Eventually, Anne invited me to join her and her
family in Dublin—it would be good for me, and it would be
good for her to have another friend to talk to, someone who understood writing. Thus began my migration, first to New York
for six months (where I finished two novels) and from there to
Ireland with a bit of change in my pocket.

Anne picked me up at the airport, and it was like coming
home to family. On the way back to her digs, she said, "Let's
pick up some takeout from the Chinese restaurant." We walked
into a fairly nondescript building, and one of the most beautiful
Chinese women I'd ever seen in my life smiled at us and said,
in perfect brogue, "Top of the evenin' to yeh! May I take yer
arder?" It was the single most perfect moment of culture shock
in my entire life.

I should also say this about Chinese food in Ireland—if they
can't get the right ingredients, they substitute. Usually a potato.
'Nuff said about that. I leave the rest to your imagination. (That
may have changed since 1970, though.)

A couple of days after I moved into the McCaffrey manse,
one of Anne's local friends—Michael O'Shea—offered to take
me and Anne's eldest son, Alec, out drinking. Michael O'Shea
outweighed me by at least fifty or sixty pounds, but I kept up
with him all day long, drink for drink. Michael's plan had been
to "take the piss out of the American." It didn't work. Knowing
a smidge of biology, I also put away two or three glasses of
water for every glass of whiskey. So when we got back to Anne's,
I went upstairs to type a letter. Still pretty buzzed, I had to slow
down to sixty words a minute. Apparently, my being able to sit
and type, despite putting away so much whiskey, was enough to
impress him that I was a force unto myself. (And yes, I admit,

the hangover the next day was pretty horrendous. I haven't done any real drinking since then.)

I stayed with the McCaffrey clan for only a couple of weeks before finding a flat of my own in Dún Laoghaire (pronounced *dun laary*), a small village nearby where James Joyce had lived. It's the site of James Joyce Tower. There's also a statue of the man. I suppose that should have been inspiring, but James Joyce was not known for his science fiction.

Shortly after settling in, I called Anne to inform her, "You have to come and meet my landlady. She's Lessa." Indeed, this feisty, no-nonsense, wiry little woman could have beamed in directly from Pern. (Actually, she was from England.) Jan was Lessa in looks and personality and that quality that western writers would call "gumption." Anne met Jan and was immediately taken with her. It was the start of a lifelong friendship. Being in the same room with them was joyous. Standing between them was dangerous.

Ireland was the rest I needed, but it wasn't conducive to my writing. I'd finished two novels in New York City, but had made no real progress on anything while parked in Dún Laoghaire. About the time I realized I was seeking out Dublin's permanent floating John Wayne film festival, I knew my time in Ireland was ending.

I went back to New York, wrote another book and a half, returned to Los Angeles, and began the process of learning how to be a real writer—one who rolls with the punches and keeps on writing. But those days of sanctuary that Anne McCaffrey provided were the lifeline, the much-needed opportunity to discover the emotional resilience that passes for maturity.

So I say that Anne McCaffrey saved my life.

It's a debt I can't pay back. But it is a debt I will pay forward.

Thank you, Anne. I love you, I miss you. I'll hoist a jar in your honor tonight. (And a couple of glasses of water too.)

DAVID GERROLD is the Hugo and Nebula Award-winning author of *The Martian Child*. His other books include *When HARLIE Was One*, *The Man Who Folded Himself*, *Jumping Off the Planet*, and the War Against the Chtorr series. He also wrote *that* episode of *that* TV series and a bunch of other stuff.

It's the twinkling eyes and the hint of a devilish grin that let you know that there's a lot more to Bob Neilson than one might first guess. He loves a good argument as much as the next Irishman, will drink whenever there's something in front of him, and, like far too many of us, was once a smoker.

He's immensely practical but still willing to take a dare—which is exactly what he did many years ago when his wife, Stacey, suggested they should open a bead store. They did, and Yellow Brick Road is still thriving nearly three decades later.

In many respects, Bob is my mirror image—if I'd be born in Ireland instead of merely a late arrival. He loves science fiction, has been active in fandom, and was one of the founders of *Albedo One*, an award-winning science fiction magazine.

He was best man at my wedding, just as his wife was matron of honor at my sister's wedding.

I asked Bob to write for this tribute because he knew Anne McCaffrey both as a fan and as an Irishman, a rare combination. Of course, if I haven't made it clear already, Bob is a rare man!

Bookends

ROBERT NEILSON

IN 1972 MY future wife, Stacey, entered Newpark Comprehensive School in South County Dublin where she met, and became friends with, Todd "McCaffrey" Johnson. Thus began a thirty-nine-year friendship that happily involved Anne McCaffrey and my family and me. Like everyone who knew Annie even slightly, Stacey's memories mostly revolve around the strength of character, friendliness, and generosity of a woman who had an immense impact on everyone she met.

The McCaffrey house, no matter which of the four over their years in Ireland, was always a safe haven, and Annie was always more than willing to take on the many waifs and strays—both animal and human—that found their way to her doorstep. Although Stacey couldn't be considered a stray, she found herself hanging out at Todd's house, where Annie provided endless coffee and toast for hungry teenagers. At the time, finances were tight in the McCaffrey household, but the hospitality was a tap that was never turned off.

There was a peculiar soundtrack to life in the McCaffrey household back then, as Stacey remembers it—the clatter of typewriter keys. She recollects one day when an excited Annie took delivery of a new typewriter—an IBM Selectric, the famous "golfball" model. Annie was always capable of taking enjoyment out of the simplest of things.

In 1981, I gate-crashed Stacey's twenty-first birthday party. Todd wasn't in Ireland at the time—he was in Germany serving with the US army—but it wasn't long until I was invited down to Dragonhold to meet her good friend Todd, who was back on leave. As a science fiction fan, I knew who Todd's mother (the Hugo and Nebula award-winning author) was and consequently was a little awed at visiting her house. The person I met was not Anne McCaffrey, famous writer, but Todd's mum, who offered coffee and other refreshments and turned a blind eye while we smoked grass, played endless games of yahtzee or liar's dice, and laughed like drains.

Over the following years, I spent quite a lot of time at the two Dragonholds. I still clearly remember driving along the hedge-lined lane to the first one; that was house number three—the first outside the immediate Dublin suburbs, the first one she owned, and, I guess, her definitive commitment to Ireland. Naturally I was filled with trepidation at the possibility of meeting a "world-famous author." The house itself was a medium-sized bungalow, nothing special (if the context could be ignored), though it had stables out in the back. Now that was impressive—ordinary people simply didn't have stables behind the house. But then, while Annie may have been many things, ordinary was never one of them.

I soon became familiar with the family and the huge cast of characters that orbited clan McCaffrey, and I sometimes wonder if there is a single one of us that is without a personal story of Annie's generosity. I don't think I can recall ever hearing a single mention of that generosity from Annie's lips, always just a remark in passing from a third party, and always told as if it were the most natural thing in the world. Medical bills or simply living expenses covered for friends and even relatives of friends, people she hadn't even met in some cases. But it was never just money; it was the care and consideration for the comfort and happiness of others that made the real difference.

Also through Todd, in the early '80s Annie met a young fantasy author from Lisburn in Northern Ireland, Peter Smyth (who writes as Peter Morwood). Peter and his then-girlfriend visited Dragonhold, and Annie took a liking to Peter and kept a motherly eye on him. When he broke up with that girlfriend, Annie turned her hand to matchmaking—an ancient Irish tradition. We even have a matchmaking festival in Lisdoonvarna each year.

It happened that a science fiction writer of her acquaintance, one Diane Duane, had also been through a breakup, and Annie figured they would be a perfect match. And how right she was. Love blossomed at about the speed of light—maybe a little below it if you really want to be pedantic—and they were married within a year. More than twenty years later, they still seem like a pretty good match.

For all of the '80s and half of the '90s, I was something of a corporate suit, so occasionally Annie would call on me for an opinion on a business matter. Now I have to admit that if Annie had a sixth sense, it was no business sense. As a writer, it could be said, she didn't need business sense. But because she was a successful writer, there were always "opportunities" cropping up. Often, they were simply a means for her to help friends and family. One such venture was the Irish Farriery Centre. You see, Annie had a friend . . . which in McCaffrey-speak is how "once upon a time" stories usually begin. And because of this friend, Annie had acquired some property. And on that property stood a (semiderelict) building. And Annie had another friend who was a farrier. And that friend had an idea for a center in Ireland to teach farriery—a badly needed facility and close to Annie's heart through her love of horses. And the building on the property could be turned into a school for farriers. Not that there was anything school- or farriery-like about it. But Annie wanted it to be right and was prepared to get people to make it so.

A very Annie scenario that unfortunately found a very Irish ending. Who would ever have guessed that farriers had internal politics? Despite Annie's best intentions and efforts, Irish farriers to this day still have to "cross the water" to England to study and qualify.

Annie would also occasionally call on me as a writer—even though I was merely a wannabe who ran a small SF magazine. Yet again, it was related to her generosity—Annie simply could never say no to requests from friends or acquaintances. And successful writers make lots of acquaintances in the business. So Annie got regular requests from authors or their agents or publishers to give their latest novel a blurb—who wouldn't want Anne McCaffrey saying something nice about them on the back of their book?

The first time it happened, she asked me to read a book that she frankly "didn't get." Most authors would have refused to blurb it or damned it with faint praise. But Annie was sure no one would ask her to blurb a bad book, and she really wanted to say something nice. And it was an award winner. I read it and "got it" and told her how much I liked it, and she took me at my word and was relieved to be able to say those nice things.

The time that really sticks in my mind involved a galley proof of a fantasy novel from an American publisher. She said nothing, simply asked me to read the first fifty-or-so pages as she had a particular question to ask. Thank goodness she only needed me to read fifty pages. Shortly before this I had seen the film *Roxanne*, starring Steve Martin, and knew that Annie had enjoyed it. So in reverence to the scene where Steve lambastes a guy in a bar for wasting the opportunity to make fun of his nose by displaying a complete lack of wit, I honored the movie with my own version featuring twenty different ways of saying how bad a book could be—there were singing elves marching through the forest for fuck's sake, and the lyrics of their songs were lovingly rendered in italic script. Annie countered with a page on which she had found, counted, and underlined more than sixty adjectives and adverbs.

Annie's problem was not that she could not tell a bad book, but that she was looking to see if there was anything of worth in there whatsoever so that she could write the blurb. In the end, I could only persuade her to politely decline the request, which she did with some reluctance.

Nothing was too much trouble for Annie, and at times when you would expect her to be focused on herself and her own needs, she always had time for others. I was reminded of this in conversation with (English SF writer) John Meaney shortly after Annie passed away. He mentioned to me how she had befriended and inspired him and how she had attempted to help his career by seating him beside Diana Tyler, her agent, at Todd's wedding as she felt it would be a good opportunity for him to hook a top-of-the-line agent. At the same wedding I was afforded the opportunity, through the good graces of the family, to interview one of the guests, Lois McMaster Bujold, for my magazine—not usually considered to be part of the best man's duties, but I didn't lose the ring or embarrass Todd in my speech, so I guess they were happy enough to give me that latitude.

At Gigi's wedding, Stacey was matron of honor, so I was alone at a distant table. But as I was a wannabe writer, guess where they seated me? Poor Diana Tyler must have thought it was a bad case of déjà vu as we discussed my novel at length. Annie and Todd (the apple didn't fall far from the tree) had been busy again ensuring that nobody missed out.

Annie's consideration for others reached far beyond her extended adopted family to her fans. She loved to meet her public and had endless patience and good humor to share with them. She was well-known at conventions all over the world, where she threw herself headlong into the action and was genuinely interested in everyone who was interested in her and her work. But it didn't stop at conventions. I remember one afternoon sitting in the bay window of the kitchen in Dragonhold-Underhill, chatting with Alec, when a strange car pulled up outside.

"Fans," Alec said, shaking his head. As her eldest, Alec always felt a need to protect his mother, often from herself. But nobody ever stopped Annie from doing precisely as she pleased. The fans, it turned out, had flown into Dublin airport from the United States, looked up Annie in the phone book—where she was proudly listed as Anne McCaffrey, Writer—and called her up, at which point Annie invited them to Dragonhold for the night. I could sympathize with Alec's viewpoint, but you simply had to smile and shrug and say, "Typical Annie."

Also typical of Annie was her excitement over her achievements and her ability to share her enthusiasms. I remember another day, yet again at that kitchen table, when a package arrived in the post. It contained books from Japan—author copies of her first Japanese translations. She ripped open the box excitedly and pulled them out to show everyone, with a huge grin spread across her face and a sparkle of glee in her eyes. They were in Japanese, and *they were printed back to front*. These books had made her day. The accompanying royalty check hardly even got a glance.

For me that table was the center of the second Dragonhold, and although I spent a lot of time in that house while I was in business with Alec in the mid-'90s, the good times happened in the kitchen. My kids would give you an argument on that one. For them, memories of Dragonhold and Annie revolve around her pool. Almost nobody in Ireland has an indoor heated swimming pool in their house, but Annie had one. My daughters, Vickie and Danielle, learned to swim in it, and while they were kids, they loved it. They still have the fondest of memories of it almost twenty years later.

Considering how much time I spent with Annie over the years, it is odd to think that I was only ever at one science fiction convention outside Ireland where she was a guest. In 2007 I was invited to Eurocon in Copenhagen to launch a short story collection. I was proud to see my name on the poster, almost like I was a real guest, especially so as the Guest of Honor was the venerable Anne McCaffrey.

Denmark took us seriously, unlike Ireland, which treats science fiction as, at best, a slight embarrassment. The convention guests were treated to a reception by the city in a beautifully appointed municipal building as though we were *real* writers—in Ireland *real* means "literary," though not necessarily good. At the reception, I snuck up on Annie from behind and took her by surprise. And she had one of those moments when she drew a complete blank. Her minder was no help—a fan volunteer who didn't know me from Adam. I was a little taken aback myself. But I smiled and said, "It's Bob." And suddenly everything clicked into place, and she said, "Bob Neilson." She proceeded to list the names of my wife and kids and my address and every other fact she knew about me. And we grinned and embraced and chatted for a while. The next day I bumped into her at the convention. "Bob Neilson," she yelled across the room. "Husband of Stacey. Father to Victoria, Danielle, and Christopher. Want the pets too?" She grinned. And the same when we met on the plane to fly home. Same wicked grin, same list of names, same sense of fun.

It was also in Copenhagen that it was brought home to me just how big a star she was. *Albedo One*, my magazine, had been allocated a free table to sell our wares, so whenever I wasn't on panels, I hung out at the table. The dealer beside us sold nothing but Anne McCaffrey collectible books and did a roaring trade until he ran out of stock. Signing sessions had been set up in the dealers' room, and as I was launching my collection, I was put onto the list of authors to sign. This I was not looking forward to, but as I watched the other authors signing a half dozen or a dozen books in their allotted hour, I felt it wouldn't be too embarrassing—I had a handful of friends from Ireland at the con who could pretend to get stuff signed in a pinch.

When my signing came along, I was paired with Harry Harrison. I was introduced to Harry by Todd in the early '80s and knew him quite well at this stage, so we chatted with a few interruptions for book signings for our hour. It was pleasant, and I didn't feel that I had acquitted myself too badly—hell, I'd have been horrified if I'd signed more books than Harry.

The next day Annie was down to sign. Just one author signing this hour as she was Guest of Honor—or so I thought. But actually it was a masterstroke of logistics by the con committee. The queue began to form before the start of the hour. Anyone who wanted signatures from the poor devils that were on the hour before had to fight their way through. I watched the signing begin as Annie smiled and chatted with each fan and signed as many books as they had brought. After a while, I wandered out of the room and followed the line along the hall and down the stairs and out of the building altogether. To me it looked as though there were more people in the queue than there were members signed up for the con. I was glad I wasn't on a panel that hour.

I grabbed a coffee and went back to the dealers' room. The hour was up, but the line was still halfway along the hall. Annie dismissed the concerns of her minder and kept signing until every one of the fans in line had had their moment with her and their signatures. By the end she was worn out, but nobody had been shortchanged. She had put her fans first as always.

Every year in October there is a craft show in the Royal Dublin Society where Yellow Brick Road, our family business, takes a stand. As the talented one in the family, Stacey runs the stand and meets our public. Last year Annie turned up at the show. She was being wheeled around by one of that extended adoptive family of hers, Anne Callaghan, and they stopped to visit with Stacey and my daughter Vickie. It had been a while since Stacey had seen Annie, and they had a long chat about old times. That evening when Stacey was telling me about her day and her conversation with Annie, she said, "I was delighted to get a chance to chat with Anne."—To Stacey, she was always Anne. "In all the years, I had never told her how much she meant to me. I told her today. I'm so glad I did."

Two weeks later Annie passed away. It was fitting that Stacey, who had been first, was the last of our family to see her. When I told her the news, she said once again how glad she was to have been able to tell Annie how much her friendship and example had meant. I hope many others had this opportunity over the past years, and I hope that Annie realized how profound an impression she made on the lives of everyone who knew her.

In Ireland we have a farewell that comes in three parts, and it is particularly fitting for Annie, I feel: May the road always rise up behind you. May the wind ever be at your back. And may you be in heaven a half hour before the devil knows you're dead.

Sleep well, Annie. It was a privilege to know you.

BOB NEILSON is married with children and lives in Ireland. In partnership with his wife, he runs a successful retail business in Dublin city. His short fiction has appeared extensively in professional and small press markets, and he has had two radio plays performed on RTE and one on Anna Livia FM. He also presented a SF radio show on Anna Livia for a year. He has had two short story collections published, *Without Honour* (1997, Aeon Press) and *That's Entertainment* (2007, Elastic Press), as well as several comics and a graphic novel. His nonfiction book on the properties of crystals is a best-seller in the United Kingdom and Ireland. He is a founding editor of *Albedo One* magazine. Visit his site at www.bobneilson.org for more information.

When I was first approached about this tribute to Anne McCaffrey, Elizabeth Moon was on the short list of people I hoped we could get to contribute. She shared with Anne a love of horses, cooking, and fencing and a military background. They got along on a level that was subtle and sublime—I think they communicated on that special "mom" wavelength or something. Certainly, Elizabeth was considered by all to be the *ideal* houseguest. When she rightly won the Nebula Award for her amazing *The Speed of Dark*, we all cheered.

Lessons from Lessa

ELIZABETH MOON

I WAS IN my junior year of college when "Weyr Search" appeared as the cover story in *Analog* (October 1967). I couldn't afford *Analog* every month, but that month the cover illustration and McCaffrey name made it essential. Once I started reading, whatever class work I was supposed to be doing languished until I'd finished.

I read the story as science fiction, not only because the story appeared in *Analog*, but because the "dragons" were so clearly not fantasy dragons but bioengineered creatures. Telepathy was then a popular element in many science fiction stories—had been for years—so the telepathic abilities of humans and dragons—or watchwhers—also didn't slide into fantasy. "Weyr Search" felt like science fiction, but particularly rich and evocative science fiction.

Another reason it felt like science fiction and not fantasy was the characters, the earthy reality of them. Retrograde societies weren't unusual in SF of the day, so the more primitive "holds" and premodern cultural behavior did not signal fantasy. Science fiction included characters whose lives were anchored (even if over a long span of time or space or both) in our reality.

But "Weyr Search" offered something new even for science

fiction: Lessa, the rightful heir of Ruatha Hold, who broke the mold for women characters in both the science fiction and the fantasy I'd read. Far from the cool, pale, untouchable elven queens or fairy princesses of fantasy, elegant in their robes, Lessa is 100 percent human. Yet she is not the beautiful but biddable helpmeet of so many science fiction stories or the rational/practical sort found sometimes in Heinlein.

Lessa, in fact, isn't anyone's ideal girl/woman in that era: intelligent and courageous and talented, yes, but also scrappy, prickly, resentful, manipulative, and vengeful. She goes against the standards of womanly behavior for both Pern and the culture in which I'd been brought up. She isn't in search of a good marriage; she wants justice for her family and for herself and is willing to do anything to get it. "Anything" includes pretending to be older and uglier than she is and acting the part of a rather stupid servant, while actually plotting to drive out—if possible even kill—the man who has murdered her family and stolen the holding. In everyday society, and in other novels, such behavior stamps a woman as wicked and worthless. And yet as the story goes on—as all the Lessa stories go on—it is clear that she is not purely selfish, a storybook villainess. She cares deeply about people and works for goals beyond herself.

Lessa resonated instantly with me. For far less reason, I had, at that time, a sackful of resentment for unfairness heaped on girls in general and me in particular. I understood instantly the drive, the ambition, the ability to choose a seemingly impossible goal and go after it in spite of disapproval and threats. I shared her personality: the hot temper, the impatience with fools, the searing hatred of injustice, the sheer blind stubbornness that pitted me against so much of that era's attitudes.

As Lessa manipulates F'lar into fighting Fax, I saw talents I didn't have (or hadn't needed). As she resists what someone else would have seen as rescue to stand up for her own rights, I saw the person I'd been in high school—the outsider determined to get and hold what was hers. A Bausch & Lomb science medal wasn't Ruatha Hold, but when told I should give it up to a boy because girls didn't need validation in science, my reaction was pure Lessa, though she hadn't been written yet. Although I'd never plotted against those I blamed for my predicament (no telepathic powers, alas), I cheered Lessa on. Lessa even had unruly dark hair—like mine—in an era that seemed to produce endless book-girls and -women with golden curls or red tresses.

But even in that first story, Lessa began to have dual effects on my life. First, Lessa validated my sense of worth as a self-motivated female who didn't fit the current ideal. What some called faults—independence, temper, prickly nature, fierce ambition for something others thought far beyond reach—needed only a little smoothing of the sharp edges—some maturity, some experience—to reveal the underlying virtues that made Lessa into a force for good in her world. Lessa was encouragement for being myself—someone who didn't fit well in any of the categories that were then, in the '60s, being so firmly defined and established.

Second, the existence of Lessa as a character in a story, with that specific personality and its development, changed how I conceived of characters I might write. I had been writing stories since childhood, and like most child writers, much of my writing was derivative, taking its inspiration from one writer after another, from varied sources scattered across genres. But at that time, none of them had shown me a female character with Lessa's vibrancy who did not end up "tamed" or "punished" into more a conventional life. So as a young writer, that part of my mind—the writer-brain, as it were—sucked Lessa in and digested her very differently than I had as a reader alone.

How, writer-brain wanted to know, had Anne McCaffrey *done* that, created such a compelling, fascinating, complex female character who transgressed—and triumphed? Was it just having a female acting in charge of her own life, from an initial position of apparent weakness? Writer-brain paused to gulp down several of the other characters for comparison: F'lar, Robinton, Manora—other women in the story who were more conventional. I read more, of course: "Dragonrider" in the December *Analog*, everything of Anne McCaffrey's I could find (I often had to wait for used bookstores). I was reading many other things as well, but the writer-mind kept circling back to Lessa and comparing her to other female characters.

Much of my learning about writing, at this stage, was scarcely conscious and certainly not analytical at the surface level. It was felt: this character was full and satisfying; and that one felt thin, sketchy; and that other one felt like a lecture on sociology. But slowly, as I tinkered with my own stories, the characters—both men and women—began to change.

Everything I read and experienced had some effect, of course. In the 1970s and '80s, more women were writing science fiction, and women's writing (old and new) gained more critical importance. I found, and read, many more women writers. Many books with women protagonists had women as victims—sometimes as victims who'd managed to survive and succeed at something, but whose lives were shaped by having been victimized.

But as I reread *Dragonflight* until the paperback was thoroughly tattered, and gradually collected the other Pern books, Lessa stood out as an early example of someone who transcends the victim role—whose life is not defined (once she becomes Ramoth's partner) by the attack on her home and her family's death. As Weyrwoman, she has authority, and Lessa can snap out orders as quickly as any Weyrleader and fly her dragon to fight Thread just as well. As she matures, book by book, her ambition ranges wider but is tempered by experience and the wisdom she gains from it: she has grown beyond Ruatha Hold, and even beyond Benden Weyr. Such a character—a woman intelligent enough, strong enough, complicated enough—could not only star in a single book, but could anchor an entire multivolume story arc.

Again, that insight affected both my life and my writing: Lessa as not just a survivor, but a transcendent survivor, as she matures through the various books, retaining the essence of the self-directed, courageous, intelligent girl, but learning from her experience, softening the jagged edges without weakening her resolve to see justice done. And Lessa as an example of how writing could unpack human experience at multiple levels.

As a writer, I was slow to develop, especially slow to develop the confidence to believe I could write anything worth publishing (despite the Lessa influence). I was forty when I sold my first story and forty-three when my first book came out. I had never written a fan letter (believing that I shouldn't bother someone in the throes of creating a book) or met other writers. At my first Worldcon, I was full of awe and almost tongue-tied in the presence of those I admired.

So it was that a few years later, when my publisher called and asked if I'd like to collaborate with Anne McCaffrey, I was momentarily speechless. Breathless. *Anne McCaffrey?* Lessa's writer? And me? Together? "Does water run downhill?" I remember saying after fighting past the disbelief, followed immediately by "Yes, of course." That collaboration, on two of the Planet Pirates books, was like a master class. Working with Anne was pure delight—she was a generous, helpful, senior partner. I could ask questions; I could ask advice; I could offer ideas, some of which she liked and we used. On the second book, *Generation Warriors*, I asked about making up a couple of new alien races. "Have fun," she said. Wow. Not only was I playing in Anne McCaffrey's sandbox, but I had the freedom to rearrange the toys. (The blue, plush, horse-shaped mathematician . . . the spiky sulfur creature.)

Then came the launch of the first of those two books, *Sassinak*, at Dragon*Con, when I first met Anne McCaffrey in person. By this time, I knew that she also loved horses and music and that she admitted to a temper. I knew enough of her history—divorce, moving to Ireland, supporting her children as a single working mother—to see connections between her and many of her characters—including Lessa.

I was both eager and scared to meet someone who had generated so many different worlds, so very many different characters. Familiar shyness lasted all the way to the actual meeting and melted instantly in her warmth. It felt like suddenly acquiring a favorite aunt I hadn't known I had.

That meeting began a friendship that persisted over the next two and a half decades, until her death. When I finally got email, we could correspond that way (much easier than snail mail or telephone, given the time difference from Ireland to Texas). We ran into each other at conventions, very occasionally: Ireland and Texas are a long way apart.

More and more, as I came to know Anne better, I saw the part of her that generated a character like Lessa, although there was, as with any author and character, more to Anne than Lessa could show—the sparkling wit, for one thing, and that wonderful laugh—the graciousness with which she hosted visitors in her home or at a dinner at a convention. If she ever felt Lessa-impatience, she never showed it.

But the core of Lessa, her blunt brevity and power, burned bright in the core of Anne McCaffrey, and one incident in our friendship made that very clear. We shared an editor at the time, and I was not convinced the editor was right about something. So I asked Anne, explaining the situation. Back came the answer, with a Weyrwoman's authority. "She's right; it won't do. Fix it." She was, of course, right.

ELIZABETH MOON has published twenty-four novels including Nebula Award-winner *The Speed of Dark*, short fiction in anthologies and magazines, and three short fiction collections, including *Moon Flights* (2007). Her most recent novel is *Limits of Power* (Del Rey, June 2013). When not writing, she knits socks, photographs wildlife and native plants, pokes her friends with (blunted) swords, or sings in the choir. She likes horses, dark chocolate, topographic maps, and traveling by train.

When Robin Roberts approached Anne McCaffrey about writing her biography, the response among the family was "Yes, please!" Anne had talked for a while of taking time off to write her autobiography and had even started it once, but writing about herself wasn't as compelling to her as writing about Lessa or Killashandra or Helva.

Robin, with an academic's eye, listened much and spoke little, and soon was embraced by Anne's much-extended family. We were quite open with her, and her *Anne McCaffrey: A Life with Dragons* is currently the best biography of Anne McCaffrey available.

We were thrilled when we discovered that Robin was made Dean of the J. William Fulbright College of Arts and Sciences, not only for her but also for what it means to science fiction and fantasy as a whole: that the literature, so often derided in the past, has moved into general acceptance.

In this essay, Robin gives tribute to the literary impact of Anne McCaffrey from an academic standpoint.

Flying in New Directions
Anne McCaffrey's Literary Impact

ROBIN ROBERTS

WHEN ANNE MCCAFFREY published her first science fiction story in 1953, and even in the '60s and '70s, women writers and women's concerns were marginalized in science fiction, as they were in the real world. As shocking as it sounds today, in the mid-twentieth century, an editor could dismiss women's writing as "diaper copy," the phrase implying not only that the pages were disposable, but also, pejoratively, that the writing focused on women's mundane preoccupations, including romance, family relationships, emotions, and children. While some women had always written science fiction, its so-called Golden Age was dominated by male writers and characters. Male science fiction writers tended to emphasize action and problem solving, with female characters serving only as dangerous distractions to the male hero. (A classic example is Tom Godwin's 1954 story "The Cold Equations," selected as one of the best science fiction stories published before 1965 by the Science Fiction Writers of America; it features a pretty and foolish young girl who stows away on a one-man spaceship, endangering the lives of many people.) Science fiction magazines were edited by men, and the readership was presumed to be male; plots, illustrations, and dismissive comments about women and female aliens revealed a suspicion, and even fear, of femininity.

Until Anne McCaffrey. Through her original and compelling worlds, aliens, and plots, McCaffrey demonstrated that women writers could write powerful and popular science fiction.

As a young woman, I remember being frustrated by the limited roles available to women in science fiction. I enjoyed reading Isaac Asimov, Robert Heinlein, and other male writers, but I yearned for heroines with whom I could identify. *Dragonflight* and *The Ship Who Sang* opened my understanding of what women could do and be. (McCaffrey's books inspired me to write one of the first nonfiction books on gender and science fiction and to teach science fiction in university courses.) I wasn't alone. McCaffrey's fiction received recognition not only from the mainstream reading public, but also from science fiction fans and her peers, other published science fiction writers. In 1978, her Pern novel *The White Dragon* appeared on the *New York Times* Bestseller List. McCaffrey also has the distinction of being the first woman to win science fiction's two awards: the Hugo (awarded by readers) and the Nebula (awarded by published writers). McCaffrey authored 100 publications, sold millions of books, and her titles appear in more than a dozen languages. Many readers who thought they didn't like science fiction changed their minds after reading one of McCaffrey's novels, and dozens of the genre's writers credit her with inspiring them to become writers.

These distinctions alone merit McCaffrey a place in literary history, but her impact on popular fiction did not lie only in showing she was as talented as any male writer, blazing a trail that other female writers could follow. McCaffrey's legacy lies in the changes she brought about in science fiction literature itself.

Science fiction has been characterized as falling on a continuum, at one end "hard" science fiction, which focuses on the sciences such as biology, chemistry, and physics, and, on the other, "soft" science fiction, which is characterized, in contrast, by its emphasis on the so-called "soft" human sciences of psychology and sociology. The term "hard science fiction" appeared in the 1950s, as editors, writers, and readers were promoting the genre for its realistic scientific premises. As more female and male writers began focusing on characterization and social sciences in the genre in the 1970s, the corollary "soft science fiction" proved a useful publishing and fan term. Soft science fiction focuses as much on characterization as on scientific issues, and is as concerned with human emotions as it is with scientific premises. Hard science fiction was associated more with male writers and characters, and soft science fiction with women.

In the Golden Age of science fiction, the genre largely focused on a scientific premise or problem, solved using technology or scientific knowledge, by a male hero in an adventure setting. The science was the center of the story. Less emphasis was placed on character development or a complicated narrative. Anne McCaffrey's work was different. While her books were emphatically science fiction, not fantasy—set on other planets or in space, in the future, and interested in technology and science, not magic—she combined the traditional science focus of science fiction with previously derided female concerns like emotion, romance, and sexuality. In doing so, McCaffrey helped science fiction gain both larger audiences and widespread acceptability. Her complex, interesting female characters, who confronted emotional trauma and learned the value of tolerance, assertiveness, and leadership, brought in female readers, expanding science fiction's readership.

The Dragonriders of Pern, as McCaffrey's best-known and most successful series, provides a telling example of her literary innovations, which are evident from the very first story set on

Pern. *Dragonflight* focuses as much on Lessa and F'lar's relationship and Lessa's blossoming as an individual as it does on the science fictional setting of a planet and the urgent puzzle of how Pern ancestors defended the planet from the invasive spore called Thread. Readers identify with Lessa's outsider plight and follow with intensity her growing assimilation into the world of dragons and dragonriders. Lessa learning to love and be loved provides a compelling narrative. That emotional narrative is intertwined with a problem with a science-based solution: how to work with dragons to protect life on Pern. How the puzzle is solved, however, demonstrates an alternative to hard science fiction's traditional engineering or laboratory solution. It is not a lab of scientists or an action hero wielding a new weapon that saves the day. Instead, the ability to interpret a tapestry and understand a song's hidden meanings provides the critical clues. Female characters' appreciation and knowledge of traditionally (in our world) feminine texts provides Pern's redemption.

The importance of these feminine domestic arts is central to many plots in the Dragonriders of Pern series. It must have been especially surprising to readers, that first time, that songs, tapestries, and stories contained the knowledge needed to save the planet from Thread. Such a solution demonstrates, to the book's characters and to its readers, that art can be as important as science, and that art and science are both essential to human existence. It suggests, less explicitly, that both men and women are essential to society and that we ignore "feminine concerns" at our own peril.

The Dragonriders of Pern also raises another "feminine concern," relationships, to a place of world-saving importance—particularly the one between dragon and rider. Dragons and dragonriders share emotionally rich and rewarding collaborative relationships, ones that are essential to Pern's survival. Rather than fantasy monsters to be feared and killed, Pern's dragons are sentient beings created by science. In them, McCaffrey took the human-animal bonds we know from our own lives a step further, radically reimagining a fearsome creature into an intimate partner. What Isaac Asimov did for robots, transforming them from humanity's enemies to our supporters and friends, McCaffrey did for dragons. On Pern, dragons are sentient, competent, and caring companions with a believable scientific explanation for their existence.

As useful partners to humans, dragons play crucial social and emotional roles on Pern beyond their contributions to fighting Thread. Emotionally, a dragon's relationship with his or her rider is so important that, in most cases, should a dragon die, the human also will die from the shock of losing his or her dragon companion. Should the dragonrider die first, the dragon will fly *between* and die also. Because of their telepathic bond, dragons and their human riders can share complete openness and intimacy and provide a model for the kind of ideal, mutually supportive relationship that humans have difficulty achieving. Certainly the emotional relationship of Lessa and F'lar in *Dragonflight* is much more complicated and fraught with difficulty than the one between Lessa and her dragon, Ramoth. Literary critic Jane Donawerth suggests that McCaffrey's dragons and dragonriders offer an alternative to traditional heterosexual relationships based on male dominance. Perhaps fittingly, then, dragons also provide a source of social power. Through their relationships with dragons, female characters on Pern have a path to leadership, something as hard won at that time in literature as in real life.

In addition to making relationships the center of her narratives, McCaffrey dealt explicitly with sex and sexuality, and did so in a way that contrasted dramatically with that of most of her male contemporaries. Sex frequently wasn't mentioned at all: for example, the justly celebrated Isaac Asimov almost completely ignores sex, and his brilliant female scientist, Dr. Susan Calvin, eschews sex and femininity. If present, sexuality in texts by men tended to be oppressive, presented in a way that made clear the female character's complete subordination to men. In 1953, Philip Jose Farmer received a Hugo Award for the novella *The Lovers*, in which a female alien morphs into a male fantasy of a sexually attractive partner. This female alien only exists to sexually satisfy a human male even though the resulting pregnancy kills her. Her offspring look like just like her, suggesting that the next generation of females will fulfill the same subordinate role.

In contrast to such portrayals, McCaffrey depicted sex as a key part of a full and satisfying relationship of equals. In *Dragonflight*, Lessa first experiences sex when her queen dragon mates because when dragons mate, their riders feel compelled to have sex also. Since the experience is not initiated by Lessa, she faces the possibility of losing control of her body. Over time, however, she asserts her dragon's ability to out-fly undesirable suitors, and with her dragon's support, is able to assert herself as an independent female, including choosing to embrace her sexual desires. By the end of the novel, her involuntary association with F'lar has become a true partnership.

McCaffrey's willingness to assert the importance of a romance of equals in her dragonriders' relationships remains an important legacy for science fiction, but the sexual complexity of the dragonrider community may have been even more groundbreaking. Dragonriders have a noticeably different attitude toward sex than other groups on Pern due to the effect of dragon sexuality on the dragonriders' emotions and actions. Sex outside of traditional relationships is common. Also, if a rider of a female dragon is male, then he may very well end up mating with the male rider of a male dragon. McCaffrey depicted these relationships positively and even includes a romantic and sexual relationship between a male rider and a non-dragonrider male, a healer. While the Dragonriders of Pern does not present a polemic view of homosexuality, on Pern, homosexuality is normal and accepted.

Through both dragon-human relationships and Lessa and F'lar's partnership, McCaffrey valorized collaboration and relationship as an alternative model of leadership. However, this emphasis on collaboration, a traditionally feminine model of cooperation, extends beyond the content of her work to the development of it. As a writer, McCaffrey chose to open her worlds to other writers in what is sometimes called a "shared universe." McCaffrey has cooperated in more shared universes than any other science fiction writer, sharing not only Pern but also many other planets and concepts with several other writers. She cowrote numerous books in the Brainship universe, the Powers series, the Doona series, and the Planet Pirates series, among others. These books, authored with mid-list and early-career writers like Elizabeth Moon and Elizabeth Ann Scarborough, to name just two award-winning authors who cowrote with McCaffrey, provided invaluable financial and emotional support. Evidence of McCaffrey's generosity, these shared universe series show her influence as a writer who could create not just one very popular world, but several.

It is always a tribute to an author's genius if her works survive her own death and seem to have a life of their own (for example, Mary Shelley and *Frankenstein*). To create creatures, settings, and plots that can successfully continue in others' hands is a great tribute to a writer's creativity. Anne McCaffrey's Pern seems to be one of these.

McCaffrey carefully planned for this legacy, first cowriting books with her son Todd before turning the series over to him before she passed. As I write, the twenty-sixth Pern novel is being published. Todd McCaffrey wrote four Dragonriders of

Pern novels before his mother died and has continued the series with four others—all have made the *New York Times* Bestseller List. Just as Anne mentored and encouraged other writers, she also developed a writer in her own family.

Pern's continued popularity in Todd's hands is, however, only one measure of Anne McCaffrey's literary legacy. Her influence has been attested to by many other writers of subsequent generations and can be seen in the work of numerous writers who later continued and further developed the motifs she pioneered. After McCaffrey died in November 2011, there were dozens of moving tributes to her importance and influence. In an interview, Naomi Novik, author of the Temeraire series, described herself as a big fan of McCaffrey's and explained how her dragons were influenced by those of Pern. Similarly, Robin Hobb, author of the Rain Wild series, recently discussed the unique features of McCaffrey's dragons and acknowledged she followed McCaffrey's lead in creating scientifically plausible and intelligent dragons. Sharon Shinn's beautiful genetically altered humans with wings and their powerful and compelling use of music in her Samaria series owe a great deal to McCaffrey's ballads and harpers on Pern, as well as the dragons. Other works that bear the impress of McCaffrey's vision range from Terry Pratchett's Discworld to Christopher Paolini's Eragon books, and include writers such as Mercedes Lackey (another McCaffrey cowriter), Catherine Asaro, and many others.

If the genre of science fiction can be compared to a hold on Pern, Anne McCaffrey surely is its masterharper, singing songs of great beauty and power. She valorized the importance and power of the arts, especially singing, through the influence those arts had on her created worlds, and she herself lived up to this vision of art, by creating characters, worlds, and stories that have had a tremendous impact on our own world.

ROBIN ROBERTS is the dean of the J. William Fulbright College of Arts and Sciences, professor of English at the University of Arkansas, and author of five books on gender and popular culture, including the biography of Anne McCaffrey, *Anne McCaffrey: A Life with Dragons* (University Press of Mississippi) and *Anne McCaffrey: A Critical Companion* (Greenwood Press).

t was the late jan howard finder who first introduced me to Lois McMaster Bujold's work. He grabbed me at a convention in the dealer's room, dragged me along after him with his never-ending monologue, picked up a copy of *The Warrior's Apprentice*, paged it to a certain spot, and said, "Read this."

I did pretty much the same thing with Mum when I next saw her. Mum always eagerly poured through Lois' latest works and was thrilled to be asked to write any quotable words of praise for her books, saying most notably, "Boy, can she write!"

In her essay, Lois explains that some of the inspiration she received and built on came from none other than Anne McCaffrey—greater praise can no writer ask for!

Modeling the Writer's Life

LOIS MCMASTER BUJOLD

THE FIRST ANNE McCaffrey tale I ever read was also one of the most memorable works of its era. Sometime in the mid to late '60s, which was my mid to late teens, I encountered the short story "The Ship Who Sang" quite by chance in my random SF reading, in a battered paperback Judith Merril anthology that Wikipedia (but not my fuzzy memory) tells me must have been the Dell *7th Annual Edition The Year's Best S-F* (1963). I remember absolutely nothing else from that anthology.

To become a starship! To live for centuries! What a geek dream that was. (The tragic romance, not to mention the galaxy-famous singing career, was icing on the cake.) To be an SF girl geek in the 1960s, before the term had been repurposed or the concept even invented, was every bit as uncomfortable as one might imagine. But that story spoke to me.

My next encounter with this writer—I did not think of her as "a woman writer" at the time—was via my subscription to *Analog* magazine, which my dad had bought for me starting in 1964 and kept up for some years thereafter. This fell in the heart of editor John W. Campbell Jr.'s classic era. The story, of course, was "Weyr Search," which (thank you again, Wikipedia) was published there in the year I graduated from high school, 1967. I still remember the wonderful, sinister, moody black-and-white illustrations by John Schoenherr. Not yet being plugged into SF fandom, I was unaware that the story went on to win a Hugo (deservedly). The story stuck in my brain without that aid. I see in retrospect that Anne found the novella length to be very friendly for her ideas, as I was much later to discover in my own work.

My own youthful first stabs—"stabs," I think, is probably the most appropriate term—at writing began in eighth grade and continued on into high school and early college. I was heavily influenced, as young writers tend to be, by the fiction I then loved. I had actually started reading adult science fiction by age nine, as I picked up paperbacks and magazines left lying around the house by my engineering-professor father, who used to buy them for airplane reading when he went on consulting trips. My school libraries, and the three public libraries that I was eventually able to sporadically access (we lived out in the country at the edge of the suburbs, and reaching any library required co-opting a parent with a car), supplied the rest. Library SF/ Fantasy collections were much smaller in those days; one could read them all up. I first discovered Tolkien when I was fifteen; *Star Trek* came out when I was sixteen. Both fell on fertile soil already plowed by Campbell's *Analog*. Poul Anderson, Randall Garrett, and Frank Herbert (through the *Analog* serialization of the first *Dune* novel, also with magnificent Schoenherr illustrations) all came to me by that route.

It never crossed my mind that my gender was any barrier to the SF writing task. I had already encountered Andre Norton in my YA (then called "Juvenile"—what's with all the renaming, anyway?) early reading days and was entranced by the "People" stories of Zenna Henderson. Female scientists and female heroes? The James H. Schmitz stories, also found in *Analog*, modeled them for me handily. (Nile Etland!) Anne's work slotted right in.

Whatever fight was then going on in the genre trenches by women writers for recognition passed far over my head as a young reader. While I have had plenty of problems in my life as a woman, which I share with other women, and the usual allotment of struggles in my life as a writer, which I share with other writers, I can't say that I've ever felt particularly impeded, professionally, by being a woman writer. The SF genre, at least in the United States, seemed a pretty level playing field by the time I strolled in.

There were causes for this, and one of the most important was Anne McCaffrey. One of the most important *reasons* was her hard-earned popularity. Other women writers may get more academic attention, but Anne hit the *New York Times* list with a hardcover SF novel (*The White Dragon*, 1978), one of the first SF writers to ever do so. I can (nowadays) just picture the response in the SF editorial community—"Hey! Rival publisher has a best-selling woman writer! Why don't *we* have a best-selling woman writer?" followed by a sudden reevaluation of their slush piles. Anne's pioneering on the awards front was vital, but it is *sales* that allow publishers to stay in business—and to take chances on new writers.

As a very young reader, to me writers were represented at most by a few not-very-illuminating biographical lines in the backs of the books. Books themselves seemed to come out of the walls; there was no authorial or critical barrier between me and what I had not yet learned to call "the text." It was all the *story*, then, seeming to bloom spontaneously in my mind's eye as I read. Writers were distant figures, not connected in any way to my everyday world. This started to change for me when I discovered SF fandom and the convention scene soon after high school. My first SF convention was Marcon, in Columbus,

Ohio, in 1968. Even then, writer guests of honor were still rather distant, up on podiums or panels that I seldom made it to. (Although I came within inches of first meeting the young Robert Silverberg in a somewhat crowded convention motel swimming pool in Pittsburgh, Pennsylvania, circa 1970, by not *quite* accidentally kicking him in the head. I'm sure our later first meeting, whenever it was, was much better.) My fling with SF fandom in this period was brief, running perhaps four years all told, but it gave me knowledge of a major go-to resource a decade and a half later when I came back as a wannabe pro.

I'm afraid I missed most of the '70s and the early '80s in SF, just the period when Anne's career was building up. I was put off SF by the dreary dystopian turn it took into the New Wave and abandoned the genre in favor of mysteries, romance, general fiction, and boatloads of nonfiction. A somewhat too-early marriage (didn't seem like it at the time—twenty-one was as old as I'd *ever been*) diverted me out of college and into the workforce, and I lost track of wanting to be a writer. But a job in patient care at Ohio State University Hospitals and a staff card that admitted me to the university library's main stacks gave me both original life experiences and a new breadth of reading that were to pay off later.

From the mid-'80s, I was back in the SF scene, this time as an aspiring, and soon actual, pro, thanks to Baen Books picking *The Warrior's Apprentice* out of their slush pile. My next brush with Anne came through Baen, who evidently brought my books to her attention; they, and I, received a most valuable promotional blurb from her. (Although I do have a memory, totally disassociated from its context, of having a writer-guests-get-together sort of lunch with Anne at some convention or another in the late '80s or early '90s. Her beautiful silver hair made me think she was older than she perhaps actually was.)

I was, at the time, watching older writers like a hawk in an effort to pick up tips not so much for writing, but for how to live a writer's life—everything from dealing with contracts and tax records and royalty reports to public speaking to managing one's time and space as a self-employed person. My particular quirk in the late '80s was office-envy. I didn't have room for a home office in my house back then; my tasks were carted variously around from the back of my dining room to my kitchen table to my living room or bedroom to the couch in front of the big window at the Marion Public Library, as chance permitted. So in greenroom conversations and the like when I met colleagues, I often ended up asking them to tell me all about their home offices, rather like a person on a diet asking someone to describe their dessert. Roger Zelazny and Anne both stick in my mind as mentioning that their home offices looked out upon mountains, a tidbit which, in Anne's case, must have come from that convention lunch. (I never imagined that I might someday see her work space.)

The marketing idea of "sharecropping" popular SF universes was just getting rolling in those days. New and hungry young writers were frequently targeted as junior partners for these arranged marriages. Sometimes, as in publisher Jim Baen's case, it was also a ploy to bring new writers to the attention of a wider audience and turboboost their careers, a hat trick he subsequently pulled off several times. Sometimes, I'm afraid, it was just because new writers were cheap. My first such invitation was to write for a YA line in an Asimov robots-universe series, an offer I found very flattering then, but, by luck or some dim sense of self-preservation, turned down. The next such invite was a *lot* harder to say no to.

I was, as I recall, on a family vacation to my brother's place at Lake George, NY, (therefore midsummer, though I don't now remember the year) when someone at Baen caught up with me with a proposal to be the junior writer on an expansion of

Anne McCaffrey's Planet Pirates series. This was not one of her books I'd previously read; I think there may have been a quick dash to the closest B&N, an hour's drive away, for a cram course. I looked very seriously at the proposal for a week or so, trying to think my way into it, but it was in competition for my very single-track brain space with my own work in progress, so I at length took a deep breath and turned it down. (If it had been in the Ship Who Sang universe, a series expansion Baen took on later, they might well have had me.) In any event, the project went to Elizabeth Moon, which she later mentioned was a well-timed break for her as her own original creativity had hit a downturn at about that time due to difficult family obligations. And the book that I would have set aside was one that went on to win a Hugo Award for best novel. So that was better for both of us. (Elizabeth's collaborative work gained her some striking covers, though.)

My next encounter with the McCaffrey clan was the result of a string of random chances. Being still in the, so to speak, financially challenged phase of my writing career, I sought a roommate to split costs with for the fiftieth Worldcon in Orlando, Florida, in 1992, and ended up with a friend of a friend of a friend whom I had never before met (the chain actually went like this: Lillian Carl—Pat Anthony—Pat Anthony's writing group). *Barrayar* was up for a Hugo for best novel that year, and I was in the usual temporarily insane and wholly distracted state of mind, which that experience tends to engender in hungry young nominees. Since I had no other guest, I invited my roommate, an aspiring writer, along to the Hugo ceremony. Todd McCaffrey was also there on his mother's behalf for her nomination for *All the Weyrs of Pern*. He did seem enviably calmer than I was, though I expect he, too, had the Schrodinger's-cat problem of holding in mind coherent acceptance remarks that one might or might not be called upon to deliver.

As it chanced, the rocket was bestowed on *Barrayar*; caught out by I-do-not-remember-what need to be in two places at once right after, I bestowed it in turn on my roommate to take back to our somewhat distant (and therefore cheaper) motel room. Todd, gentlemanly, ended up assisting her with the awkward chore, and, apparently, an acquaintance was struck up.

The next I knew of all this was when I was invited to say a few words at their wedding in August of 1994. In Ireland.

I was still in my broke phase and recently divorced, although closer to climbing up out of poverty than I could have fore-seen at the time. (I have always regarded my writing income as fairy gold, not to be relied upon.) I was also in a time crunch, readying my fifteen-year-old daughter for departure to an AFS year in the Netherlands, on money mostly borrowed from her maternal grandmother. But—Ireland! Anne McCaffrey's place! I delicately angled for an airplane ticket, stomped both financial and maternal guilt in the head, and accepted.

It was a marvelous trip, filling what had been a blank space on my mental map of the world with memories of unexpected beauty and fascinating details. A kindly neighbor down the road put me up—I still remember her hydrangeas, my first encounter with that strange litmus flower, and her Jack Russell terriers, my first encounter with that breed of dog—and I was able to visit Anne's house several times. You can bet I was paying very close attention. Modeling, by that time, had finally become a conscious process for me, not least because it was so much a part of how I had learned to write. How did another female writer, also divorced and towing a family, put it all together and achieve success? Such practical career-maintenance skills are not taught in any literature or writing class. What does doing life well look like?

Her place was not, contrary to fannish legend, an Irish castle, but a comfortable, rambling house built in the local modern style. (All right, the indoor swimming pool was probably not Irish standard.) Also not entirely standard, though more common in rural Ireland than around here, were the stable, arena, and pastures, although, Vorkosigan-like, Anne had clearly mastered the art of finding the most superior minions for help. Help! What a concept! (My life was very much do-it-all-myself-or-it-won't-get-done-at-all at that point.) Also, Maine Coon cats and kittens!

The first things to seize my eye upon entering were naturally the Michael Whelan original paintings for some of Anne's best book covers lining the hall leading onto the living room. But I did get a glimpse of her office—basically a modest back bedroom repurposed but, as advertised, looking out the window upon, if not exactly mountains, some very green hills. Also of great interest was the way she kept her foreign-publications-records file as an organized library of author's copies, lining one whole wall of an upstairs hall/room. As is very common for writers, academics, and serious fans, her personal library overflowed into spaces and climbed walls not, perhaps, originally architecturally intended for such, but properly internally organized. Her kitchen seemed a dream of space and modernity—I'd been living in a narrow slot of a kitchen last remodeled in the late '60s, dark and cramped and shabby in avocado and gold. To paraphrase a line from a movie, my not-so-subliminal response might be summed up: "Waiter! Bring me a life like that woman is having!"

Todd's tales of their earlier and more straitened days in Ireland both put this success into perspective and gave me hope. An old McCaffrey family line quoted—I'm not sure if it was originally from Todd or his sister—"Gosh, Mom, wouldn't it be nice to have pancakes for dinner just because we *liked* them?" rang a plangent bell. Substitute "French toast" in my household's case.

As an added bonus, after the wedding Todd took a day to drive a carload of us around to see both some of the lovely Irish countryside, including the ruins of an ancient monastery, and to drop in on Diane Duane and Peter Morwood. This gave me a chance to glimpse yet another version of how-writers-can-live, as they were then domiciled in a fascinating old thatched-roof cottage. Peter, magician-like, conjured an excellent spicy chicken dinner for his late and lingering guests. I enjoyed the sense of a widening of my possibilities. I'd had a similar benefit from visiting C. J. Cherryh's home in Oklahoma City a bit earlier, in 1990, when I was a guest of SoonerCon. How may writers live? How can we learn from each other how to do it better, by all measures?

It is really only in retrospect, writing this essay, that it occurs to me how much the Ireland trip had to do with my gathering the gumption to uproot myself, library, pets, and children and leave Marion, Ohio, for Minneapolis the following year, when an unexpected media-rights-sale windfall made that escape possible. Looking around, I see I have achieved the foreign-rights library, the cool paintings on the wall, and the back bedroom office looking out into green space, granted that mine is an overgrown railroad cutting rather than mountains—though I rather like the Soo Line trains, twice a day. Also, if not minions, at least I have a cleaning service every other week and someone else to cut my rather difficult lawn. Modeling. It's how humans learn.

The trick of it is to model from the *best*.

I last saw Anne in person at the 2005 Nebula banquet in Chicago, where the Science Fiction and Fantasy Writers of America honored her (and themselves) by bestowing upon her their Grand Master Award, and I carried off my second Nebula Award for best novel for *Paladin of Souls*. It was a most happy concatenation of events, as I thought of *Paladin* as very much my chick book. Grrls rule! (As my younger friends would phrase it.) We were at different tables for the banquet, so I didn't get to talk to her very much, though I did get a chance to lean over her shoulder at one point and say, "And it's about time!" What I remember most clearly were not her acceptance remarks—nor, God knows, my own—but how she was so warmly surrounded by her very supportive family and how Todd and the grandkids present welcomed her back to their table by a raucous shower of colorful silly string, the closest they could come to both indoor fireworks and Pernese Thread.

Because a writer's life at its best includes balance between the professional and the personal, and Anne clearly had a knack for both.

LOIS MCMASTER BUJOLD was born in 1949, the daughter of an engineering professor at Ohio State University, from whom she picked up her early interest in science fiction. In addition to her Vorkosigan Saga science fiction series from Baen Books, her fantasy from HarperCollins includes the award-winning Chalion series and the Sharing Knife series. Her work has been translated into twenty-one languages.

Wen Spencer's first book, *Alien Taste*, was thrust upon me by Anne McCaffrey when I arrived for one of my annual visits to Ireland. "You've got to read this!"

I did. Fortunately, there were already two sequels in print, so when I finished the first at some dark hour in the morning, I could snag the second off the bookshelves of the hall library and continue.

When I mentioned Wen Spencer later to some people in Pern fandom, they told me in lowered voices, "You know she started out writing Pern fanfiction."

That was one of the benefits of writing fanfiction about Pern that no one had ever considered. It was learning this story that started the re-think on Mum's fanfiction policy: if writing fanfiction led to such brilliant writers, then it seemed something to be encouraged (within the limits of propriety and copyright). I'm very glad to have Wen Spencer here in this tribute; she holds a special spot in our memories of Pern.

All the Weyrs of Pern

WEN SPENCER

I WAS BORN in 1963, in the literary equivalence of the middle of nowhere. From as young as seven years old, I knew I wanted to be a writer. More specifically, I wanted to be a writer of fantastic stories. The place and time of my birth, however, meant that this ambition was something on par with aspiring to be a wizard. My parents were supportive but as clueless as if I wanted to do magic.

How do you write a science fiction novel? How do you create a world other than our own? How do you make a fantastic world richly layered? How do you create and maintain conflict for the entire novel instead of just stringing together fights with monsters? My parents had no idea. My high school teachers taught me how to craft a sentence and how to type on electric typewriters (state of the art at the time). They gave me scores of famous short stories and classic novels to read. But how to actually craft a science fiction novel? They were totally ignorant of the process. My only guideposts were *Writer's Digest* magazines and occasional books on writing I'd find in the library and memorize. All of these assumed that you were writing literary short fiction, not science fiction novels.

Somewhere in the mid-'70s I found Anne McCaffrey. Since

her first novel, *Restoree* (still a personal favorite), came out when I was four, I'm no longer sure which of her novels I discovered first. I know by 1977 I had tracked down all that she had written. I can vividly remember waiting for *The White Dragon* to come out. I was fifteen at the time, and it was the first novel I ever bought in hardcover.

It wasn't until the 1980s, though, that Anne changed my life.

I had spent my teenage years attempting to write short stories and submitting them to magazines like *Asimov's* and *Analog* and *Omni*. The professional markets were black holes to drop stories into. Each story generated identical form rejection letters. Was I submitting anything near what you could call a short story? The badly mimeographed form letters gave no clue. How did you move from a few thousand words of a short story to a novel? How did you create an entire other world? Nothing I could get my hands on explained the mysterious process.

I went to college and minored in English Writing. I took every undergraduate fiction class that they gave. The professors all forbade me from writing science fiction, and none of them tackled novels. Four years, and I was left just as clueless as I started. When I graduated, computers were just appearing on office desks. Word processing was in its infancy. The internet was yet to be commercialized.

I've watched other people write endless short stories, submit them to professional markets, and slowly lose faith in their abilities because they were beating themselves against immovable rocks. There was a chance I might have followed, eventually giving up hope on being a writer.

In college, though, I had made one very important friend. Her name was June Drexler Robertson. She loaned me her extensive collection of science fiction novels. She taught me *Dungeons & Dragons*. She tutored me in physics and Greek mythology. And she knew the coolest people. They were fen, as they liked to be called, using the irregular plural of "fan" to mean only one particular type of fan, a person that attended science fiction conventions.

Originally, fandom was only focused on books and mostly ignored television and movies. This was, in part, because there was so little of it. *Star Trek* changed that. After it was canceled, its fans were desperate for more. Largely ignored by the programming staff of regular science fiction conventions, they gathered together in the hallways to discuss their favorite shows. They started to write stories based on the *Star Trek* characters in what became known as fanfic and passed it around to each other. Finally they started to hold their own conventions, nicknamed by the other fens (with a sneer in their voice) as media cons. The sneer came from the fact that unlike other conventions, they were often run by for-profit companies that paid the actors of canceled TV series to appear. In 1978, the media con subculture started the fan-run MediaWest Convention in Michigan.

At MediaWest, there was a large and hungry crowd of fen looking for more of what it loved. The authors of fanfic no longer had to pass out stories to one or two friends that they met by chance; they could now sell it in the dealer's room. These were borderline to outright illegal magazines, infringing on copyrights willy-nilly, hand-typed, mimeographed, and badly stapled. These "zines" were tailored for the masses, featuring the main characters of television shows, and thus tailored toward stories that were collected to be sold. They started with *Star Trek* and expanded. They included *Star Wars*, *Blake 7*, *Battlestar Galactica*, and *Man from Uncle*, just to name a few.

People—well, actually, mostly women for some reason—who had been lost and alone in their hometown could find like-minded fans just by standing by the table selling "fanzines" of what they liked. To stay in contact, they created fan clubs.

A new form of fanfic developed out of these clubs. Instead of focusing on the main characters of the work, each member had a chance to live in the fictional world via a new and original character that was wholly their own creation. They could be an ensign on the *Enterprise*. They could be a viper pilot on the *Galactica* or its sister ship, the *Pegasus*. They could be a wolf rider elf in Wendy Pini's Elfquest universe.

Or they could be a dragonrider on Pern.

Pre-internet, the Facebook of fen were APAs, or Amateur Press Associations. Each member of an APA would type up a page or two (or more if they had the time and money) and duplicate their pages as many times as there were members. Content ranged from book reviews to essays on current trends to personal journals. If an APA had thirty members, each member would make thirty copies of their section. Remember that while there were photocopiers available, they were expensive, often a quarter a page at a time when a can of soda was thirty cents. Since mimeographs had been around forever, people often used old machines they'd bought secondhand. The members would mail the copies of their section to a central mailer. She would collate everyone's sections, create a cover and an index, bind all the pages together into a magazine, and mail it to the members.

The fanfic clubs created a hybrid of the APA. They started up newsletters where each member would write a section and mail it to the editor. Dues would not only cover the cost of mailing the newsletter but also the copying cost. The editor was often the person with access to some type of cheap duplicating machine.

Up to 1984, I was totally ignorant of most of fandom. That summer, though, my friend June Drexler Robertson turned to me and said, "Your family has a large farm, doesn't it?"

My reaction was probably the same as yours is now. *What? Huh?*

June had joined a Pern fanfic club. She didn't have to explain
Pern to me; I had all of Anne's books. It was "fanfic club" that I
needed explained. It turned out that all around the world, fans
of Anne's were finding each other and creating clubs where they
could live on Pern via shared fiction.

Sharing, however, meant that not everyone could be a
queen rider that could hear all dragons. (Yes, almost every new
member had to be told that they couldn't hear all the dragons
nor that they could automatically be a queen rider; otherwise,
the weyr would have been fifty queen riders and two or three
very happy but exhausted bronze riders.) Since fictional leadership somehow overruled common sense, it turned out that for a
club to function, the people who ran the club had to take up the
key positions. The Weyrleader, Senior Queen, and Weyrsinger
went to the people that created the club, covered costs when
dues fell short, scoured conventions for new members, collected
material for the newsletters, copied them, and mailed them.
That way a member wouldn't be telling the "club officers" that
they could buck the system because "the Weyrwoman said I
could."

Every new member was encouraged to think beyond Lessa
to create a different kind of character, often to fill a gap in the
weyr. Journeyman harper was the favorite second choice. Once
a talented author took over a craft and their story appeared in
the newsletter, other members would drift toward that choice.
Woodcrafting became popular in our club after Melissa Cran-
dall took over the weyr's woodshop and wrote sections so vivid
you could nearly smell the sawdust.

Another overlap of fiction and reality was the location of
the club. The clubs were fiercely territorial despite the fact that
technology made it difficult if not impossible to coordinate the
fictional worlds. Once a club laid claim to a weyr or a hold,
they would defend it from other clubs using it as their home.

I think that it came from the fact that different clubs would come up with slight variations on the world, and they didn't want to be confused with other clubs with a radically different spin on Pern.

Ista Weyr was the first fan club with its leadership based in New Orleans. Fort Weyr was a close second. When all the northern weyrs were taken, the Southern Continent was divvied up into wholly fan-created slices. After that, new clubs decided to move forward in time. Fort Weyr Tenth Pass was a totally different beast than Fort Weyr Ninth Pass.

While the initial meeting of members had been at conventions (because there was no internet to provide a way to find each other otherwise), the clubs began to hold Gathers. My friend June was looking for a campground for the third annual Gather of her club and remembered that my family had a farm with a large open field perfect for camping.

We had thirty-some people that summer of 1984. I was twenty-one, fresh out of college, still desperate to be a writer, but unsure how actually to go about it. I was skeptical of this whole "fan club" idea, but the members all shared my love of science fiction. They had Anne's book memorized. They had made giant papier-mâché eggs with little statues of dragons inside for candidates to impress. (They crack like gunshots when you smash them open.) We ate roast wherry (turkey) and homemade bubbly pies and sang late into the night, led by the Weyrsinger who played the guitar. It was a lot of fun, but I wasn't hooked yet.

Toward the end of the weekend, someone handed me the club's little ten-page newsletter called the Harper Beat. It was created by pasting text onto eleven-by-seventeen-inch paper, photocopying it, and folding it in half, so it created a booklet. One page was a report from the Weyrwoman, who was the club's founder and president. The vice president was the Weyrleader, and his report was called Kreelings. They talked about club memberships and activities and their daily lives. I ignored those two columns. What hooked me was that the rest of the news-letter was a story. Eight pages of fluff from the Weyrsinger filled with everything I loved about Pern. The dragons. The fire-liz-ards. The weyr.

"June says you write. Why don't you write something for the newsletter?"

I had never considered writing fanfic before. I had no desire to create stories set in someone else's world. The fan club, though, offered two things I couldn't resist: an editor and an audience.

They explained Anne's rules to me. At the time you couldn't use any of Anne's characters nor could you set any story in Benden Weyr. A club whose members were air force pilots with "silver dragons" triggered a rule that only Anne's stan-dard five colors could be used. Men couldn't ride gold dragons and women weren't allowed to ride bronzes. And of course, we weren't allowed to sell our fiction.

I sat down and tried to write the persona I had used all weekend. He was a brown rider from another weyr. His weyr-mate had recently died, and his grief had caused him to come in conflict with his wingleader. The trouble had escalated to a knife fight. He'd won the fight only to be transferred out before more trouble could follow. He was an angst-ridden, battered man. I wrote him coming to the new weyr and handed the "story" to the editor, Julia Ecklar. (Yes, the club fostered two John Campbell award winners. Julia won the award in 1991, and I won in 2003.)

"It's nice," she said in a tone that clearly meant that it was barely acceptable. "It's just not a real story. It's a vignette."

"A what?"

"Vignette. Slice of life. A *story* is when a hero has a problem. See, in my story, the Weyrsinger discovers the problem in the first scene. In the second scene, he attempts to fix the problem and only makes it worse. Third scene, he attempts again and fails. Fourth scene, he resolves the problem. That's a story. I'm practicing telling a story with only four scenes, but you can take more."

This triggered a great deal of rereading famous SF short stories to verify that she was completely correct. (Her method of limiting the number of scenes turns out to be a great way to focus on what a scene is about and why you're writing it.)

Well, I couldn't wrap my brain around what kind of difficulties would face a middle-age widower bonded to an animal the size of a small jet. I was twenty-one and still working on the whole first serious boyfriend thing. I scrapped the brown rider and came up with a new character, one whose problems would be easier to grasp. His name was Zachafiddel, but he was nicknamed Zac. He was a twelve-year-old apprentice beast herder who took care of the flocks of wherries that the dragons fed on. He was new to the weyr, ignorant of how things worked, and had an abusive journeyman.

I wrote up a short story and sat nervously as Julia read it. After a few minutes, she sighed and handed it back. "It's still a vignette."

It took two more attempts before I grasped "story." The newsletter was published every other month, so I managed to write six stories before the next annual Gather. I basked in the glow of people telling me that they liked my writing and loved my character. Zac grew up as time passed, becoming a journeyman beast herder, and then searched as a candidate. Eventually he impressed a bronze and changed his name to Z'del.

The club grew, and what the members read in the newsletter encouraged them to also write stories about their characters. Like me, several were learning the craft before breaking out into their own fiction. We had solid writing skills. What we lacked was the ability to take it to novel length in a world of our own creation.

Anne had created a rich and detailed world. The wonderful thing about fanfic writing is that you're free to ignore world-building at first; your audience knows all the cool details that the creator laid into place. I could write about my character stripping off his wherhides as he walked into his weyr, uncovering the glows to light his way, and then using soapsand to bathe without having to invent and explain anything. I could focus on getting my character through four scenes to set up and solve a problem.

Once I got short story structure nailed down, I discovered that I could create two levels of conflict. The surface level would be a simple world problem that gave my character something to do while he struggled with inner emotional conflict. The two could be thematically connected but otherwise unrelated. The mental lightbulb went on while I was writing a story about Zac attending a Gather immediately after walking the tables and becoming a journeyman. He's been charged with keeping all the boys he'd been an apprentice with under control. He's distracted, though, by his girlfriend asking him to move in together.

The outer conflict is trying to have fun with his girlfriend while keeping track of the younger boys in thick crowds, breaking up fist fights, and chasing accidently freed herd animals. These are all things out of his control; he can only react to them.

The internal conflict is trying to cope with being "adult." What decision does he make in regard to things he can control? How grown up does he want to be? Does he try to be responsible or does he focus on having fun? Does he really want to be in a relationship as serious as living together?

For the first time, I realized that there could be a disjuncture between what a character was doing and what he was thinking. Zac could be trying to dance with one eye out for his apprentices, but what was going on his mind wasn't *step one, two, three, spin, clap . . . was that a wherry?* No, no, he was thinking *Move in together? Oh shards, what do I say? What do I say?*

None of my college courses or writing books ever explained conflict in this manner. I don't think I would have easily made the realization writing short stories set in worlds of my own creation. I would have been too caught up fighting with world-building to pay attention to that fine point.

With this freedom, there was also this wonderful feedback from Julia explaining where I'd gone wrong with a story (often demanding rewrites until I got it right) and the general membership telling me that I was great. (I wasn't actually "great," but I was writing exactly what they loved: Pern.) Even in the age where we were photocopying all the stories and mailing them to the membership with regular postage, the feedback was rich and heady.

Anne was six books into Pern when I started to write fanfic. Once I got a handle on the basics of storytelling, I wanted to expand my story arc, to reach more toward novel length via a series of related short stories. But to grow, I first had to understand Pern. How the weyr and holds worked together. How they came into conflict. How the crafts fit in.

Pern at the basic level is man versus nature. Thread would destroy all life on the planet if given a free rein. The dragons, while full of wonderful beneficial abilities, came with negative side effects, from the dangerous awkwardness of hatching, to the uncontrollable mating flight, to the perils of going between. I quickly learned that primal forces result in simple conflicts with fairly straightforward plots. The character has only one choice: do or die. It made for exciting action scenes. A longer story arc, however, required complex conflict to support it.

What Anne did so ingeniously was set up a three-branch society structure of dragonriders, holders, and craftsmen. They
desperately needed each other to survive, but were in constant
conflict on multiple levels. In addition, each branch was hierar-
chical in nature, so each group also contained conflicts within
itself.

While many of the dragonriders might have started as hold-
bred, the very nature of being searched and then impressing
conveyed a sense that they had been elevated above the normal
man. If they didn't feel that way, their dragon telling them that
they're the greatest thing on the planet would soon convince
them. They then risked life and limb to protect the planet. It is
natural that they would assume that they were owed a comfortable life, if not the best of everything. And they brought their
living "jet fighter" to any meeting to back up their demands of
being supported by the holders and crafters. Given their dragon
and an open field, they could win any one-on-one fight. It led
to a certain "oh *yeah*, me and my *fire-breathing* dragon will take
on you and your flashy runner" arrogance to their interactions
with the holders and crafters. Their sense of entitlement, however, did not sit well with the other two.

The fact that there are five different dragons—gold, bronze,
brown, green, and blue—creates division within the weyr. Anne
set up that there was only a handful of gold dragons per weyr
during the earlier passes and a score or so of bronze. The riders
of these colors could and often would suddenly find themselves
in leadership positions. A senior queen dies, a bronze unex-
pectedly wins a mating flight, and the weyr's highest positions
would suddenly change hands. It meant that candidates for
these dragons had to be vetted carefully. There would be fierce
and often bitter competition for the gold and bronze dragons,
and people would be disappointed to be rated "just a blue."

Because the dragons control who sleeps with whom, the

weyr's society had to be free of moral judgment on sexuality. For the weyr to function, a person couldn't be shamed for acts that the dragons forced them to commit. This included women having children with multiple partners and same-sex pairings. Nothing put this into perspective more clearly than a dice game we came up with to play at the club's Gathers. People would often announce that their dragon/fire-lizard was rising for a mating flight to create a random element to their story fodder. For pure bragging rights (the clubs were mostly women after all), people would attempt to "catch" the rising female. Bronzes were given the best odds, but browns and blues would occasionally win due to a combination of who was competing, when the flight was announced, and pure luck. Add in the fact that Anne wrote of males on female green dragons that rose in mating flights every few months, and homosexuality had to be considered as a natural consequence.

The title "Lord Holder" goes far to understand the moral mentality of the larger holds. The lord holders supplied the world with food and shelter. They were kings, complete with armies, and expected to be in charge. They tended to see craftsmen within their territories as talented servants, to be fed and housed only as long as they produced. As with kings of old, they are concerned with passing on their wealth to their heirs. Since a man can only be sure that he's providing for his children if a woman only has sex with him, the holders value female monogamy and morally view sex as "for procreation only." All sexual freedom is considered perversion. They viewed the dragonriders as morally corrupt mercenaries.

Within the holds were dozens of levels of society, from the lord holder's family, to "cot holders" who headed up satellite households, to drudges. In Anne's books, each lord holder dealt with those under him differently. In the Harper books, the Half-Circle Sea Hold is staffed mostly by extended family. (Yes,

I know that it's not a major hold, but it serves as a point of reference.) Under Fax, Ruatha's drudges were slaves living on the edge of starvation, constantly beaten. Under Jaxom, the same drudges lived more like maids and butlers of an English manor.

The crafters had the short end of the stick on Pern. Intelligent and guarding over the ancient knowledge of their past, they nonetheless needed the food and shelter that the lord holders controlled. Steeped in lore (especially the harpers), they respect the dragonriders but rarely can openly act against the will of the lord holders. In order to protect their craft, they need gifted children, which means the child's parentage doesn't matter. There are indications that the crafters have a less rigid sexual moral code than the holders.

The social structure of the crafts, however, was very rigid and constantly marked by the rank knots that the crafters wore. Competition between individuals was often fierce for coveted positions of higher rank. Piemur is made a target not so much because he is small but because his intelligence quickly put him on the fast track in the drumming heights. Judging by Menolly's testing to become journeyman harper, the merit advancement protected the craft against its knowledge base eroding, but a great deal of politics went into any promotion. It seems to indicate that walking the tables also controlled who had power within the craft.

(Interestingly, the clubs chose to echo Pern's political structures. New members often were asked for real-life experience to match up with fictional ability. For example, the beast healers of one club wanted writers who had some veterinary medicine training. In addition to knowledge, the new members were vetted as to how well they played with others in the shared world prior to being able to claim a higher fictional rank. I joined an online role-playing club and applied to be an apprentice beastherder. The person playing the master beastherder interviewed me to see if I was knowledgeable enough to be an apprentice. Since I'd been raised on a farm, I surpassed even their level of understanding of what herding animals required. I was only allowed to apply to be an apprentice. If I proved myself over time, they would allow me to advance to apprentice and then to journeyman.)

Thus Anne became my teacher in world-building. Looking back, it's almost like she took my hands, ran them over the bones of her world, showing me the layers so I could do it myself. The key lay in simple complexity. With a handful of sentences scattered through the first book, she set up the basic structure of weyr, holds, and crafts. From the lord holders to the drudges, from F'lar to the lower cavern workers, from Master Robinton to the apprentice harpers—all three branches of Pern society are sketched out to be later filled in.

As a writer of fanfic, what I was doing was filling in at even smaller details. Anne stated that there was a beasthold at the weyr for the animals that the dragons fed on. There are mentions of a lake and the feeding pens. I took my own knowledge of farms, animals, and butchering animals to weave a reality. It made me realize that that was what Anne was doing in every book. In *Dragonflight,* she created Master Robinton and the concept of harpers. In *Dragonsong*, she added in the details of the harper hall based on her knowledge of boarding schools and opera.

Step by step, I was learning more and more about writing. After dozens of independent short stories that only occasionally shared plot points, five of the fan club's writers decided to write one massive joint story about a Threadfall that goes horribly bad. We gathered at my house and created a plot line. We would write the same event from the point of view of our character. Everyone's first scene would be the morning of the Threadfall as the weyr prepares to fight, and would introduce our character's individual conflict. A second scene would establish the location of everyone as the dragonriders met the leading edge of the fall. The third scene would detail the cascading disaster that would have dragons falling from the air. A fourth scene depicted all the characters reacting as the enormity of the disaster struck them. The fifth and six scenes showed the struggle to save the day and then deal with the aftermath. The last scene wrapped up each character's own personal storyline as it had been detoured by the accident. Seven scenes times five characters gave us thirty-five scenes for a total of 50,000 words, which is the technical definition of a novel.

At the time, my character Zac was the journeyman in charge of the beasthold. He'd been recently searched, which meant that someday he would have greater responsibility than just taking care of a couple hundred wherries and a handful of troublesome apprentices. Would he be able to handle the duties of being a dragonrider in a fighting wing? Would he be able to instantly react to protect not only himself and his dragon, but his wingmates and all of Pern? What if he impressed a bronze and one day became a wingleader? As the wounded came flooding in, he suddenly found himself as the person in charge on the ground. It made him realize that he had what it took to stay collected while making life-and-death decisions.

A whole Christmas tree full of light bulbs went off in my head. For the first time I understood the structure of a novel. It was this simple unit I'd been practicing over and over, just expanded. The four-scene short story was in truth echoing the basic building blocks of a novel: setup, complications, resolution, and wrap-up. Each of these four blocks can be treated as separate subbuilding blocks. For example, the setup itself can be broken down to the character's discovery of a problem (setup), the elements that complicate that problem (complications), the character coming to terms with—and thus the reader becoming fully aware of—the scope of the problem (resolution in terms of setting up the story arc), and the first plan of action that the character takes to resolve the problem (the wrap-up that leads to the four subblocks of the complication). It all clicks together like fictional Legos. A novel with multiple viewpoint characters would only need a few scenes of each building block to tell each character's story arc, just like we did for the Pern fanfic novel. A novel with only one viewpoint character would need several problems presented to the character, each problem being given its own story arc to interweave with the others to create a long enough story to qualify it as a novel. If I did this in a world that I created, then I would have something to sell.

And that's what I did. The hardest part of it was walking away from the rich and heady praise that I was getting from writing fanfic. What made it bearable was that during several failed attempts (and then many successful novels afterward), my first readers have all been members of Anne's fan club. They were willing to give me the benefit of the doubt and read my original work. And because I'd read their fanfic, I knew they were good and creative writers in their own right.

In 1989, the club pooled resources and rented a van and drove down to Atlanta to see Anne at Dragon*Con. We had taken a big banner that I had made for our Gathers, and we hung it from our hotel room's balcony, where you could see it from the atrium, announcing to the entire con that Anne's most rabid fans were there. I had a hardcover copy of *Dragon's Dawn*, and I stood in line to get it signed. Not to me, but to my Pern character, bronze rider Z'del, because through him, Anne had totally changed my life.

Just like my first attempts at short stories, it took me several tries to produce a publishable novel. Thanks to my experience with writing fanfic, though, I was confident that I would succeed; I just needed to keep trying. When I received personal rejection letters, I was actually delighted because it meant I had nearly succeeded and that obviously next project I'd reach my goal. In 2001, my first novel, *Alien Taste*, was published. To my ultimate fangirl joy and delight, I learned that Anne had read my novel and loved it. I *grinned* all day and called everyone I knew to let them know. No other review or award that I've received has meant as much to me as Anne's praise.

———————————

WEN SPENCER won the John Campbell Award for Best New Writer in 2003. She has written ten novels, several of which have been translated into German, Japanese, and Russian. She lives in Hawaii near a volcano with a massive caldera much like the weyrs described in the Pern novels, only lava is spewing out of hers. She now considers Anne's famous short bio as a coded warning to new writers that they will have to write endless bios about themselves.

Anne McCaffrey was first introduced to Bill Fawcett back in 1984 when he was working with Mayfair Games. The folks at Mayfair were science fiction fans and wanted to make a Dragonriders of Pern board game.

As I was big into board games, Mum made me point on the project, and I found myself proposing names for all the minor holds and designing their colors and liveries. It was while we were working on the board game that Bill suggested that I write a piece to put inside the advanced rules booklet. This piece became "Threadfighting Tactics on Pern." (That same piece later went into *The Dragonlover's Guide to Pern* as "Training and Fighting Dragons.")

Shortly after that, Bill met this really nice lady, and at some point while they were dating, she took a very small dinner on which Bill remarked diplomatically. The lady—Jody Lynn Nye—said, with a twinkle in her eye as she punned, "Well, a waist is a terrible thing to mind."

When Bill reported this to me later, he added, "And that's when I *knew* that I had to marry her!"

Bill and Jody have been family ever since. Their connection with Pern fandom grew not just from the board game and *The Dragonlover's Guide to Pern* but also from two choose-your-own-adventure books that Jody penned in the Pern universe, *Dragonfire* and *Dragonharper*. During the past several years, Bill and Jody have been found regularly at Dragon*Con, often at the dedicated *Weyrfest* track.

The McCaffrey Effect

JODY LYNN NYE AND BILL FAWCETT

SCIENCE FICTION FANS are a passionate group. They come together, either at conventions or online, for the love of a shared vision of the future. The books or movies they love are, for them, a momentary escape from mundane life. While most fans restrict their involvement to reading or viewing their favorites, some devote themselves more deeply, perhaps wearing costumes, learning invented languages, and forming hierarchies as depicted in their favorite stories. Few, though, have formed a community as cohesive, widespread, or ongoing as those who have read Anne McCaffrey, and particularly those who love the Dragonriders of Pern series. As not only devotees of Anne's body of work but also creators therein,* we have had the rare chance to experience this phenomenon

---

* Bill was one of the owners of Mayfair Games and was on the design team that developed the *Dragonriders of Pern* role-play game (and, not incidentally, employed one Todd McCaffrey to help work on it). He packaged not only the Crossroads game books, *Dragonharper* and *Dragonfire*, but also *The Dragonlover's Guide to Pern*, as well as a number of novels coauthored by Anne and less established writers in some of her other universes. Jody wrote *The Dragonlover's Guide to Pern*, *Dragonharper*, and *Dragonfire*, as well as coauthoring four of those other books; writing a solo sequel to one, *The Ship Errant*; and penning short stories for a few of Anne's own anthologies.

firsthand, to sit down and get to know those who are deeply affected by it: Anne's fans. We asked a number of longtime fans for the reasons they are so devoted to Anne's work. They shared their thoughts and feelings about being part of the community that has grown up in the last few decades, which we've pulled together with our own, in hopes of sharing a sense of that community with you.

Welcome to Pern

One of the reasons for this phenomenon is the way Anne's stories give the ordinary person a chance to become great. Most fiction focuses only on heroes with extraordinary talents. Among the legion of science fiction readers are scientists, computer programmers, test pilots and astronauts, environmentalists and biologists, yet the great majority are ordinary people—usually more intelligent than the average, but not the geniuses or heroes that are the usual protagonists of novels and movies. On Pern, however, there is a chance for the ordinary man or woman to step forward and be great—anyone can impress a dragon. To do so is also to acquire a lifelong companion who hears only your thoughts and is utterly devoted to you. In this simple relationship, Anne shows an understanding of two longings experienced by many readers: the desire to belong to someone (or some*thing*) who will give unconditional acceptance and the desire to be given power and responsibility (the care and riding of a dragon) that is at the same time manageable. Anne's words express thrillingly what it feels like to form that relationship with a dragon, unshakable and unbreakable unto death.

Not only has the ordinary man or woman gained a devoted and powerful friend, but he or she then becomes a member of a support group that cares for dragons and risks their lives with them. We see unconditional acceptance by the community, as well, and they want to be a part of it. Science fiction fans in particular, by virtue of their intelligence and awareness of the isolation that often provokes, long for that inclusion. In Anne's books, they see a special group to which they can belong. That is an attractive quality that draws those readers back again and again.

Few authors offer a viable social model for the common human being. Anne McCaffrey's Dragonriders books appeal to a particularly devoted readership partly because of the way these books portray people living on Pern. Though their lives might be lived under harsh, even primitive conditions, the characters are able to survive, thrive, and create. The cultures are so rich in detail that it is possible to reconstruct a semblance of life in Hold, Hall, or Weyr—in ruling and administration, craft guilds, or dragon husbandry, respectively. Life on Pern is hard; characters are always fearing what may fall next from the skies. Yet, those characters live and love, sing, distill wine and spirits, and tell stories, gathering together in groups for mutual support and pleasure, enjoying the homey touches missing from more technology-oriented future sagas.

Like J. R. R. Tolkien in the Lord of the Rings saga, Anne scattered songs and poems throughout her books. Music and storytelling run a close second in fans' hearts to the dragons themselves. From the beginning, the Harper Hall has been the favorite guild, and its longtime guild leader, Masterharper Robinton, a favorite character (especially Jody's). All of these elements add texture, depth, and color that we drink in along with the adventures and romances. You might *exist* in the worlds created in some series; you could *live* on Pern.

Especially when they were first written, Anne's literature also might have been the first that young women—and men,

too—had found in which strong, interesting female protagonists have adventures of their own and are in charge of their
own fate. That was a welcome change from most SF of the
time, when female characters often seemed to be helpless and
stupid, or were depicted as less-effective men with breasts. Not
only that, but the cultures from which Anne's characters spring
are cooperative and interactive, values usually associated with
women. Anne's heroes and heroines do not seek solo glory.
They know themselves to be part of a greater whole in which
every person has his or her role. As Charlotte Moore, longtime
track head of the Worlds of Anne McCaffrey at Dragon*Con
(and author of another essay in this collection), said, "the consistent theme in *all* of [Anne's] work is the importance of connecting to someone else—human or otherwise—as a means to
find one's self."

Reading about these compelling relationships, we readers
crave to be part of something like that as well. It seems natural
for fans to begin to emulate the communities they read about.
The first Weyrgroups began to arise in the 1980s from a core
of fans who loved the books and wanted to touch that sense of
community within themselves. But a community, or any organization, takes its cues from the people at the top, or in this
case, one person: Anne McCaffrey herself.

Meet the Weyrwoman

For many fans, it was not just Anne's work that attracted them
and earned their loyalty, but her personality as well. Back in the
1970s or '80s, the followings or readerships of other authors
such as J. R. R. Tolkien may have been more vast, but they
did not have the benefit of the author participating directly in

their activities. Anne enjoyed interacting with her fans. She was friendly and open with people, never making them feel as if they were wasting her time (not to say that she suffered fools or self-aggrandizers). She always listened patiently to nervous young fans who stood in line to get her autograph, focusing on them and making them feel that what they had to say was important. That isn't so extraordinary in the science fiction/fantasy field, which boasts a goodly share of nice people who write books, but Anne went beyond the usual. In the days before the internet, when social media was primitive and computers were slow and difficult to manage, Anne answered all her letters herself and participated in online discussions. Unlike many writers, she was an extrovert who was comfortable reaching out to others. Her assertive personality broke down the reserve of many a shy fan, winning their lifelong devotion. Because she was inclusive and fearless by nature, she formed friendships with her readers. She dined with them, visited with them when she traveled, and invited them to drop in on her at her home in Ireland. She made them feel comfortable in her company and in that of her other fans.

Having the privilege of knowing Anne McCaffrey over the years, it is easy to see how Anne's personality was an inspiration for her fandom. Her inherent faith in people and their goodness came through in the plots and characters. She honestly believed in people, giving them the benefit of a doubt, and often her trust, until proven wrong. Anne also cared, cared deeply, for many people. She often opened her home to someone in need. A few of those she took in literally continued to live as part of the Dragonhold household for months or years. As a part of her general faith in people, Anne was amazingly nonjudgmental. Whatever your faith, or lack thereof, your beliefs, orientation, or personal quirks, you were welcome in her world.

This same worldview can be seen in her books as well. Many

years before gay men and women found acceptance in larger society, Anne made them an integral part of weyr life.* In no way
do Pernese discriminate against others because their skin is a
different color or because of their sexual orientation. For those
readers who belong to often-targeted minority groups, Anne's
books provide literature in which, as Dr. Martin Luther King Jr.
hoped for the greater society, people are judged by the content of their character. Her characters don't always act perfectly;
they're very human. But in general, everyone strives together
for the common good.

Anne never preached or even asked you to agree with her
views, but she lived them. In her books she brought to life characters that shared her tolerance, optimism, and kindness. Because she was sincere about being inclusive, fans who did not
feel welcome in other groups often found their way to hers.

ANNA LEE SMITH:

"And the books taught important values that I didn't see, or feel,
being taught anymore: honor, integrity, morals, acceptance, openness, courage . . . Not just the Pern novels, but all of them. They were
the common thread through all of her books. She imbued her characters
with these characteristics and that's what drew me to them all."

CHARLOTTE MOORE:

"Anne's stories are rife with the promise of redemption for out-
casts and the misunderstood. They're about hope, perseverance,
trust, and friendship . . . Anne McCaffrey fans want to believe the
world is fundamentally a good place, that people can mean well and
do the right thing."

---

* The riders of green (female) dragons, except for a girl named Mirrim, are
men. When these dragons mate, it is with male dragons whose riders are also
male. Pernese society does not discriminate against green riders. They are just
dragonriders like all the others, courageous and competent defenders.

Impressing Your Dragon

Like the characters they so admire, McCaffrey devotees tend to be willing to share and cooperate for a greater good. SF fans in general are intelligent and curious, but not as often are they as open to others as Anne fans. It's difficult to say whether the less well-socialized among them have not yet found Anne's books, or if they have but didn't like them because they did not find a voice that speaks to them. Yet, those readers who do find their way into the fan group find that sought-after inclusion they do not find in their other lives. Once included, it behooves them to learn to be inclusive as well. This last-named is sometimes a stretch; it requires trust, something that has been beaten or teased out of many SF fans in their more mundane existence. But to extend that trust among Anne fans is to be rewarded with the joy of having someone to share your passions.

Anne's fans are a diverse group. They come from every walk of life: children and adults, professors and shelf stockers. It's not uncommon to see college students having passionate discussions (and arguments) with doctors, lawyers, computer programmers, dog-walkers, stay-at-home parents, test pilots and astronauts, environmentalists and biologists, real estate agents, and copywriters. What they have in common is a love of a good story, well told, with compelling characters that behave under extraordinary pressure in a way that the readers admire and hope that, under similar circumstances, they too would respond.

A sense of humor is almost a necessity to appreciate Anne's literature. She had a marvelous understanding of the natural ups and downs of life and of those moments that bring a twinkle to the eye. She often used levity to balance against the utter seriousness of life on Pern. Her audience appreciates that. As many of her fans are serving or retired military, they understand the dragonriders' foxhole humor. A moment of lightness helps to relieve the pressure of a terrifying situation. Anne's fans love a funny story and share a capacity for finding humor even during difficult times.

GILLIAN HEWITSON:

"That was the thing about Anne Fans. They tended to be fans of everything else too, and the ones I've gathered up (who are among my best friends now) are all kind, generous, funny, geeky, and caring. Something about Anne's work seems to draw people like that in. Her books strike a chord with my sort of people."

HISHAM EL-FAR:

"I often find myself comparing the behaviour and character [of] the interactions amongst Anne's fans, with that of the other major group of fans and enthusiasts I interact with. Compared to the (at best) rowdy, loud, and aggressive Xbox LIVE gaming community, Fans of Anne McCaffrey are paragons of virtue and honour (but few would dare cross us)."

We reached out for input to those who have been long-time fans and devoted members of the community. Those to whom we sent our questionnaire not only answered, but passed it along to others. Not only did they share the experience with one another (as good Pern people would), but their proactivity meant that we got to hear from people we might not have known about but whose input we also valued. It was the sort of win-win situation of which Anne would have approved.

Among the questions we asked were: Have you noticed traits in common among your fellow Anne fans? What are they? The answers were amazingly similar and also universally positive.

HANS VAN DEN BOOM:

"Love of fantasy/sf in particular and reading in general are almost a given. A willingness to get into the matter like you usually only see with fans of the great epic fantasy series, like Tolkien's and such, maybe. As for the rest, you got them all, lovable and stupidly irritating. Shy and outspoken. Come to think of it, the diversity of the fans (especially on the forum boards I was and am admin/moderator for) is what strikes me time and again. From all over the world, rich and poor, male and female, with low and high education, the diversity is enormous and despite that, online it seems one family, and on the occasions that I met them in a group in real life, that actually stayed through, which is amazing if you think on it."

LESLIE TILLEY:

"We believe!!! And see Anne's creations in real life all the time."

LINDA EICHER:

"We all (Anne's fans) tend to believe imagination is good for the soul, I think. That while no world is perfect, there is beauty and creative thinking, and that the majority of humankind isn't just in it for themselves."

Widening the Search

As early as 1978, fans in the United States began to hold unofficial Gathers, named after Anne's term for a fair or fete, modeled after the medieval festivals. In her books, her characters attend Gathers on special occasions. The real-world Gathers resembled medieval fairs, where they ate food mentioned in the books and sang the songs Anne had written. As Anne was a musician her-self, her poems and songs were easy to set to music. In Europe, fifty or so fans met in Blackpool, England, for the first British Gathers. The fans who attended completely occupied two small bed-and-breakfast establishments and indulged in improvised song, discussion, and good humor over a weekend. They wrote lyrics devoted to "McCaffreydom" to popular tunes, such as *Jerusalem* and *Rule Britannia*; they had sing-alongs with mi-crophones, solo performances, and plenty of dancing. The dis-cussions were just as stimulating and intense and sometimes very funny.

HARRY ALM:

"For several years after X-Con in 1978 [where the Alms first met Anne—ed.], Marilyn and I hosted a New Year's party, which we called the Turn's End Gather, with a theme of Pern, and Anne's writing, and science fiction, and anything else that caught the attention of the attendees at the time. One year, our friend Todd Voros, one of the original members from Milwaukee and Anne's X-Con, in his persona of F'lox, brown Quelith's rider, came up with an idea to raise marks for the weyr and allow the weyrlings to become entrepreneurs; unstated was his idea to make a profit for himself from their activities. Person-ally, I thought he was trying to institute Junior Achievement on Pern, but my character of L'renz, Ista's weyrleader, did not have the cul-tural referent for that idea. In any case, F'lox's idea was to produce fire lizard pooper scoopers to sell to all of the people who obtained fire lizards after F'nor and Menolly found them. When he presented the idea to the Gather, the unanimous and simultaneous reaction, liter-ally, everyone saying the same thing at the same time, was, 'No, no, F'lox, everyone knows that fire lizards go between.'"

As in other fandoms, readers who were part of the established fan groups became so deeply involved in Anne's characters and story lines that they wanted more stories, perhaps in the mainstream timeline, or perhaps along a side channel, where Anne's plots had not gone. After some thought, Anne gave permission. She didn't offer a blank check, however; she established ground rules for where the stories could and could not go.

Being able to write Pern fanfiction gave the readers a feeling of pride in ownership that they were not able to obtain in most other series; other authors discouraged it, sometimes out of caution over copyrights, and sometimes because they had been burned by disrespectful fans. Anne trusted her fans to respect her wishes and copyrights, and for the greatest part, they have honored that trust. Having a stake in their favorite world made them even more enthusiastic participants than ever. Individual fan groups arose all over the world. Most of them were named for weyrs, either canonical or original (Ista, Kadanzer, Theran, StarRise, etc.). A few were purely social groups, where fans could get together to talk about their favorite author and her books, but most were founded around writing their own Pern-based fan fiction. Marilyn Alm, who with her husband Harry Alm founded the Ista Weyr group, obtained permission to begin the Canth/Wirenth timeline in 1978, the first official fanfic offshoot from Anne's main timeline.

MARILYN ALM:

". . . one of the questions I had for Anne was, 'Oh, why, oh why did Wirenth have to die? Why couldn't Canth have flown her?' Anne's reply was, 'Well, at the time I was writing *Dragonquest*, I couldn't figure out how to have Canth fly Wirenth and have Kylara get hers, and it was more important to have Kylara get hers.' We said, 'Hmm,' and went back to our room and consulted all five of the Pern books then published. And came back to her with questions. Our questions involved several 'What ifs?' and 'Is this feasible on Pern as you see

it?' and then we gave her our scenario. Anne looked very thoughtful,
and then said, 'D@mn. It would have worked.'"

Anne herself never read any of the fan-written stories for two
reasons. She never wanted to find herself accidentally incorpo-
rating someone else's plot or alternate timeline into "canonical"
Pern. Nor did she want the fan writers to feel pressured that the
real Weyrwoman was looking over their shoulders. It was another extension of trust. As a result, the fan base policed itself.
As new members joined in and penned their own stories, they
were informed as to the rules. Instead of feeling as if they were
under an onerous authority, the fans felt as though they were
part of the universe.

Jody's book *The Dragonlover's Guide to Pern* came into
being because it occurred to us that by that time (1988), Anne
had created so much background material on Pern that a good
gazetteer was possible. When Bill put out feelers among the
fans for whether or not we should do it, the response was overwhelming: "Yes! Now!" We knew that it would be a grand tool
for the fan writers, as well as a lovely, illustrated introduction for
new readers to get to know Anne's brilliant and complex world.
Doing ten days of interviews in Ireland with Anne for the
Dragonlover's Guide to Pern, it soon became apparent to us
that even parts of Anne's world that had not been thought out
in detail when she wrote them to make the story work were
often subconsciously consistent. Based upon their reading of
Anne's internal timelines, Harry Alm and Eric Webb codified
the Threadfall charts, doing mathematically what Anne had
done more or less instinctively, and discovered that she was
working from an accurate mental model. (When Mayfair did
the *Dragonriders of Pern* role-play game, they used a University of Chicago math grad to analyze the Threadfall data,
and it held up perfectly.) Marilyn Alm brought in mapmaker

Niels Erickson to draw the charts that Anne later used in *Dragonsdawn*.

Anne encouraged fan involvement in her research and always announced who had given her facts and figures. Her easy confidence in her work allowed her to consider other people's ideas as readily as her own. If someone proposed a notion that she liked as well or better than one of hers, she adopted it (with fair warning!) for the official canon. (Some of Jody's innovations in the two Crossroads books became part of Pernese history—and she couldn't be prouder.) That open spirit inspired her fans as much as her work did.

When websites and bulletin boards became easier to access and use around the turn of the millennium, Anne's son Alec created one of the internet's first online communities, the Kitchen Table website and Kitchen Table Live chat group, in 2000. Anne frequently invited fans to visit her at her home in Ireland; even drop-ins could count on a friendly greeting and a cup of tea at Anne's kitchen table. The Kitchen Table website was an online extension of that. Three fans, Hans van den Boom, Cheryl Miller, and Anneli Conroy, were invited to become site hosts, to welcome and mediate between participants. The boards covered conversations about each of Anne's books in turn. People talked about their favorite characters and scenes.

Anne herself participated in the chats. The fans appreciated the gift of her time and attention. She was playful with her fans, allowing herself to be a little silly, perhaps a bit ridiculous, and inviting others to be the same. Anneli Conroy mentioned an instance when Anne visited the Kitchen Table Live not as herself, but pretending to be a cat. (That's why the good humor in her literature finds such resonance among its readers. It's not pasted on—it's true.)

The hosts kept the discourse civil, so the KTL, as it came to be known, was a safe place to have those discussions (and arguments) in the round that were otherwise impossible except at conventions, Gathers, or meetings—especially impossible considering that the participants logged in from all around the world. Hans, Cheryl, and Anneli hailed from, respectively, the Netherlands, the United States, and Great Britain. Constant communication fostered further trust and friendship among the participants. Deep friendships formed among the fans.

CHANTAL GAUDIANO:

"My life has been immeasurably improved by finding Anne's literature and meeting other fans of her work. I have made friends among other Pern fans whose longstanding friendships are precious to me. I regard them as a second family, and a couple of them I regard as sisters of my soul. I have learned and shared wisdom with them, shared tears and joys with them. If Anne McCaffrey were still alive today, I'd tell her that I could never thank her enough for providing a common ground for me to meet such exemplary, brilliant, and fun people."

LINDA EICHER:

"Because of my love of Anne's stories, I went looking for other people who enjoyed her books like I did and I found the *Meeting of Minds* fan forum and the Kitchen Table forum. The result of finding those two Anne McCaffrey fan forums, I also found not only wonderful friends . . . but also got to finally meet Anne herself. I drew the members of MoM, and then Anne herself. After seeing one portrait of her, she wrote to me asking if she could have it . . . I have made the most wonderful friends in the world, and have had the privilege of meeting the wonderful woman herself . . . and knowing I was able to give her back a small amount of the joy she had given to me over so many, many years."

ANNELI CONROY:

"In the early days of the Kitchen Table, one man traveled the

world staying with friends from the bulletin board. It was the kind
of link that meant that a stranger can spend two nights on your sofa
without your having to worry—'hey, he's an Anne fan.'"

Nothing is perfect. Even Camelot had its rough spots. At one
point, the KTL shut down, but the hosts opened up two new
websites, A Meeting of Minds (hosted by Cheryl Miller) and
Anne McCaffrey Fans (hosted by Hans van den Boom). At first
the fans separated between the two, but over time Anne's influence and the general friendly feeling among the group eventually brought about a détente.

Though the new sites were run entirely by fans, they have
also reached out to writers who for one reason or another had
become associated with Anne. We have been asked several times
to stop in for scheduled chats, but also have been made very
welcome should we log on any time we happen to be free. A
Meeting of Minds also has provided Jody with a thread of her
own to post in. The same courtesy has been extended to other
writers associated with Anne, such as Elizabeth Moon, who co-
wrote two of the Planet Pirates novels with Anne, *Sassinak* and
Generation Warriors.

And what do the fans themselves get out of the equation?
The name of Cheryl Miller's website describes it well: a meeting
of minds. Like-minded readers are able to meet, either in person
or on the web, others who feel the way they do about the work
of their favorite writer.

Flying Between Hold, Hall, and Weyr

Conventions and ordinary mail fostered the first of the devoted
fan communities. Then they were supplemented, though not

superseded, by electronic forums. As CompuServe and Oracle gave way to reliable email and the internet, communication became easier. Online role-playing grew more widespread. Fanfiction moved from paper zines to electronic sharing. The community has diffused, but whenever it meets, it seems to be as strong as ever. This closeness is seen most readily at Dragon*Con, held every Labor Day weekend in Atlanta, Georgia. (In spite of its title, Dragon*Con was not named for Anne's work, though she was its first and favorite guest of honor.) Other fandoms have their associations, such as the Star Wars-inspired Stormtroopers, who like to hang out in large groups at conventions, but rarely have organized interaction outside of a fan event. Dragon*Con has a shared programming track devoted to the worlds that Anne created, most especially Pern. Fans return year after year, even after Anne's passing, to celebrate what she has created and what they all share. Thanks to Facebook, Twitter, and all the other online media, the community never has to be out of touch.

No official celebration had been planned for the fortieth anniversary of Pern in 2003, but her admirers banded together under Hans van den Boom to produce *40 Years of Pern*, a book of essays by fans and fellow writers alike, including Bill and Jody. When Anne attended Eurocon in Copenhagen that year, as Anneli Conroy put it, twelve to fourteen fans from five different countries "kidnapped" Anne for Chinese food and presented the first copy of the book to her. Needless to say, Anne was deeply touched. Her fans were proud to give back to Pern's creator appreciation for what she had given to them.

Like Camelot, the golden age of McCaffrey fandom may be a glorious time that we will look back on with nostalgic longing. While her books are still with us, she is not. The McCaffrey Effect may not be as powerful without Anne's presence, but the legacy of openness and acceptance that she promoted through her books always will be. We regret that that special connection with the writer herself is no longer possible. Time passes. The lives she changed remain changed. The fans whose lives she touched still love her work and will continue to give it to others to enjoy. It is up to those privileged souls to keep the joy alive by being open, accepting, curious, inclusive, and cooperative—by reaching out to those who are not yet a part of the group and giving them the same kind of welcome that Anne gave to them.

———————————

Best-selling science fiction and fantasy author JODY LYNN NYE describes her main career activity as "spoiling cats." When not engaged in this worthy enterprise, she has published more than forty books and novels, largely humorous, some in collaboration with noted writers in the field, such as Anne McCaffrey and Robert Asprin, and more than 110 short stories. Her latest books are *Myth-Quoted*, nineteenth in Asprin's Myth-Adventures series, and *View from the Imperium*, a sort of Jeeves and Wooster in space. She is married to Bill Fawcett.

BILL FAWCETT first met Anne at Mayfair Games. He has been writing and editing SF since his years at Mayfair in the early '80s. He has edited or co-edited more than forty science fiction anthologies including a Nebula anthology. As Quinn Fawcett, he has coauthored the Mycroft Holmes and Madame Vernet mystery novels. His nonfiction books include a book on UFOs, two oral histories of the US Navy SEALs, and ten nonfiction books on mistakes in history. He is also a game and computer game designer.

Bill Fawcett had a great idea: get Anne McCaffrey to outline some story ideas that she didn't particularly want to write on her own but that would continue the universes of her other worlds. The idea was part of a larger strategy to pair established authors with up-and-coming writers so as to get a good book, name recognition for the new writer, and a story that otherwise wouldn't have been told. It was very much in keeping with Mum's credo, "Never just return a favor—pass it on!"

And with that were born such stories as *Crisis on Doona*, *Sassinak*, *The City Who Fought*, and *The Ship Who Searched*—the last cowritten by Mercedes Lackey.

Since that book, Mercedes Lackey has gone on to become a major force in the world of science fiction and fantasy, and we're very glad to have her in this tribute.

The Ships That Were

Optimism, Dystopia, and Anne McCaffrey's Brainships

MERCEDES LACKEY

IT'S REALLY TEMPTING for critics to try to read things about the writer into a writer's work. And yes, sometimes things in the work really can apply to the writer herself—heaven knows that Anne McCaffrey was fun and funny to be around, and . . . well, if not *obsessed* with food and cooking, certainly was good at it. And she loved music, opera especially, and was a classically trained operatic singer, which she used to great effect in her Crystal Singer series.

But when it comes to things that are more internal than external—attitudes and leanings—believing you can judge the writer by the story becomes a very slippery slope indeed. Not to name any names here, but I know several writers whose work would suggest that they are great, open people to be around, the kind of people you would like as friends, and in reality, they are anything but open—often curmudgeonly and reclusive— and would be the kind of folk that would cause problems at your parties, whether they had overimbibed at the punch bowl or not.

That slope is particularly slippery in Anne's case because she tended to lay a veneer of her own cheerful personality over the top of even the most depressive situations when she wrote, making it easy for the superficial reader to think that she was depicting something that she was not. Take, for example, the aforementioned Crystal Singer series. Lovely premise, how Crystal Hunters seek the rarest and most precious of their quarry by singing for it and listening for the echoes, then use voice-controlled machinery to cut it. It sounds very beautiful, and what a potentially idyllic life for a musician who has failed to make his or her mark *as* a musician. But then there is the dark side . . . a symbiotic spore may make you a master singer, give you a hugely extended lifespan, make you virtually immune to disease, and heal almost any injury—or it may deafen, mutate, or kill you. And eventually, it will render you sterile, destroy your memory, and drive you insane. There is a dark heart to this paradise.

This is true as well in the Brainship books and stories, one of which I had the honor and pleasure to cowrite with Anne. The emails and notes we exchanged gave me a unique look at the background of these books, a background that might not be apparent to a casual reader.

Anne was never one to dwell on negatives. Her emphasis was always on how her protagonist overcame her barriers, not on waxing emotional about her troubles. But let there be no mistake about this: although the doctors in the books present the disabled-child-to-shell-person-slavery as a highly positive thing, and even though the shelled themselves are presented as being cheerful, generally contented people, the universe of the Brainships is, at least for the shell people, an often-hellish dystopia. How could it not be? It is a universe where, if your infant is deemed sufficiently handicapped and is not smart enough for the shell program, he or she is summarily snuffed out. A universe where even if the handicapped infant is deemed "worthy," he or she is promptly enrolled in a program of indentured slavery under the guise of "saving" his or her life. Annie was well aware it was a hellish dystopia, and did not in the least approve of it. She could have made everything about this situation positive—except the part about being indentured, since that was integral to the plot. This was her world and her choice to make it a kindly or unkindly one, and she paints the brutishness of the "euthanasia" of "unacceptable" infants in obviously harsh strokes; those strokes just happen to be brief. Unlike some who style themselves primarily as dystopian writers, who would proceed to wallow in just how hellish it was, depicting page after page of weeping parents being informed that their child was not fit to live, Annie did what she always did—she cut straight to the story. She wasn't a dystopian writer; she was a storyteller. She wasn't interested in setting the stage beyond what she needed to get the story started, and for her, the important part was not the setting, but the characters and what they did within that setting. I'm pretty sure (although I never had a chance to ask) that she was at one with Heinlein's amused scorn for those writers who "sell their birthright for a pot of message." She never saw her job as that of a preacher. Her job was to tell stories.

In the case of "The Ship Who Sang," the story that introduced the Brainship universe, her job was to tell Helva's story.

Bear in mind, I am not entirely sure just which part is chicken and which part is egg here. Knowing Annie, and having watched her work when she was briefly considering taking part in C. J. Cherryh's Merovingen Nights shared world series along with me and several other writers, I think Helva herself might have been (no pun intended) the "egg." At least in the instance of Merovingen Nights, Annie came up with the character first and designed the setting to match what she wanted out of the character. I think Helva probably came first, and in order to justify Helva's physical state—a woman with the body of a spaceship—Annie invented a world in which such a state was possible.

Annie was not one to allow her characters to wallow in angst for chapters at a time. Her characters faced rotten situations head-on and took steps to get themselves out—as Lessa does in the Pern series, going from kitchen drudge to Weyrwoman, mostly propelled by her own determination. Helva was no exception. After the usual treatment—medication to stunt her growth, several surgeries, education, and special training—she emerges fairly early in the book ready to take on her first assignment as a Brainship and with a steel-hard determination to pay off her debt.

This is a theme that runs through the entire book: the heavy, crippling debt that the shell people are saddled with. Annie never ignored that, nor the implied slavery. She made sure that theme continued to be present in the background of every story—when Helva speaks with other ships who are saddled with unappealing "brawns" because they cannot afford to reject one, or in Helva's conversations with planet- or station-bound shell persons—underscoring the simple fact that, no matter how pleasant some parts of the society Annie created are, this *is* a dystopia. A very pretty dystopia, and a dystopia where most people have good, or even exceptional, lives—but one that functions at the expense of others who have had no choice and no say in being made slaves.

Annie was far more interested in how Helva dealt with and circumvented that dystopian culture than she was in railing against it. That is both in keeping with Annie's character and Helva's. Handed lemons by life, both of them would opt to make a lemon soufflé rather than rail against life or the authority that determined all they were to get was lemons. Neither were revolutionaries—and why should they need to be? They also serve who scout the way out.

The Brainship universe also looks more dystopian now than it would have when *The Ship Who Sang* was first published as a novel. The technology available to us today—and the world that disabled children are born into—is very different and much more advanced than any writer at the time could have dreamed. When Annie was writing the books, for instance, there was no such technology as ultrasound, no fetal testing, no way of knowing if a child was even going to be born alive. That context matters in how we understand the universe.

Annie, unlike Isaac Asimov or even Poul Anderson, her contemporaries, was *not* particularly interested in the bleeding edge of technology; when she needed something for a book, she would talk to an expert in that field, but otherwise, she pretty much ignored the techie stuff with a bit of writerly hand waving. Technology was a tool for her, not a be-all and end-all in itself. She put in what she needed for her *story*, and that was that. Properly so: remember that for her story and character came first, setting after, and technical details, so long as she didn't contradict herself or make some logic blunder or plot hole, were somewhere out in the distance. Annie was anything but a technophobe, but as someone who made a living as a computer programmer, I can tell you that she wasn't really interested in the details of technology unless those details would enhance or propel her story.

Actually, given the stories that Todd tells about her, I suspect that, even outside of her writing, she wasn't remotely interested in how technology worked so much as what it could do for her. Not that odd, even for a science fiction writer. I've lost count of the number of SF writers I know who are perfectly comfortable rattling off tidbits about nanotech or the complexities of bubble computers, but who are utterly baffled by the innards of their own cars.

It's also always wise to consider the real world that a writer is working in when you consider the work that they are writing. Even if technology had been Annie's primary interest, the technology of 1969—the year *The Ship Who Sang* was published as a novel and the last time she made changes to Helva's story—in no way hinted at the advances (especially in electronics, miniaturization, and medicine) that we take for granted now; very few would have dared to predict technology in the far future as advanced as the things we handle every day.

Let me take you back to 1969 for a moment.

Man had just set foot on the moon. The computing power that was necessary to send man there required entire buildings to house. Hard to imagine, then, that a computer capable of running a spaceship would someday fit inside the CPU of a moderately complicated digital watch, with room to spare. Even *2001: A Space Odyssey*, released in 1968, showed us a HAL 9000 that was several stories tall. Intel had only just invented the first microprocessor. When asked if there would be computers in the home (something Isaac Asimov and Ray Bradbury had both already envisioned), Intel engineers suggested that there might one day be "a dozen or so" people who were interested. The idea of a PC was considered ultrafuturistic, and even Asimov envisioned most of its working parts being hidden away in a separate room or embedded in the walls. While science fiction writers of the time had no problem imagining interstellar travel, a solid portion of them balked at the idea of a ship being able to carry enough computing power to run itself. It made more sense to imagine that a ship's "computer" was the brain of a living human instead. A human, even with extensive life support, would "always" take up far, far less space than a multistoried computer—and be less likely to fail.

As for communication of large amounts of data over vast distances, that didn't seem even remotely possible. By 1969, the first computer-to-computer message had been sent over ARPANET (Advanced Research Projects Agency Network), but it was a classified military project that very few people knew about. There was no internet. Plenty of science fiction writers still bought into the idea that any data you would need on a spaceship, you had better bring with you.

The first artificial heart transplant took place in 1969, but the machine that powered it was outside the body and was about the size of a large desk, and it worked for only three days until a donor heart was found. The procedure was insanely expensive. In fact, a lot of medical procedures that we take for granted as affordable these days were insanely expensive—more than expensive enough to make a future where one might need to indenture oneself to pay for them plausible. In 1969, people died all the time of things we now consider treatable. Heart attacks, stroke, cancer . . . they were pretty much death sentences. Very few people were put on life support: coma patients, usually. Most children born with severe birth defects died. Compassionate, excellent doctors were known to take steps to make sure they did.

Though it had been several years, the specter of the thalidomide babies still haunted the collective psyche of the world. Thalidomide, an antinausea and sedative drug that was introduced in the late 1950s to be used as a sleeping pill, was quickly discovered to help pregnant women with the effects of morning sickness. It was sold from 1957 until 1962, when it was withdrawn after being found to cause many different forms of birth defects—everything from missing limbs or shortened limbs to congenital defects of the heart, lungs, and internal organs. In Germany alone, 10,000 babies were born affected by thalidomide. Many were too damaged to survive for long. Those that

did required constant care. Although there were no thalidomide babies in the United States, *Life* magazine and other publications there covered the story extensively and graphically. I
strongly suspect the images of those children, widely dissemi-
nated in the media through the '50s and late '60s, influenced
Annie considerably—as did the stories of how desperate parents
were trying to cope. Annie says in *The Ship Who Sang* that shell
persons would never have traded places with those who were
born "normal," and when she does, I suspect she had those
images in the back of her mind—because certainly, as Annie
describes them, the shelled are, in many ways, far freer than
their "brawns."

This was a difficult time for anyone with a disability, whatever its origins. In the early 1970s, people with disabilities
lobbied Congress to put civil rights language for people with
disabilities into the 1973 Rehabilitation Act. The act was actually vetoed by President Nixon because of the cost. "Supporters
would have the American public believe that each of these bills
would further an important social cause," he said, "but they
neglect to warn the public that the cumulative effect of a Con-
gressional spending spree would be a massive assault upon the
pocketbooks of millions of men and women in this country."
And though the 1973 Act included language prohibiting dis-
crimination on the basis of disability in federal programs,
people with disabilities did not achieve broad civil rights until
the enactment of the Americans with Disabilities Act (ADA) in
1990. It is not difficult to see where Annie got her dystopian
vision from. Not only were there no disability rights advocates
of consequence between 1965 and 1969, when Annie was first
writing the Brainship books, but one could scarcely imagine
that anyone would *allow* such a thing. In 1965, disability *was*
depersonalizing; the severely disabled were warehoused away
from the eyes of the public, institutionalized for the duration

of their lives, while parents were encouraged to forget that they existed and "go on with their lives." It's an attitude that invokes horror nowadays, but was perfectly commonplace back then. In even imagining that some severely handicapped infants would be given a chance to live outside the walls of an institution, Annie was far more enlightened than most people, and her imagination extended far beyond that of the vast majority of her peers.

I have to wonder whether, if they had been given the choice offered Helva's parents, the parents of those thalidomide babies of the late '50s and early '60s wouldn't have seized on such a fate as a blessing. There were no cleverly engineered harnesses to help lift an adult-sized handicapped person in and out of bed. There were no cordless phones or television remotes. There were no ramps, no lifts, and virtually no one had any notion of installing them. And of course, it is not *just* the gadgets that make life easier for the disabled in the modern world; it is the *attitude*.

When Nixon vetoed earlier versions of the 1973 Rehabilitation Act, it made scarcely a ripple in the general populace; the disabled weren't largely thought of as deserving the same rights as the able-bodied, or, for the most part, as capable of living productive lives. In contrast, in Annie's world, shell persons were respected and played an important role in society. Not only did their parents' choice to shell them allow them to live, it permitted them to live relatively well. They were cared for and appreciated for their skills.

Annie had always maintained that she was never going to revisit Helva's world, but never is a long time, and in 1992, Bill Fawcett persuaded her to come back to it and this time to invite some friends. And this is where I came into the picture.

The first rule of working in someone else's world is don't change the canon without permission. However, I wanted to do something a *little* different with my incipient shell person, Hypatia. I wanted to have the technology extended to someone who wasn't an infant because I wanted to inject a little dissonance into the notion that "shell persons would never exchange their place with the able-bodied." While that might be the case for those who were encased as infants—what about someone who had been able-bodied first?

Annie had maintained in the first books that the traumas involved would drive an adult insane, and I didn't want to break that rule. But what about a hyperintelligent child, a little prodigy—a genius, in fact? I posited that to Annie and gave her my arguments, and to my relief, she agreed. The reason I wanted this was because I wanted my protagonist to have the memories of what it was like to have a working, natural body and to strive for something beyond Helva's goal of emancipation. I wanted Hypatia to be the person who looked for a way for shell people to achieve real mobility. This was 1991, after all, and views and technology had changed vastly in the twenty plus years since the original book was written.

However, this was still a dystopia. When Hypatia is paralyzed and offered the chance to become shelled, it is with her parents' full knowledge of the fact that she will become indebted and indentured. I was writing in Hypatia's point of view, and at the point where she is paralyzed, she is far too wrapped up in her own troubles to pay any attention to her parents' reactions—but one can imagine that they are suffering the worst of torments—knowing that their daughter is paralyzed for life— complicated by the situation they are caught in—the choice they have to make for her, knowing if they choose to shell her, the experiment can end very badly, and even if it ends well, she will be an indentured servant for a very long time. I've known a few archeologists in my time, and they are far from wealthy people. I imagined them struggling with the question of what to do. Hypatia required full life support and would for the rest of her life. How could they afford that? Would one of them have to become Hypatia's full-time caretaker? If so, which one? All this, of course, was going on in the background.

Like Annie, I was bending the circumstances to serve the character and story I wanted to tell. The main difference is that, in 1992, I was fully aware that rights were being eroded. Not only could I envision Annie's dystopia coming to pass, but in the wake of Ronald Reagan's forays into the dismantling of the "social safety net," threats to privatize Medicare and Medicaid, closing institutions, "mainstreaming" the disabled and mentally ill, I was more than half convinced it *would* come to pass. I had seen the streets suddenly populated with the mentally ill, suddenly "mainstreamed" and declared fit to function in society as a result of Reagan's policies, when they really should have been in a secure living space where they could get proper treatment. I could easily imagine rights being rolled right back to the bad old days. After all, in the Ayn Randian world of Reaganomics, the rights of the corporation took precedence over those of the individual. If the individual was more of a "taker" than a "maker," then, in the words of Ebenezer Scrooge, he should "die and decrease the surplus population"—which fit right in with Annie's dystopian future.

But I am not a particularly dystopian writer either, so I wasn't going to wallow in the misery any more than Annie did.

Nor would Hypatia. Like Helva before her, Hypatia was not the least interested in accepting what she had been ordained to be. Like Helva before her, she was going to throw off her chains.

And like Helva, she was going to go where no shell person had gone before. If that's not the definition of ability, what is?

Annie had a vision; I was privileged to be invited into it.

Annie had a universe; I got to play in it. And Annie's characters had a resolutely cheerful attitude in the face of terrible adversity. I hope I managed to convey the same.

Annie's approach to the world was to meet it head on, accept the challenge, and find a way over, under, or through it. That approach truly was made explicit in her writing. Even in the face of dystopia, Annie—and her characters—would never accept anything less than winning through.

MERCEDES LACKEY is approaching 100 books in print, with five published in 2003 alone, and some of her foreign editions can be found in Russian, German, Czech, Polish, French, Italian, Turkish, and Japanese. She is the author, alone or in collaboration, of the Heralds of Valdemar, Elemental Masters, 500 Kingdoms, Diana Tregarde, Heirs of Alexandria, Obsidian Mountain, Dragon Jouster, Bedlam Bards, Shadow Grail, and other series and stand-alone books, including the Secret World Chronicle, based on an ongoing Parsec-nominated podcast series at www.secretworldchronicle.com. A nightowl by nature, she is generally found at the keyboard between 10 P.M. and 6 A.M. You can visit her website at www.mercedeslackey.com.

At one point Anne McCaffrey was thinking of collaborating with someone on a new project, and I said, "Why not Annie Scarborough? You two get along so well." I think that was the start of the Petaybee series.

We had first read Elizabeth Ann Scarborough back with her *Song of Sorcery*, *The Unicorn Creed*, and *Bronwyn's Bane*. Annie has a great sense of humor, an amazing talent for punning, and a brilliant mind.

Annie and Anne continued to collaborate right up until Anne's death. They both had a love of music, and I'm glad that Annie chose to write about that here.

The Dragonlady's Songs

ELIZABETH ANN SCARBOROUGH

 Oh, tongue, give sound to joy and sing
Of hope and promise on dragonwing

— DRAGONSONG

ANNE MCCAFFREY HAD a passion for music.

She was a musician whose first memorable gift was a piano, and a serious singer who trained as a soprano for roles in light opera and musicals. She was preparing for a singing career when someone—a tenor, according to *Dragonholder*, the autobiography she wrote with her son Todd—decided she was a contralto. In that range, flaws in her voice emerged (as they did in the voice of Killashandra Ree, the heroine of one of her later novels, *Crystal Singer*). Anne channeled the emotion she had once put into her music through her characters and her writing and continued singing for fun and enjoying listening to others. There was always a guitar at her house for anyone who cared to play it. And music played a critical role in much of her writing—especially in her twenty-six major works about Pern and its dragons.

Anne lived for most of her adult life in Ireland, where

traditional traveling musicians called harpers and storytellers, or *shanachies*, still hold honored places in the nation's heritage. Much of Ireland's preliterate history and myth might have been lost except for these "entertainers." And as a fellow musician and storyteller, Anne understood both the power of music to tell stories and the power of stories to show the importance of music as a culture-bearing art form.

Anne often told fans she chose dragons as Pern's biggest protagonists because "dragons have always had bad press." She proceeded to provide them with good "press," not just in our world, through her books, but on Pern in the form of the Harper Hall, which literally sang their praises and tales of their heroics to everyone on the planet throughout its post-technological history. In fact, next to the dragons and Threadfall, music, and the way it is used by the harpers, is probably Pern's most distinctive feature. Anne created a civilization in which music was, as it once was in Irish culture and in other Earth cultures throughout history, the circulatory system of society. The dragons may preserve the planet, but music is what makes the world go around.

Pern isn't the only world in which Anne used music in her storytelling. In *The Ship Who Sang*, Helva's music is, like Anne's, opera and operetta and is part of the world Helva creates within her hull. On Ballybran, Killashandra's trained operatic musical tones are used to cut crystal. But while music is a form of self-expression for Helva and a utilitarian tool on Ballybran, music on Pern is pervasive. The reason is important to the overall narrative of Pern.

Pern is a post-literate world. Early on in Pern's colonization, the technology settlers brought with them began to fail for lack of fuel or resources, or else became irrelevant to life as the descendants of the original settlers know it. By the time the series begins, reading and writing, previously eclipsed by computer technology, are no longer available to most inhabitants.

With no written communication to inform people of events past and present, the harpers, who travel from hold to hold, are the newscasters and the message carriers of their planet. They do more than just play music; they provide information and education for the people they visit.

Although the Harper Halls are very selective and their tests quite strict, vocal quality is not the only or even the most critical qualification. Singing and/or playing is important, and being a good storyteller is essential, but it is also necessary that a harper be a good listener and something of an investigator in order to learn about events so they can be remembered, dramatized, and retransmitted as songs. The harpers' songs often celebrate or mourn recent victories and losses, particularly the brilliant deeds of the dragons and their riders, and by compressing these complex adventures into comparatively short songs ("it's only forty verses and I won't detain yez long"), they help the news spread quickly and be remembered easily. Because of the harpers, the culture of the heroic dragons and their riders is preserved and brought forward, just as the culture of Camelot was preserved by bards long after its enemies brought it down. Because of the songs and stories, Camelot remains. Without them, not even the name would remain. Similarly, without the harpers, the history of Pern would be forgotten.

When the supercomputer AIVAS is discovered, making much of the wisdom of the pre-Harper Hall past recoverable, there is no need to fear that the years between colonization and rediscovery of AIVAS will be lost. It's been well-recorded in harpers' songs. (It helps that the same class of people who compose and perform dragon-related songs are the ones who help assimilate the "new" knowledge as well.) At some future point in Pern's development, reading and writing would probably have made a comeback, but meanwhile, it's a story with a rhyme, a chorus that repeats itself, and a catchy tune or haunting melody that keeps the dragon lore—and everything else—fresh in the hearts and imaginations of the young and the memories of the old.

Diplomacy is also a necessary trait; Pernese harpers are often guests in the homes of powerful and influential people who may use them as impartial sounding boards for critical decisions. Their input, especially that of Master Robinton throughout the earlier books, is sought after and valued in many cases. (Perhaps this is partly because everyone wants to be remembered well in the ballads that they hope a harper will someday compose about them.) Master Robinton at times seems to take on the role of a spy and at others, a diplomat. This seems a natural role for someone who knows and understands more about the planet's history and how its problems have been discovered and overcome in the past. Also, as a performer, Master Robinton and the other harpers are used to "working" audiences, to getting and keeping a crowd's attention. The manipulative skills a harper needs are useful in local politics as well.

None of this is entirely separate from the harpers' function as entertainers. In a world without books, letters, or newspapers, as in medieval days when live entertainers were the only readily available diversion, any change, including juicy gossip, serves as entertainment. People provide what entertainment there is, be it harpers with songs, traveling actors, or games devised by both children and adults for relaxation. News and stories from other places, stirring songs of derring-do, songs making fun of foolish behavior or decisions, are wonderful sources of entertainment. New tunes to whistle, new ballads to sing, new scraps of news presented, perhaps, with a new viewpoint are all welcome diversions. The skilled harpers provide all of these nourishing entertainments for the holds and weyrs.

Although traveling harpers act as a sort of musical glue to hold the far-flung communities of Pern together, not all harpers travel or continue traveling after a certain age. Some take up permanent residence in hold or weyr, acting as teachers and historians and inspiring new generations to dream of things they otherwise might not. Think of Menolly's desire to become a harper, in defiance of the life her family and her hold want her to embrace. It's due to the influence of old Petiron the harper that she knew some of the history of Pern, giving her a broader perspective on what her life could be.

In other words, harpers are the culture bearers of Pern, from their personal influence as teachers of young people like Menolly, to their planet-wide influence as recorders and transmitters of history and culture. Harpers' music is about, by, and for ordinary people, not something apart. Unlike contemporary times, where the majority of life is devoid of music except for that on recordings or in concerts by professional musicians who are personally unknown to their listeners and sung about people equally unknown to them, on Pern, harpers often live with their audiences, and music underscores life from the cradle to the grave. Harpers' talented fingers dip into almost every phase of life on Pern.

Whether or not a harper is in a specific scene or chapter, each Pern book generally includes some reference to music, and chapters often start with a chorus or verse from a song. Thanks to the harpers, every Pernese person knows at least some songs. They are part of each citizen's childhood and upbringing. Just as American children learn the "ABC" song, Pernese children receive their society's most basic information in the form of songs.

For instance, in *Dragonflight*, Lessa knows from songs of old that the warlord who has taken over her hold, orphaned her, and made her disguise herself as a kitchen drudge, is imperiling the hold by disobeying the ancient rules about keeping the grounds free of vegetation that will spread fire during Threadfall, even though she has not seen a Threadfall during her lifetime. Since Threadfall is unpredictable and occurs only once in a generation or so, it's crucial that the people of Pern, as a culture, remember how to fight it and prevent it from damaging their homes.

The Harper Hall trilogy and the first three Pern books contain most of the songs characters refer to in later books. The songs serve not only as examples of the harper's art, but to move the plot forward, foreshadow events, and convey those events' emotional impact. In subsequent books, for the most part, these earlier songs are quoted. Sometimes, as with "The Ballad of Moreta's Ride" (which we first learn of in *Dragonflight*), those original songs served as impetus for Anne to tell the story behind them, as she did years later in *Moreta, Dragonlady of Pern*.

Anne made up Pern, but she didn't entirely make up harpers. There are sources she drew from among harpers' counterparts in our world. Earth has a long tradition of musician/storytellers—in Ireland, Scotland, and England, but also in the rest of Europe and in Asia and Africa—and these court musicians and storytellers, like Pernese harpers, entertained, taught, and even served as informal political advisers. The equivalent of the European minstrel in the Tsongan tribe of Africa, for example, held a special place politically; the Tsongan fool (or *jongleur* in French) was the only person allowed to criticize or make fun of the king/chief of his tribe, rather like a musical political cartoonist.

Anne's Pernese harpers most closely resemble their counterparts, also called harpers, from her beloved Ireland. One of the most famous traditional Irish harpers is Turlough O'Carolan (1670–March 25, 1780). Blinded by smallpox, he traveled throughout Ireland with the help of a guide and a horse, living in the homes of patrons, composing songs and melodies for them. Quite a few of these songs are titled "Planxty _____ " (Gaelic for "thanks to" or "a tribute to") followed by the name of the host or patron who was providing for O'Carolan while he composed, played, sang, and entertained.

This isn't the only time Anne has used the Irish music tradition in her work. In the Petaybee or Powers series, Anne and I crossed the folk traditions of the Inuit with those of the Irish, as the culture was a mixture of the two peoples. Like Pern, Petaybee is a post-literate world. Inhabitants use songs in their rituals when they commune with their planet and also to talk about their personal experiences. Following Inuit tradition, most songs are owned by the person who made them and only that person can sing them without permission. On Petaybee, songs are a way of establishing individual identities on a sparsely populated world where people spend much of their time heavily bundled or isolated from each other by severe weather conditions. They have no harpers, but everybody makes up and sings songs during communal celebrations, so their lives also have "background" music. The Irish tunes make the personal Inuit songs easier for the mixed population to sing.

Pern's music draws heavily on the tradition of the bards, minstrels, and harpers of medieval times on Earth. While serving similar purposes to their predecessors, Pern's harpers have some marked differences in their approach to the bardic tradition.

In his book *The Songman, A Journey into Irish Music*, Tommy Sands, one of the foremost contemporary songwriters in Ireland, writes of this bardic tradition in Ireland that it

is one of the first and greatest forms of preserving and sharing culture . . . the complicated and beautiful stories of unbreakable spirit . . . developed a degree of sophistication with the addition of meter and rhyme. More influential than even the poetry, however, were the great storytellers and musicians that passed

on legends and histories from tribe to tribe. Enigmatic entertainers, these sages communicated carefully constructed tales
through lyrics and rhyme without cultural prejudice or politics.
Wearing the colors of all lands, but under the thumb of none,
these men of strong voice and heart became known as the bards.

Like the bards Sands describes, Pern's harpers are great storytellers and musicians who, as discussed, pass along histories
from hold to hold and weyr to weyr. However, though they
owe allegiance to no specific hold or weyr, they are not entirely
independent agents, as the early bards were, because they are
part of a guild structure that trains and educates them in their
music studies and also in the duties the hall expects of them.
No raggedy wayfarers, Pernese harpers often seem to have assignments, almost like government agents, and go from one
place or another (sometimes by dragonback, a great privilege
among nonriders) to suss out a situation.

While Pernese music carries on the bardic tradition in many
particulars, the ideas expressed in the songs of the planet are
more sophisticated, less full of primitive beliefs, magic, or superstition than the Child Ballads, a comprehensive collection
of 305 Scottish and English songs once sung by medieval minstrels, gypsies and travelers, pub singers, court performers, and
ordinary people as they worked and played. (The "child" in
"Child Ballads" was folklorist Frances James Child, who published the annotated songs as *The Scottish and English Popular
Ballads* between 1882 and 1898.)

Pernese harper ballads lack, for the most part, the *Jerry Springer
Show* aspects of many of the older ballads and the body count of
those Scottish and English ballads. Most of the deaths recounted
in Pernese songs are those of riders and dragons who die during
Threadfall, more akin to Arthurian knights than to the characters
of murder ballads, such as sisters who kill each other over a man,

brothers who kill (for various reasons) men their sisters love, or spouses slaying each other because of sexual betrayal. Pernese ballads offer no tales of unquiet graves or locking hearts "in a box of golden," though there are laments for dragons or human friends who've gone between. While the songs do a terrific job of conveying emotional experiences such as the joy of riding a dragon or impressing one, the grief when a loved one disappears "between," or the fear of Thread, we don't see many examples of other emotional content. There are few more personally emotional tales of "passion, bloodshed, desire, and death . . . everything, in fact, that makes life worth living," as the bartender in *Irma La Duce* put it.

This strikes me as odd, when I think about it, since Anne has written romantic stories on Pern and her other worlds and was a passionate and earthy sort of person. Anne's musical passion was first and foremost for opera. It and operetta, like the old ballads, are used to tell a story, but the songs within them are usually only one fragment of the story or are told from one viewpoint, using the music to display vocal pyrotechnics and convey the emotions of the characters involved in the story. Certainly Helva, the spaceship with a human brain, sang that way, often from sheer joy and once, at the loss of her friend and pilot, from overwhelming grief. (The story is one Anne could never read aloud without crying, especially when she got to the part where Helva sang at the burial of her beloved. Though it doesn't say so in the story, the song was Taps, and the story was her way of expressing her grief over the loss of her father.)

But while the harpers perform songs about personal experiences, and we have one or two about death, there are no more romantic love songs than there are songs about magic, and no tales of violence committed when love goes sour. These were stock-in-trade of the early Earth minstrels. Many of Pern's songs are more akin to the American work song about John Henry than to the older songs. The stories the harpers tell through their music do not seem to be fictitious, in most instances, or even parables, but instead descriptions of real occurrences.

Some Pernese songs do have themes and structures similar to medieval riddle songs and magic ballads. Unless the magical tasks in the latter are performed in a specific way, something unpleasant may happen to the person assigned them. For instance, they could be required to follow their dead lover back to the grave. In one version of the song now known as "Scarborough Fair," the singer says, "Tell him to make me a cambric shirt without any thread or needlework." Like the other verses in the song, the instructions are for impossible tasks. In the days when superstition ruled peoples' lives, songs sometimes taught preventative lessons and incantations. The common elements among them all is that they are simple to sing (they have a lot of repetition and rhyme) to make them easy for the listener to learn. But while Pernese songs may contain directions for the listener to avert death and destruction, the similarity stops there. Harper songs drill into inhabitants the need for preventive measures of a pragmatic nature to protect all within the range of the Thread (or whatever) from a very material disaster.

The rationality of Pernese song lyrics stems from the culture's postmodern roots. The differences between the ballads of Pern's Harper Halls and the ballads of old (and of many fantasy novels) make sense when you realize that the Pernese harpers are retrofitting their repertoire to suit a world whose original settlers had been scientific types who saw enough wonder in the universe as it is without embellishing it with further magical mysteries.

There's another kind of song in our world that instructional Pernese songs resemble even more closely, called teaching songs. Teaching songs set rules to rhyme and add a tune, making them easier for children to learn and remember. The "ABC" song is one of these. Similarly, "Old MacDonald Had a Farm" teaches children about animals and the sounds they make in an easy, repetitive musical rhyme. "This Old Man" is a counting song, rhyming each number with an object, as in "This old man, he played two. He played knick-knack on my shoe," and so on. Another simple form builds from one object to its relationship in the world: "On this hill there was a tree/on the tree there were some branches/on the branches there were some twigs . . ."

On Pern, a classic example of a teaching song is a good tool to teach kids about—what else? Dragons and dragonriders! This little round, which we first encounter in *Dragonflight*, contains information about the movement and color of dragons, what they do, who they do it with, and what their motivation is, all in a few lines:

> *Wheel and turn*
> *Or bleed and burn*
> *Fly between,*
> *Blue and green.*
> *Soar, dive down,*
> *Bronze and brown.*
> *Dragonmen must fly*
> *When Threads are in the sky.*

This song about how to handle the dangers unique to Pern, which first appeared at the beginning of "Weyr Search" (later turned into the first chapter of *Dragonflight*), is another perfect example:

> *Drummer, beat and piper, blow,*
> *Harper strike, and soldier, go.*
> *Free the flame and sear the grasses,*
> *Till the dawning Red Star passes.*

Anne had tunes in her head while she was writing the lyrics to Pern's songs, she said, but like many tunes not written down, they more or less fled after the lyric was written. While Anne was a lyricist, she was not a songwriter and wasn't all that interested in personally sitting down and composing repeatable tunes for her words. Nevertheless, they were songs, and she knew they had tunes—and should have tunes. She wanted people to be able to hear them.

Anne knew that to fulfill their purpose in Pernese society, most of the songs would need to have fairly simple tunes, easy to sing in the context of the story and also easy for her fans to sing, as she knew they would. She felt her two young musician friends, Tania Opland and her husband, Mike Freeman, would understand what she wanted. And in fact, it made sense to Tania that such a musically inclined people had scientifically advanced ancestors. As she explains her understanding of the unusual relationship between Pern's space-traveling legacy and its harpers: "Many studies in our own culture have demonstrated the close link between early musical training and aptitude in maths, sciences, and technology. It helps those parts of the brain develop. So (on Pern) we end up, centuries later, with a high percentage of vibrantly creative and intelligent people." So Anne asked Tania and Mike to write the music and to arrange, perform, and coproduce with her two CDs full of Pernese harper songs: *The Masterharper of Pern* and *Sunset's Gold*.

Anne liked the CDs so much she originally hoped to add their first Pern CD, *Masterharper*, to the book when it was released, since music is such an integral part of Robinton's story. This didn't happen, despite Anne's pleasure in it and her feeling that this was how the songs would sound. (The publisher apparently imagined something a little less medieval and a lot more rock 'n' roll. But a teaching song can't be overpowered by the music, and while "Oh baby, baby" might fit into a chorus instead of, for instance, "Hey nonny, nonny," the words are the most critical element of the bardic ballads, both medieval and Pernese.)

I asked Tania why the duo settled on the melodies they chose for their work with Anne.

"Mike wrote the melody for 'Red Star Passes' in his sleep," Tania wrote from Ireland.

He says he went to sleep with the words in his head and woke up with the melody. His conscious thought beforehand was that we could use something with a more "contemporary" feel since, after all, the colonists arrived on Pern with all the musical traditions of Earth up to the time of their departure. There's even a mention in one of the prequel novels of a group of musicians who would have been first or second generation on Pern playing an old favorite called "The Long and Winding Road." Don't know for sure if she meant the Beatles song, but why else use such a familiar title for a piece of incidental music?

My approach to writing the music had been based mainly on inspirations from early and liturgical music, to match the very medieval feel of the culture as it was described in the books.

A couple of the songs were heavily influenced by many childhood Sunday mornings, where singing together was, for me, the most meaningful expression of family and community that church had to offer. "The Duty Song" was meant to be very hymn-like. I also had Annie's description in one of the books, which had the melody being handed off between the sopranos, altos, tenors, and baritones.

Another hymn-inspired melody: "By the Golden Egg of Faranth. By the weyrwoman wise and true . . . " The rhythm of those first two lines reminded me so strongly of the song

I know as "Of the Father's Love begotten"—a 5th century Latin lyric set to an 11th century melody and translated to English in the 19th century—that I had to use that as the basis for my composition.

In view of the fact that Pern has no religion, the use of liturgical music in some cases seems odd, perhaps. But much of medieval music (on which many bardic ballads are based) is closely intertwined with religious music, and it does indeed reflect the period of Pernese culture, which feels medieval but with significant differences in both the songs and the planet's history and culture. And although Anne often said there was no religion on Pern, there is definitely spirituality. People are born and die and speculate about what lies "between" and beyond death, as expressed in the song sung by Robinton and Piemur in *All the Weyrs of Pern*:

> *Get up, take heart—go, make a start,*
> *sing out the truth you came for.*
> *Then when you die, your heart may fly*
> *to halls we have no name for.*

Likewise, it would be pretty hard not to be awed by something larger than yourself when your best friend, who can read your mind and whose mind you read, is a humongous dragon. And Thread! That alone is enough to send more primitive souls into paroxysms of genuflections to the Red Star and probably drive them to staking out a few maidens for sacrifice to Thread as well.

But the unusual thing about Pern is that they don't. Some Pernese are greedy or stupid or crooked, but they do not revert to magical beliefs and superstitions or try to use them to manipulate each other. These people were descended from those with the skill to morph a native beast into a telepathic dragon to protect them from Thread, which they recognized as a natural, if inconvenient, cosmic phenomenon. If their technology declined, their intellect remained sharp, if less informed of matters their ancestors comprehended.

More than pretty songs that entertain by stirring the emotions, Pernese music stirs the intellect and inspires the soul.

For Anne as a writer, the songs may have provided her a way to make shorthand references to past events in other books she'd written about this complicated society. Along with moving the story along, her use of music connects characters and places with a repetitive refrain, providing a Greek chorus that defines the scene at hand and even relates it to an earlier one where the same song was sung. For Pern natives, maybe the same connection occurs, and a song from another event brings to mind a former solution. Even if the new problem is unfamiliar and the lyrics don't hold a solution, the song at least tells the listener that Pernese people before them have faced seemingly impossible troubles and, with great ingenuity and perseverance, overcome them, even if it took inventing a new species of dragon or moving a star from its orbit to do so. Like the stirring ballads of old, harper ballads inspire the people of Pern and give them hope and courage, for they come of a people beloved by dragons. What can possibly be beyond the ability of such people?

In addition to writing twenty-two solo books, including 1989 Nebula Award–winning novel, *The Healer's War*, ELIZABETH ANN SCARBOROUGH co-wrote sixteen books with Anne McCaffrey, including the Petaybee series (the Powers trilogy and the Twins of Petaybee trilogy) and the two Barque Cats books, *Catalyst* and *Catacombs*. She also joined Anne and Margaret Ball in creating eight of the books in the Acorna series. Scarborough lives in Washington state with two black cats and a lot of beads, and occasionally entertains wandering minstrels.

F ather, have ya got a blessing for a horse?" said Anne Mc-
Caffrey to Richard Woods, OP, sometime during their first
meeting. Anne had shortly tried her hand at raising racehorses, and this was the occasion when Nickel Run was first
due to run. Richard rose to the occasion and produced some
good words, but sadly Divine Providence demanded otherwise
for poor Nickel.

Though the whole Dragonhold lot—a group of horse-mad girls
who had attached themselves to Anne in the early '70s and
grown into women who remained her close friends—were wary
of a Dominican priest, Richard wooed them all. He continued to
woo them and me when I met him. Richard is the sort of person
who gives religion and the Catholic Church a good name.

Anne had given up on the Catholic Church in the midst of the
Second World War when her father was missing somewhere in
the Atlantic Ocean, her little brother was getting ready to die of
osteomyelitis, her older brother was in Hawaii awaiting possible
invasion, and she herself was sent down South to a boarding
school. Conversations with Richard seemed to have changed that,
so much so that Anne came to write "Beyond Between," decided
to be buried rather than cremated, and had a cross on her casket.

Richard wryly commented that Anne had either a
"Presbytolic" or a "Catholitarian" funeral service. My brother,
sister, and I asked if Richard could say something at her
service, and he found the most excellent words of both praise
and comfort.

Religion on Pern?

RICHARD J. WOODS

"IF YOU COME to the church, you've gone too far." That pretty much sums up Anne McCaffrey's approach to organized religion.

Anne once told me that she came from Catholic stock, but separated from Rome over a number of issues long before I met her. Nominally, she was Presbyterian, a wise choice for the Republic of Ireland, where she had moved with two of her three children in 1970. In the end, her funeral was conducted warmly and well by a retired Presbyterian minister, Rev. Jim Carson. He had been her choice, and it was the right one. (Jim asked me to give a reflection at the service, which I was honored to do. But that's another story.)

Because Anne had excluded religion from her Pern stories in particular, many fans and even some professional critics assumed that she was an atheist. Some celebrated the assumption; others denounced it, for instance, as, "Anne's hatred of religion and morinic [sic] view on religion as an evil destructive force. The people of Pern are not human, since every one of them are atheists."* She did have many atheist fans, who peppered

---

* http://karimblog123.blogspot.ie/2012/08/anne-mccaffrey-example-of-stupid-being.html

the dozens of McCaffrey (and other) forums with their views, not least in the "Atheist OUT Campaign" string on the New Kitchen Table page.*

But Anne was not an atheist. Her attitude toward religion, including religion on Pern, was more nuanced than might appear from blogs and brief reviews, however, and it was especially so toward the end of her life. Thereby hangs my tale.

The Dragonlady of Wicklow

I first met Anne in 1981. I was working on a book about trends in contemporary culture and spirituality, especially the implications of some ground swells in regard to an apparent revival of neo-Celtic themes in music, literature, and art. Although I had read the Dragonriders trilogy and the Harper Hall trilogy, I was still unaware that Anne was laying the groundwork for a vast science fiction saga. I was inclined to see her stories more as the exploration of an alternative medieval world with Celtic undertones. And I was very fond of dragons. Always had been, and it wasn't all that trendy then.

Thus armed with happy ignorance and eagerness, I took advantage of a trip to England, where I was conducting research at the time, to visit Ireland and, if possible, to interview Anne McCaffrey. I wrote, she wrote back, and I was invited to come around. I still have the postcard she sent. At the time, Anne lived in Kilquade, a tiny village between Bray and Wicklow Town. It was not easy to find. Hence the phone call. Scribbled at the bottom of the card are some instructions I jotted down:

---

* http://annemccaffreyfans.org/forum/showpost.php?p=1024665&
postcount=126

"Road to Bray, right at Loch Garman sign, 7 mi to sign Kilpedder (L), sign to Kilquade, ½ mi down rd, 3 gateways, R L R, last house, church = too far . . ." That would have been tiny St. Peter's Church, which (she told me later) had a wall dating back to the ninth century. Hence the name, so characteristically Irish—Kilpedder, Peter's Church. (I never figured out who Quade was.)

When I finally arrived at Dragonhold, I was ushered into a living room full of dogs, cats, and people—Anne herself, and a few close friends, Derval Diamond and Maureen Beirne among them. Later I figured out they were there in case "the priest" tried to strong-arm her into some kind of confessional debate. Fortunately, that was the farthest thing from my mind, and we got along well enough that she invited me back. Later, she told me, it was not all that common an occurrence. When my book came out, I dedicated it to Anne. And I did go back.

Gradually, I met more friends and family—"the daughter," as the Irish say, Georgeanne (Gigi) and her brothers, Todd and, eventually, Alec. Anne's widowed sister-in-law (once removed), Sara Virginia Brooks Johnson, came to live with her shortly afterward, and Geoff Kennedy, a friend of Gigi's from earlier days, was a frequent visitor. Fast forward to Geoff and Gigi's gorgeous wedding in the little parish church of St. Patrick in Glencullen, and then Todd's wedding, his daughter's baptism, and two funerals. By then you might say I had become the unofficial weyr chaplain of Dragonhold.

Somewhere along the way, "Anne" became "Annie." Over the next thirty years, we engaged in a mainly epistolary exchange but at times worked together on projects of mutual interest. When I was able to visit, we plotted and schemed story ideas, went to movies, and enjoyed bodacious family feasts at Christmas and whenever the occasion might be made to arise. Part of the fun of working with Annie was that the "brilliant ideas" we concocted over these sessions served mainly to stimulate her imagination and rarely glimmered even faintly between the lines of print. But that's why we did it.

Once in a while religion came up, but it was hardly a topic of everyday interest despite the wonderfully flinty observations of the redoubtably Protestant Sara Virginia. She, however, was Methodist, like my grandpa. We had that and gardening in common (she was an expert gardener), and she had been a nurse. We got on.

Teaching at Oxford half the academic year during the 1990s gave me a good opportunity to ferret out odd bits of information for Anne, perhaps most usefully in regard to the development of horseshoes in sixth-century Britain, which she used to good effect in her young-adult Arthurian novel, *Black Horses for the King*. She put more "religion" in that than any other of her books, which was historically appropriate. She ran a few of the scenes past me to make sure she got details right. She did.

As we were otherwise separated by the Irish Sea, the wide Atlantic, and half the United States, we initially exchanged real letters every few weeks, but with the advent of email, the dialogue quickened prodigiously. I archived most of the messages, and fortunately so because they have a way of clarifying events that might otherwise pass unremarked or misunderstood in other biographies and interviews, including the matter of religion on Pern.

McCaffrey, Religion, and a Planet Called Pern

Though religious matters never occupied much line space in the hundreds of letters and emails we exchanged, scattered clues and asides illuminate some of the more obscure zones in accounts of the development of the saga. In February 1998, she wrote, not without a touch of gentle irony, "As I said the other day, I do not like organized religions but that doesn't mean I am not religious in my own way and form."

On a number of occasions—accidents, the injuries and illness of friends, sudden deaths, and similar challenges—she would briefly request that I put in a word with the Lord. And I believe she did as well, in her own fashion. No doubt more a polite suggestion than a plea, but the Lord did not seem to mind. However, churchgoing was reserved for Very Special Occasions, especially weddings, baptisms, and funerals.

If organized religion was an unobtrusive and very infrequent guest at Dragonhold, it was totally lacking on Pern, an absence that hardly went unnoticed. Many science fiction writers and fans are vehemently skeptical, but others range from the spiritually curious to outright Bible-thumping evangelical. So for one reason or another, Annie found herself constrained on occasion to render an account of the apparent vacancy in her best-selling series.

When asked by one interviewer why the people of Pern were not overtly religious, Anne explained,

> As you probably realize, during a terrible war situation people either cling as their last hope to the religion of their choice, or they become agnostic, losing their belief in a Good, Kindly [and] Wise Deity who has allowed such atrocities to happen to innocent people.
>
> The colonists who went with Admiral Benden and Governor Boll were of the second type, especially from groups who had suffered from atrocities committed BECAUSE of religion: notice what's happening in Kosovo and Iran. What happened to the Mormons in the USA? So no ORGANIZED religion was brought to Pern and none was set up. There is,

however, a strong ethical code among the colonists and by this they govern their lives and interactions. Not even Thread was allowed to alter these precepts.[*]

Anne was well aware of the role "organized" religion played in bloody strife, not least in Northern Ireland, as well as in other global hotspots. She—along with her Pern colonists—deliberately precluded that from marring what was planned to be a permanently peaceful new world, at least in that respect. There would be plenty of malice, greed, hate, and violence, of course—what would fiction be without them?—but not as the result of religious conflict. Not on her planet! I suppose it could be argued from this that Anne's evaluation of what religion ought to be was, in fact, too lofty. She was hardly a utopian, but she had high ideals.

As we learn from Emily Boll's speech in *Dragonsdawn*, eliminating organized religion from Pern had been deliberate from the earliest phases of the colonists' planning:

> "We may not be religious in the archaic meaning of the word, but it makes good sense to give worker and beast one day's rest," Emily stated in the second of the mass meetings. "The old Judean Bible used by some of the old religious sects on Earth contained a great many commonsensible suggestions for an agricultural society, and some moral and ethical traditions which are worthy of retention"—she held up a hand, smiling benignly—"but without any hint of fanatic adherence! We left *that* back on Earth along with war!"

Though admittedly smug, Emily's statement effectively summarized the colonists' rationale. Anne's own explanation

---

[*] http://pernhome.com/aim/anne-mccaffrey/frequently-asked-questions/

(supplied after the fat hit the fire following the publication of "Beyond Between" in 2003) provided some personally meaningful detail:

> I figured—since there were four holy wars going on at the time of writing—that religion was one problem Pern didn't need. However, if one listens to childhood teachings, God is everywhere so there should be no question in any mind that he is also on Pern. Thus, there is a heaven to which worthy souls go. So, without mentioning any denomination of organized religion, I figured that both Moreta and Leri deserved respite after their trials . . . and that's where "Beyond Between" is.*

Personal comments from earlier emails cast a bit more light on her attitude, such as this revealing aside from September 1996:

> Actually, I usually do counter the lack of religion by the presence of a high tone of spirituality on Pern—when pushed by Baptists to do so. I'm currently reading a Dave Duncan which has a veritable pantheon of gods/esses for all sorts of purposes, each with a color and a creed and an ability to interfere with mortals similar to the games that went on at Mt. Olympus. Well, it makes a nice change from galleying McCaffrey.

(Anne spent considerable time proofing galleys of her prodigious output.)

One of the more exasperating aspects of deliberately eliminating organized religion from Pern was the reaction from people Annie sometimes referred to charitably enough as "nuts," but with whom she often undertook a dialogue,

---

* http//www.writing-world.com/sf/mccaffrey.shtml

sometimes a spirited one, so to speak. A few correspondents were content to denounce her for promoting atheism. She didn't, of course. She ignored religion and simply left God out of the discussion (so did J. R. R. Tolkien in The Lord of the Rings, of course, but I don't recall readers accusing him of atheism).

One of the more strenuous objections came from a fellow with some cultural anthropology background who maintained that every human culture and society on Earth had evolved some kind of religion. It is intrinsic to human civilization. Ergo, over the centuries, some kind religion would have evolved on Pern. So where was it?

Didn't exist, Annie said. Had to, said he. The dialogue became heated, and Annie finally called in the weyr chaplain (me) to see if I could get this fellow off her case. Eventually, we had to invite him to go elsewhere with his rants.

I had some ideas of my own, based on accepted notions of religious development, which I had run by Annie's watchful eye back as early as 1986. They did not convince her, and I didn't expect them to, but we enjoyed the repartee:

what with persons bugging you about Religion on Pern, I would LOVE to sit and chat, since that is my area. (Not Religion on Pern, but Religious Studies. About which, also cf. below, as they say . . .) Don't fall for the stuff about the Primal Egg. Neither culture (nor religion) on Pern [would have] evolved from scratch (so to speak), but would be a descended (but transformed) version of whatever religion(s) or religious feelings the first colonists had. I.e., much more likely a historical religion (e.g., like Judaism, Christianity, and Islam) than a nature religion, dragons notwithstanding. It is also likely that the holders would have a religious code different from and in some respects hostile to that of the

Dragonriders—more mercantile/agrarian (*a la* later Judaism) than nomadic/herder/warrior (*a la* Islam). But they would be shoots from the same stem. And in each case there would be some vestige of built-in demythologization from the Olden Days, probably in the form of a pervasive skepticism. The Dragonriders would probably have a more developed notion of luck/fate/grace because of the precariousness of their work, while the holders would be more complacent and, in good times, downright atheistic. In any event, the Pernese would not worship mythical dragons or Eggs. They're too smart. I doubt if there would be a formal priesthood, either, although a kind of Zen-Buddhist monasticism might have sprouted among the Riders, just as Zen was cultivated by the Samurai. Something also worth pondering re: the Dragonriders would be the Shintoist-Zen cult of the Japanese pilots of WW II, including the suicide ethic. In short, a modified form of ancestor worship in which figures like Moreta would function like hero-saints and martyrs along with their dragons. A kind of semi-polytheism under the umbrella of a vague monotheism (sounds a bit like some forms of Catholicism!). . . . (I could go on for a long time, but mercifully won't. But someday let's do.)

We did, on occasion. In 1996, she provided another telling comment after I reported on a chatroom debate I had with a particularly truculent correspondent (who was eventually cut off by the monitor):

Glad you survived the CHAT—they can be fun and there're usually a couple of awkward ones—I get them, too—and usually have to repeat what I've said earlier online . . . glad the electro cops could step in. Didn't the ass know that the Dragons ARE the religion on Pern?

Cussing

Absent organized religion on Pern, the matter of profanity also posed something of a problem, if one more literary than political. For reasons deep and dark, religion (next only to sex) seems always to have provided humankind matter for its most outrageous and, therefore, useful expletives, frequently curses involving the inappropriate use of the Lord's name or ingenious (and obscene) references to sacred body parts. The retrospective volume *Dragonsdawn* does find the original colonists swearing colorfully, if not frequently, including some vocabulary that would have seemed out of place in the original Pern stories. But even these hardy pioneers seem temperate in employing the usual religious epithets, giving the more heated exchanges a kind of Victorian hue. But it is cumbersome even to be mildly profane when there is no *fanum* to be outside of.

I did make a few lame suggestions in a note from 1997: "Shards! Okay, so your Pernese are a pretty nice lot. They are still human, right? By the Burning Thread of Firstfall! By the First Egg!" Annie came up with some alternatives, but "scorch it!" and "fardling" just don't carry the conviction that one might expect from sweaty, battle-hardened Dragonriders just in from a tough bout of flaming Thread. Did I mention that although Annie had her tougher side, she was a genuinely gentle, kind, and caring person?

On February 27, 2000, she wrote,

Have thought of one idea—with many of the "common herd" a bit dubious of Aivas and the good he's already done/will do/ has files on—suspicions arise. Of course, because Aivas helped save the planet from the fireball, 'By Aivas, he helped' becomes a vouchsafe for surety. So, whether he wants to or not, Aivas becomes a talisman . . . better than the 'By First Egg.' Do I know what I mean by all that?

Speaking of Aivas, the Artificial Intelligence Voice Activated System buried by the first colonists and recovered thousands of years later by Jaxom and Piemur in *Renegades of Pern*, the computer got the best line when it came to religion or at least the Bible. Toward the end of *All the Weyrs of Pern*, Aivas cites the Book of Ecclesiastes (or do you say *Qoheleth*?) to ease Master Robinton's final moments of life in one of the finest scenes of the whole series:

> "'To everything there is a season, and a time to every purpose under heaven,' Master Robinton."
>
> "That is poetic, Aivas."
>
> There was one of those pauses that Robinton always thought was the Aivas equivalent of a smile.
>
> "From the greatest book ever written by Mankind, Master Robinton."

Of course it's possible to read more into this passage than Anne intended. A number of readers have cited it as evidence of an underlying spiritual, if not religious, conviction. Considering previous offhand statements, this would not be too far off the mark. It at least shows that while organized religion had been precluded from Pern from the earliest phases of planning, the colonists had not entirely forgotten the positive religious heritage of humanity. Annie had her Bible at hand. She knew where to find things.

Going Beyond Between

Anne's deeper spiritual inklings came more strongly forward in her final solo work, a short story that launched a number of heated reactions.

It started off innocuously enough. Although she had handled the religious references and chapel scenes in her earlier historical novel *Black Horses for the King* well enough to pass muster, and her allusion in *All the Weyrs of Pern* is evidential of her positive attitude toward the spiritual aspect of religious tradition, she came closest to tackling a genuinely religious, or at least metaphysical, theme in "Beyond Between." We exchanged a folder full of email about this short story, which she referred to originally as "Moreta's Ghost." Its genesis provides a literally haunting glimpse into her attitude toward matters religious and spiritual.

Late in 2001, she had been invited by Robert Silverberg to submit a ghost story for his forthcoming anthology *Legends II*, which was originally to be entitled *Shadows, Gods, and Demons.* Dutifully, she set out to write a genuine ghost story, and for characters and theme she went back to one of the most deeply felt and successful of her Pern novels, *Moreta: Dragonlady of Pern* (1983). Anne worked on the story for over a year, but when "Beyond Between" appeared, it proved to be arguably the least well received of all her stories. Even some of the trade reviews were surprisingly abrasive.

Moreta's weary disappearance "between" at the end of the novel admittedly came as a shock to readers at the time, although Anne had long since established that if dragonriders failed to envision a point of emergence from the spatial-temporal dimension through which dragons could pass, they would be trapped there and inevitably perish. Still, the surprise loss of a powerful and engaging heroine was deeply disturbing to many readers and to her editors as well.

In an interview with Lynne Jamneck published online in 2004, Annie commented:

> When I wrote *Dragonlady* and allowed Moreta to go between and not come out, there was quite an outcry, including one from Judy-Lynn del Rey, my editor. She thought Moreta could have mistakenly gone to the future, or the past but that she was still alive.*

But Anne's decision to follow up on Moreta's fate, as well as that of other riders who had disappeared "between," gave her the opportunity to explore both personal and fictional issues regarding life, death, and immortality that mattered deeply to her. The losses of relatives and friends over the years weighed on her, especially those of her elder brother Mac and her friend Johnny Greene of the Foreign Legion (recalled in several novels by characters with J.G. in their names), as well as those of neighbors, clients of Dragonhold Stables, and her own household staff. Her favorite and supportive Aunt Gladdie had died years earlier, and Annie's crusty companion and expert gardener, Sara Virginia Brooks Johnson, "Sis," went to her rest in 2001 as did her friend and fellow author Gordon Dickson. She didn't talk about these losses a great deal, but they clearly remained with her as a challenge to her sense of destiny and the place of friendship in this world and beyond.

Still, surfacing these concerns in a published story, even indirectly, was bold, a move perpendicular to the customary

---

* Lynne Jamneck, "An Interview with Anne McCaffrey," http://www
.writing-world.com/sf/mccaffrey.shtml

tone of the Pern canon, and perhaps surprising given her general reticence about religious themes in previous works. Over the months of its gestation, we exchanged dozens of messages about the story as Anne struggled to express her sense of the indestructibility of the human spirit. As the canon was jealously guarded by ardent battalions of self-appointed sentries, departures could prove hazardous. And such divergence was even more flagrant than getting the color of a dragon's (or dragon-rider's) eyes wrong.

On January 13, 2002, she wrote, "Bob Silverberg was, for him, ecstatic about me doing a Pernese ghost story so I'm taking that one past both Todd and Gigi for input." And three days later, "Did 6,000 words on the ghost story yesterday and will reread to see how I like it now it's cooled off a bit." Two days later, the tally was up to 16,000, but some health setbacks and plot problems began to slow the pace.

In February, Anne wrote, "Todd, Gigi, and I are going to brainstorm to see if I can get a story up and running. As I said last evening, Todd has queries about why am I writing this? I dunno, and he pointed out that I already had a Helva ghost story which he likes. And it's a case of parameters."

I wrote back cheekily, "But the Moreta story is also a helluva good ghost story if still in the early stages of development. It's important for what it says about Between, too. It's *not* just a ghost story. It really advances the understanding of Pern's second-most interesting feature."

In mid-March, she had begun to feel that she had hit a roadblock but was determined to press on: "I had the most fascinating dream wherein I was telling myself I was dead and I haven't finished Moreta's ghost so how can I leave yet? Ciao now, Padre. Add Joan Harrison [Harry Harrison's wife] to your prayer well."

As the story neared completion, Gigi and I agreed that as

it stood "Beyond Between" ventured too far beyond the pale of Anne's normal reserve concerning the supernatural. We advised her to tone down some of the descriptions. A number of "New Age" touches suggested by friends of that persuasion seemed more metaphysically luminous and beckoning than "ghostly."

The final version was a more subtle statement, but also stronger after Gigi's judicious tailoring. After reading it, I wrote in July, "I read 'Beyond Between' last night. It's great! Trimmer and more pointed, but sufficiently ambiguous to be an excellent ghost story. Gigi did a masterful job tidying. It's a story you can be proud of."

I was not exactly in the majority in that regard, and I was stung by the cattiness of some of the reviews after "Beyond Between" appeared in print. Annie, fortunately, did not pay much attention to such notices as a rule, though she was aware of the groans of literary dismay. Had her turn to the supernatural gone too far?

Devoted fans seemed reluctant to comment, but a number of reviews ranged from tepid to vitriolic. *Publishers Weekly* dismissed it as "an ill-conceived explanation of what happens when a dragon fails to return from Between, [that] strikes the book's lone sour note." Another reviewer opined that "As she is already dead, a story of Moreta's further adventures was simply disappointing both as a Pern story, as well as just being a story that was not terribly interesting despite my love of Pern." Even less forgiving was this diatribe: "Anne McCaffrey . . . had no business being in this book. McCaffrey is writing almost everything including her grocery lists by proxy these days, and it shows. She may very well have at one point been a master of this genre, but her time has passed, and she is embarrassing herself." And, again, "The only total bomb in this [collection] was McCaffrey's short story explaining what happens to dragons that become lost between. Even fans of the Pern novels should skip this one."*

"Beyond Between" certainly exposed a raw nerve here and there. Anne's narrative powers had undoubtedly been lessened by a number of recent health problems. But I suspect that the real venom arose because she had also crossed a well-defined line in the minds of some, perhaps many, readers. No one actually ventured to say as much, but the displeasure seemed unusually savage. In any case, "Beyond Between" did not garner much praise, to put it mildly.

Still, "Beyond Between" expresses something of Annie's struggle to come to terms with significant losses in her own life. It was written as Anne approached the last years of her own life and the final days of many others important to her. Damon Knight died the following year, and Joan Harrison died later that year, too. Annie's American agent and friend, Virginia Kidd, died a year after that, in 2003.

The following summer Annie's mentally troubled niece, Karen, who had moved to Ireland some years earlier, died suddenly. I was in Ireland at the time and was able to preside at the funeral, held at Our Lady Queen of Peace Church in a Catholic parish in Bray where Karen had become a member and received sympathetic care and attention from the church's outreach group. The parish priest graciously turned the church over to the family for the funeral mass. He and the parish staff couldn't do enough for us and wouldn't take a cent as a donation for their pains. As we left the church, Annie stuffed a fifty-euro note into the poor box.

---

* See http://www.amazon.com/Legends-II-Dragon-Sword-King/product-reviews/034547578X/ref=cm_cr_pr_viewpnt_sr_4?ie=UTF8&filterBy=add FourStar&showViewpoints=0, and http://www.amazon.com/Legends-II-Dragon-Sword-King/dp/product-description/034547578X/ref=dp_proddesc _0?ie=UTF8&n=283155&s=books

Annie continued to write over the next several years, but declining health slowed the pace, which in her heyday had been prodigious. Collaborations with Elizabeth Ann Scarborough ("the other Annie") and especially with her son Todd, who was emerging as a fine writer in the Pern tradition, became more the norm, a development not viewed favorably by some readers, who had complained before at collaborations Anne had undertaken with promising writers such as Margaret Ball, Mercedes Lackey, Elizabeth Moon, Jody Lynn Nye, Elizabeth Ann Scarborough, and Steve Stirling.

Anne did not publish again under her own name only. In the summers to come, we met several times over tea and her favorite "biscuits" to blue-sky plot devices for *After the Fall*, the last of her Pern novels (although she finished a first draft several months before her death, it is unlikely to be published in the form in which she left it).

To Everything There Is a Season

Annie died of a stroke suddenly and, of course, prematurely, on November 21, 2011, just before Thanksgiving. I grabbed a quick flight to Ireland and arrived in time for the wake and funeral. The service was not held in a church. No surprise there, and there was standing room only at the funeral home in Bray. Annie looked great in her favorite purple chiffon dress. I'm sure she would have enjoyed herself. The service started with Bach ("Sheep May Safely Graze") and ended with Brahms' "Academic Festival Overture"—Annie's favorites. Alec gave a short but eloquent eulogy, and later, after Celine Byrne (the rising young opera star) sang "It's a Wonderful World," Jim Carson gave a homily based on 1 John 4. If it seemed almost impromptu at points, he cleverly packed a lot of "religion" into it, and no one seemed to mind.

So yes, religion on and off Pern was a nuanced affair for Anne McCaffrey. Organized religion was kept at a distance—an interstellar distance on Pern, if less so at Dragonhold-Underhill. But the deeper and more mysterious dimensions of life, even on Pern, did not escape notice. Anne loved life, all of it, and lived it full stop. And she had a great ride. If it wasn't on a real dragon, she at least got to swim with dolphins in Key West and rode her favorite horses till arthritis got the better of her.

A Psalm for Annie

Jim Carson had called shortly after I arrived in Ireland the day before Annie's funeral and asked me to provide a short reflection on her favorite scriptural passage, Psalm 23, which she had selected for her funeral months before. I was grateful for the invitation, but with only a few hours to prepare, found myself perplexed. I bounded awake at 3 a.m. with most of it clearly in mind. This is how it went:

> The Lord was her shepherd. No one else could have gotten away with it so long. If she did occasionally want—it was her own amazing generosity that led to it. A couple of times, she asked me for a short-term cash loan because she had literally given away every coin in her purse. An authentic Christian, she also preferred anonymity, and I know that in making some truly heroic donations, she insisted on not letting the left hand know what the right was doing.

Although they became home to a collection of remarkable horses, dogs, and cats, her pastures were always green. On the other hand, the waters around her were not always still, in fact rarely so, but with a guiding hand, she sometimes seemed to walk on them. Her faith was not little.

Annie had a way of choosing the road not taken, which today is too often the path of righteousness, but she would be the first to guffaw at the suggestion. She was the least hypocritical of women and hated even the semblance of evil. She didn't fear it, but often railed against it. Nevertheless, she was not always a strict judge of human character because she preferred to believe that people were more righteous than, in fact, they were. When she was cheated, it hurt, but it failed to make her bitter or lessen her faith in human decency.

Even so, I'm sure she's had a few words with God about his staff, who did not always comfort her as much as they should have, but it's sometimes hard even for God to get good staff these days. I was chuffed when back in 1981, she did not find me totally wanting but invited me back to Dragonhold as a kind of an occasional weyr chaplain. We sometimes even talked about religion, the Church, and, yes, God . . .

Annie didn't always wait for God to prepare a table in the presence of anyone, much less enemies—if she had any. She got there first. And if her cup occasionally overflowed a little with good Chardonnay, it was more often the cup of kindness and mercy that made her blessed with family, friends, colleagues, and that strange cloud of witnesses called "fans," over three

> million of whom quickly tapped into Google about the death of the Dragonlady of Pern, who has found a lasting dwelling place not only in the Lord's house but in those millions and millions of hearts.

Born and reared in New Mexico, RICHARD J. WOODS did undergraduate studies in Washington, DC, New Mexico, and Iowa before joining the Order of Preachers (Dominicans), a Roman Catholic community of priests, brothers, and sisters. He earned a PhD in the philosophy of religion (Loyola Chicago, 1978), MAs in systematic theology and scholastic philosophy, and an STM (master of sacred theology) from the Dominican Order. For twenty-seven years, he taught on the graduate faculty at Loyola University Chicago and also taught undergraduate theology and philosophy, and since 1981, has been adjunct associate professor in the Department of Psychiatry at Loyola University Medical School. From 1991 to 1999, he was lecturer and tutor at Oxford University, and he held the Dominican lectureship at Emory University in 1999. He has written thirteen nonfiction books, coauthored a novel with Anne McCaffrey, and published three novelettes. He has edited four anthologies in religious studies and has authored articles in spirituality, theology, health care, sexuality, and Celtic studies. His last book, *Meister Eckhart: Master of Mystics*, was published by Continuum/Bloomsbury in 2011. Currently, he is professor of theology at Dominican University, River Forest, Illinois.

In many respects, Chelsea Quinn Yarbro is to horror what Anne McCaffrey was to science fiction. She holds numerous awards, many of them lifetime awards, including the rather charming "literary knighthood" from the Transylvanian Society of Dracula. I knew her first, respectfully, as Ms. Yarbro.

Whenever she and Anne got together, they would make it a point to disappear and compare whatever occult notes they'd made since their last rendezvous. They always had a marvelous time together.

Annie and Horses

CHELSEA QUINN YARBRO

ASIDE FROM WRITING, Anne McCaffrey and I shared a love of opera and horses, and were as likely to talk about "horses we have known/know" as we were to discuss the state of the publishing industry. We met infrequently over the years, but when we did, eventually we'd end up at horses, and we'd exchange stories, suggestions, anecdotes, tips, and other horsey things.

After she had moved to Ireland, her stable became a major focus of her non-writing life, and the horses she owned or boarded were increasingly part of the framework of her life.

Annie *got* horses as well as loved them. She could read their personalities and characters from their demeanor and behavior, and dealt with them accordingly. Most of the time, she wanted cooperation rather than dominance with horses; when this wasn't possible, she tried for minimal conflict with them, but maintained the position that the human was in charge.

About twenty-five years ago Annie and I attended the same book fair in Las Vegas, and one night over dinner, after debating the proper time to use draw-reins, we got into a lively discussion on bits, from snaffles to trammels. We ended up with her thoughts on the Kimberwick and mine on the short-shank elevator (high port with copper roller). The rest of the group had got that dazed look, so we changed the subject, to everyone's relief. At that same book fair, at another break in the evens, we ended up discussing saddle-pads.

We would from time to time exchange tales of our horses—she had more stories because she had more horses—and she was always an excellent source of information on problems. When my Norwegian Fjord mare Pikku became stall-sour during one wet winter, Annie recommended going on a short trail-ride in the rain with friends. It seemed to ease her irritation, and it's not the thing that a Californian like me would tend to think about, but Annie in Ireland was in a much better position to deal with that kind of situation.

What was most clear about these conversations she and I had was that Annie respected her horses and held them in great affection, even the annoying and headstrong ones. There was none of the kind of boasting that sounded as if she took credit for the abilities of the horses; instead she spoke as if she had been able to bring out some ability of her horses, which was as much to their credit as hers.

Once I asked her if I was right in detecting an equine undercurrent in the nature of her dragons, and she said that horses were easier to study than dragons—a clever answer that was neither confirmation nor denial; sometimes I wonder if she ever drew a line between them. Not that such a view of an imaginary creature does not have roots in known creatures—coming up with something that is truly devoid of any influence from actual human experience may be possible, but communicating it to others would take heroic amounts of work. Many have tried it, but most have not actually succeeded to pull off such a feat of the imagination.

Occasionally Annie and I would discuss our views of Pern: as the creator of the world, she always had the final word, as it should be, but I had some reservations about Pern as science fiction, although none at all as high fantasy. I know Annie saw Pern through a science fiction lens, and in narrative technique she was absolutely right. The turning from conventional magic for biology for the basis of that world is refreshing. And I had no trouble with equine dragons qua dragons, but I had reservations on equine dragons in terms of the economics of the society where they existed, and which was set up to tend to the dragons as a crucial defense system for the preservation of crops and forests. Knowing how much it costs to keep one horse, extrapolating what a number of her dragons would cost in coin or goods-and-services to maintain goes well beyond the kind of agrarian society that apparently prevails on Pern; the kind of social structure she offers in those books is far more like early fifteenth century Europe than a more urban society that rose, along with a middle class, some two centuries later. Pern, being more Plantagenet than Tudor, is therefore highly dependent on farmers and other agricultural workers, who would either be bound to the land or to the landholder in order to provide feed for and upkeep on dragons, which is only sketchily present in the series.

When we talked about this, she often said she wasn't interested in economics, or in what kind of labor might be involved, but in the need for dragons as participants in such circumstances as she used in her stories. And I admire the complexity of the stories, particularly the great use she made of the interaction of dragon and rider, which sustains the tone of the stories from book to book—no mean accomplishment for any writer. I may have had quibbles about her vision of Pern, but none at all at how well she held all the disparate elements together book after book. They are her stories and she is the one who calls the shots.

At one of the Brighton Worldcons (I think it was '87), Annie gave a Devon Cream Tea in her suite, and over crumpets and scones and jams and jellies and Devonshire cream, we, her guests, heard about her horses and her stable; it was apparent that Annie was deeply happy with her life, with her work, and with her horses. She enjoyed all three components of her life, and she wore her fame with aplomb—or if she didn't, it certainly looked like it. It is always reassuring to see writers gain recognition and gratification at the same time, and to be aware of it without lording it over their colleagues. I was glad for the example of professionalism she set for newer writers; I was delighted for her achievements, even those that had to do with horses rather than Hugos. I was sad when we lost her, her stories, and her great collection of characters—the ones in print and the ones on four hooves.

A professional writer for forty-five years, CHELSEA QUINN YARBRO has published over ninety books in a variety of genres as well as nonfiction. She has received the Grand Master award from the World Horror Convention, the International Horror Guild's Living Legend award, the Horror Writers Association's Life Achievement award, and has twice been nominated for an Edgar Award. She lives in Richmond, California, with two sublime cats.

Anne McCaffrey loved Michael Whelan's covers—and so did the fans. One of the things that sets Michael Whelan above some other cover artists is that he reads the books before he illustrates them, and that brings a level of detail to his covers that really makes them shine.

When Isaac Asimov, one of Anne's favorite people of all time (they were utterly hilarious together), passed away, Michael Whelan was commissioned to do a memorial cover for *Asimov's* magazine. Not long after, some of the comps were on sale at a Worldcon. I saw one in particular, and I phoned Mum right away. She said, "Get it."

"It's going to go for a lot of money, what's my limit?"

"Just get it."

I got it, and it was hung on the door of Mum's office from that day on.

It's both fitting and an honor that Michael agreed to do the cover for this piece. Here Michael has kindly shared sketches and notes on the creation of the many famous covers that helped introduce readers to Pern.

Picturing Pern

MICHAEL WHELAN

IN THE THIRTY-SIX years since I painted *The White Dragon*, I've done more book cover illustrations than I can count. For each book cover commission that was completed, there were anywhere from two to twenty-five concept sketches (or "comps" as they are known in the trade). These are small renderings of potential approaches to a particular cover painting, done for the art department and marketing people at a publisher so they can have a hand in selecting which approach would best serve the sale of the book. Sometimes, too, it would often happen that a book was so engaging that I couldn't decide on just one scene to single out for the cover. In such cases, I would do several comps and leave the decision up to the publisher and author.

When I became acquainted with SF conventions and fantasy and science fiction fandom, I was gratified to learn that there were collectors eager to own some of these preliminary pieces when they were available, and so most of my old comps have disappeared into private collections. Also, in the early years of my career, I neglected to document many of them, so my personal archive of these preliminary works is regretfully less complete than I would like. Still, I did manage to photograph or scan enough of them to provide a peek into the alternative ideas behind my works for Anne McCaffrey's Pern novels.

My approach to creating concept sketches has always been dictated by my subjective feelings about the book they were concerned with. Since I believe that the arrangement of lights and darks is the most important part of an image, and that the color scheme is the most malleable part of a painting, the majority of my comps over the years have been in monochrome— that is, either in black and white or limited color, sometimes with a suggestion of the warmer and cooler colors I thought might work well for the final image. However, on many occasions the colors were there in my mind when the idea for an image came to me; in such cases, I would go ahead and do the comps in color.

The preliminary works shown here are culled from six of the Pern cover art projects I worked on. All of these were painted in acrylic.

It was like winning an illustrator's lottery to have the opportunity to contribute to such important and popular books, books that were both a joy to work with and which inspired some of my most popular cover paintings. Anne's generous and steadfast enthusiasm for my work throughout the years is something I will always treasure and feel grateful for.

Pern Cover Concept Sketches

THE WHITE DRAGON

My introduction to the world of Pern came with *The White Dragon*. When I was asked to take on the assignment, I was unfamiliar with the books, so some catch-up was involved. As legions of McCaffrey fans will attest, that was no hardship!

After thoroughly reading *The White Dragon*, my primary concern was to come up with an exciting design that worked for the whole book, not just the front cover. The easiest way to do this, I felt, was to wrap some drawing paper around an actual book and draw the design directly onto the mock cover. This is just what I did, using pen and ink to sketch in the shapes. Later I added some loose color notes as accents to give the people at Del Rey Books an idea of where I intended to go with it. After the publisher okayed the idea, I was off and running on the actual painting.

What you see here is a scan of that original piece of drawing paper I folded around the book.

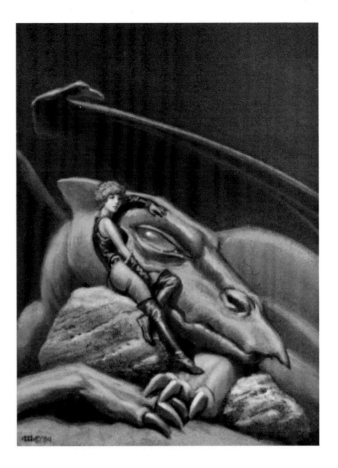

MORETA, DRAGONLADY OF PERN

Pleased with the success of *The White Dragon*, Del Rey subsequently commissioned me to do cover paintings for more Pern novels: *Dragonflight*, *Dragonquest*, and other books through the years as Ms. McCaffrey wrote them and as I was available. Each of these assignments had its peculiarities and problems.

For example, a month and a half before beginning work on a painting for *Moreta, Dragonlady of Pern* (1983), I had broken my painting hand in my karate class. When I went to the emergency room I kept hold of a pencil so they could build the cast so that my hand and arm were in a position that would allow me to continue working as soon as possible. Two other commissions and these concept sketches, all painted in acrylics, were done while I was burdened with that cast; it was something of a trial of patience getting through the work. Fortunately, when it was time to begin the painting for *Moreta*, I had healed enough to permit removal of the cast. The joy I felt in my newfound freedom of movement is what inspired the sweep of intense color in the sky seen in the final cover painting.

DRAGONSDAWN

Dragonsdawn was special for its emphasis on the fire-lizards of Pern, and I welcomed the chance to paint them in a cover illustration. The actual cover painting went well enough until the last few days, when I found I was having great difficulty visualizing the look of the water at the foot of the painting. Before I could finish it, I had to leave on a prearranged family

vacation to the United Kingdom. While touring Wales, we visited Three
Cliffs Bay, and I took the opportunity afforded by the spectacular location
to walk a bit into the surf and look back toward the beach. I could see then
where I had gone wrong in my painting at home. I looked long at the scene
and tried my best to memorize it; when I got home, I was able to complete
it in short order and send it to the publisher.

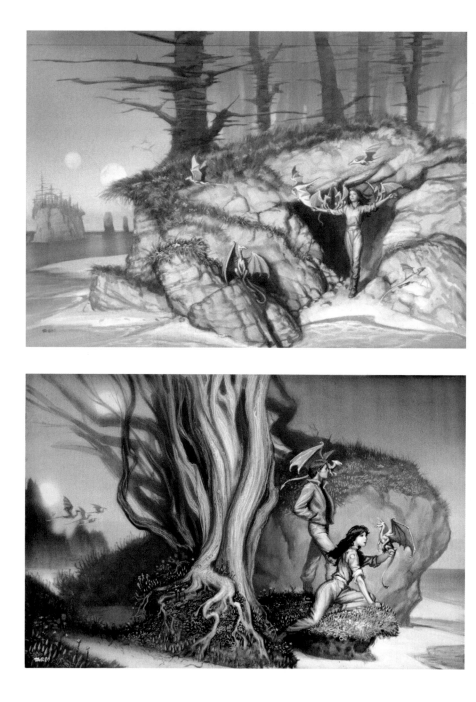

RENEGADES OF PERN

My cover painting for *Renegades of Pern* was slated to be the last one I could reliably deliver before the anticipated birth of my son, Adrian. It was going badly when, a week before his due date, I admitted defeat and started over on a new painting. Day after day, I labored to get the work done before the baby arrived and my time would be lost. But he was considerate enough to wait a few extra days, allowing me time to finish; I delivered it a mere day before Adrian himself was. A close one!

ALL THE WEYRS OF PERN

Due to a scheduling conflict, I had to begin work on the cover to *All the Weyrs of Pern* before Anne could finish writing the first draft of the book. Judy-Lynn del Rey had told me that I didn't need to read the book to do this cover anyway, since Anne had a specific scene in mind for me to paint. Anne phoned me to describe the scene in detail while I took notes. As we were talking, I ended up telling her about a dream I'd had the night before of a scene with several dragons atop eroded peaks in a huge crater valley filled with dense fog. Her response was enthusiastic: She said, "Let's do *that* one!" We agreed in the end that it would be best if I simply did comps

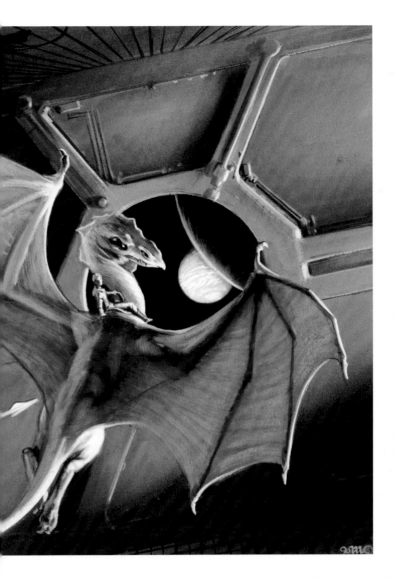

of each of our ideas, and then she and Judy-Lynn could take their pick. As it happened, they chose my dream idea!

I would have been happy to paint any of the concepts floating around for this book, but it was an added treat to not only see the idea I dreamed about come to fruition, but also to have Anne write it into the book.

The first two sketches here I made from the description Anne gave me over the phone that day. When Smart Pop approached me about doing a painting, I thought of those sketches. It felt fitting that we use an idea of Anne's for a tribute to her and Pern . . . and those sketches became the basis for this book's cover.

THE GIRL WHO HEARD DRAGONS

With *The Girl Who Heard Dragons* I was most concerned with featuring the heroine of the story front and center. Though I usually try to avoid having characters face away from the viewer, the selected scene did just that. To compensate, I strove to make her pose as expressive as possible. Though I asked our secretary, Heather, to pose for my preliminary sketches, the figure in the comp that was chosen for the book cover was made up. I brushed in a full-size study of the figure on acetate and used that as my "model" while I did the full-size painting.

Since 1976, MICHAEL WHELAN has been one of the world's premier fantasy and science fiction artists, the first living artist to be inducted into the Science Fiction and Fantasy Hall of Fame. He currently devotes most of his time to his gallery paintings, but during his career he has created more than 350 book and album covers for authors and artists like Isaac Asimov, Anne McCaffrey, Sir Arthur C. Clarke, Stephen King, the Jacksons, Sepultura, and Meat Loaf. His clients have included every major U.S. book publisher, in addition to such diverse companies as National Geographic, CBS Records, and the Franklin Mint. Recent book covers seen on the top of the bestseller lists include Robert Jordan's Wheel of Time novel *A Memory of Light* and Brandon Sanderson's *The Way of Kings*.

Alec Johnson is Anne McCaffrey's eldest son. There were times when Alec was also the person who put food on her table, back in the dark days before *The White Dragon* became a best-seller and we started eating pancakes for dinner because we *could*.

Since the summer of 2011, when she had to pass on Dragon*Con because of another mini-stroke, Mum was worried that she would pass on before she got "to see my two sons again." She was looking forward to having Alec over for Thanksgiving; I would arrive the week before Christmas so as to spread out the holiday cheer.

She passed away while Alec was still clearing customs. He flew to Ireland expecting his mother and found a funeral. Even so, he rose to the occasion and wrote a memorial for her, which he delivered eloquently at the service.

Here now he writes just as eloquently of the legacy he received from his mother.

Red Star Rising

ALEC JOHNSON

ONE OF MY earliest memories of family life with my mother was a time when we were gathered around the television watching *The Wizard of Oz*. Mom loved it as much as we did, and I've lost count of the number of times we watched it together. I'm reminded of this because of the Tin Man and what the Wizard told him about the heart he longed to possess: "A heart is not judged by how much you love, but by how much you are loved by others." By this measure there is no limit to my mother's heart.

I'm so proud that my mother led her life in such a manner as to have earned the admiration of so many, and it is altogether fitting that she be remembered in written tributes, including many gathered in these pages. As her eldest son, the privilege of writing and delivering her eulogy was given to me. She deserved nothing less than my very best effort, and that is what I confidently delivered that fair day in November. Yet as important as it was for me to rise to the occasion, I've come to realize since that the most fitting tribute I can pay Anne McCaffrey is the manner in which I lead my life, while honoring, through use, the many gifts I received from and through her. I've been a progressive activist my whole adult life in large part because of her influence. And never for a moment did I fail to enjoy her full support for my efforts. Let me elaborate.

Like many of my mother's admirers, I'm a big fan of Dragonriders of Pern. The courage, resolve, and dedication of the dragonriders inspired more than admiration. They inspired emulation, and I'm sure this had an influence on my future activism. I was also impressed by the example of Lessa's strength and wisdom, along with that of the many other strong women who sprung from my mother's remarkable imagination. The world I hoped to live in embraced strong people regardless of gender. My feminism, like the rest of my activism, has deep roots.

When I first read *Dragonflight* many years ago, I'm sure I never thought I'd find parallels between Pern and life on Earth, but today I do. When F'lar first saw the Red Star rising in the sky, he fully understood the threat it signified—an existential threat to all life on Pern. Here on Earth there is no Red Star rising to warn us about the tremendous danger we're beginning to face. Global warming* is real, happening now, and every bit as much a threat, this century, as Thread falling through Pern's skies in the world of my mother's imagining. And here on Earth, just as on Pern, there are many who refuse to recognize the threat, choosing to ignore it at their peril. Unlike Pern, however, humanity here is beset by the largest corporate players on Earth, the fossil fuel industry† that works its colossal betrayal through many of the largest governments on Earth. It's almost more than a bronze rider can cope with. Almost.

I was a teenager when I first read *Dragonflight*, and like many I longed to be a dragonrider myself. I recall asking Mom what kind of a rider she imagined I was, and she told me I rode

---

* Climate change, climate disruption, a rose by any other name signifies the same impending disaster.
† Six of the ten top corporations on Earth are fossil-fuel based.

a brown dragon. Knowing that the biggest dragons ridden by men were bronze, I requested and received an upgrade. And more than once during a demonstration or a direct action I've wished I could summon such a giant friend. Yet I recall reading somewhere that in China's distant past the dragon symbolized the people in their power. And a dragon of this kind I've witnessed many times, first when I was sixteen.

It was 1968, and I had traveled to Washington, DC, to participate in what remains the largest political demonstration I've ever witnessed, an anti-Vietnam war rally that reportedly had somewhere between 400,000 and 700,000 people attending. I recall stepping off from the Lincoln Memorial walking toward the Washington Monument. The path before me was filled with people all the way to the monument. When I arrived at it, I turned to see where I had come through, and the entire space had filled again with people. I'd never seen so many people in one place before in my life. It was an experience both electric and awesome. And while this went far toward propelling me on the path I've been on ever since, the real turning point came the following year and had much to do with Anne McCaffrey.

In the 1960s we lived on the North Shore of Long Island, and I attended North Shore High School in Glenwood Landing, New York; drawing on the local accent, many students referred to it as "Nausea High." In my senior year the school district was horrified when heroin was found on our high school campus. Our district was lily-white and quite middle to upper-middle class economically. Many regarded heroin as something that only happened in dangerous places like New York City, and a good deal of panic ensued. The school board invited students to share our concerns about this unexpected problem. What we delivered to the school board was equally unexpected, surprising them and the entire school district. And it wouldn't have happened without Anne McCaffrey's help.

Before I continue with this story, it's important to recall the context we were contending with at the time and the profound influence it had on my generation. It was the end of the '60s, and many of us were steeped in the youth counterculture. The Vietnam War cast a very long shadow over my entire experience in high school. From the time I was fifteen, high school felt like a conveyor belt that was going to deliver me to an early grave in a distant jungle. Every week the news relayed the body counts of our troop losses and estimated "enemy" casualties as if it were some kind of macabre sporting event. And then there was the civil rights movement. I had grown up being assured that I lived in the greatest nation on Earth, especially loved by God because we were the "home of the brave and the land of the free." Watching pictures of African-American school children being fire-hosed by white southern sheriffs sorted poorly with this gilded view. I was inspired by leaders like Martin Luther King Jr. and Malcolm X. I admired the bravery of the Freedom Riders, Students for a Democratic Society, and the Black Panthers. And I wasn't alone. A whole cadre of students at Nausea High shared my views, and together we responded to the school board's request for comment on the heroin crisis with more than a dozen pages of political and cultural critique that ranged far beyond the crisis in question to the larger issue of the strange and alienating world we were asked to take our place in. This document came to be known as the "Green Manifesto" (GM).

Although I was not one of the authors of that document, I can certainly lay claim to being one of its publishers and a most ardent distributor throughout the school district. More than forty years have transpired since the GM was published, and I cannot remember precisely what its pages contained. I'm sure it included much about the war, concerns about civil rights, and many concerns widely shared by the counterculture we all identified with. The reference to "green" had nothing to do with environmental considerations and everything to do with the fact that the paper it was printed on was green. Ten thousand copies were printed and distributed throughout the district, and it was a tremendous experience for all the students involved, all the more so when we beheld the collective jaw-dropping reaction of the school board and the firestorm of concern it inspired among parents in the district. It was an extraordinary introduction to the power of activism and democracy in action. It set my feet firmly on the path of a lifetime of activism (some of which I'll share presently). And the fact that it was printed at all was because I was the son of Anne McCaffrey.

The reason we were able to produce and distribute so many copies of the GM was because of a fringe benefit Anne McCaffrey enjoyed as secretary-treasurer of the Science Fiction Writers Association (SFWA). Mom printed their newsletter and somewhere along the line had acquired a Gestetner mimeograph machine for that purpose. We were overjoyed and more than a bit surprised when Mom not only agreed to help us print the GM but also proceeded to buy many cartons of green paper for the purpose. I can't remember how many days it took us to print and collate all those copies, but it was a labor of love, the fruits of which just got better and better.

In hindsight, my mother's support for our activism wasn't all that surprising. She always encouraged the young adults in her life, whether they were her offspring or not. Wherever we lived, our house quickly became a sanctuary for teens, who flowered in the environment my mother created so naturally. I should mention that she wasn't that great with very young children, and my early years were a trial for us both, but from the time I was about fourteen, and for the rest of my life, I could always confide in her, trust her, and be confident in her belief in me.

And I never doubted her love was absolute and unconditional, a gift I enjoy even now that she's passed away.

During this period when I was trying to make sense of my world, pondering so many contradictions between the myth of America and the reality I found increasingly impossible to ignore, I encountered a quote from Bertrand Russell where he declared, "I would rather be mad with the truth than sane with lies." This had a tremendous impact on me and has probably done more to shape my life than any other English sentence I ever encountered. And it was through many conversations with my confidant/ mother that I came to make that declaration my own.

The Vietnam War was a test, not only for my generation and myself, but for my family. Anne McCaffrey was the proud daughter of a career military man, Colonel George Herbert McCaffrey. Her views about service were heavily shaped by him and by the experience of having both him and her eldest brother, Hugh "Mac" McCaffrey, serve in and survive World War II. At first she regarded the draft for Vietnam as being no different than the similar call that brought her relatives to war in 1942. My father always supported my desire not to serve in Vietnam, and in fairly short order, my mother came to see that the war was a "bright, shining lie." In 1970 she had moved to Ireland, where draft evasion wasn't a crime and therefore not an extraditable offense, and so my short-lived exile began there in 1971. Early in 1972, the draft lottery I was subject to happened; I "won" the lottery, which meant my selective service status was changed and I was no longer subject to U.S. military service.

I remained in Ireland for several years and had a number of adventures. I was a trawling fisherman, and later a rabbit-hunter on the Great Blasket Island, the southwesternmost part of Ireland. I finally wound up working for the Simon Communities in Belfast—an organization that served as a "safety net" for all those who fell through Britain's existing social safety net—where I got to witness civil war firsthand, even surviving a bomb blast that exploded across the street from the shelter I worked in. Employment opportunities were scarce, however, for an alien resident living in the very impoverished Republic of Ireland in the '70s, and by 1973, I had returned to the States.

That was the year of the first OPEC oil embargo, and I got to live through the rest of the '70s, a period marked by a lackluster economy that resulted in large measure from that oil price shock. I was able to make the best of it and during that period served as the last business manager of *Liberation Magazine* and went on to found the 100 Flowers Bookstore Coop in Cambridge, Massachusetts. I was also the residential director of a halfway house for ex-mental patients, drawing on my earlier experience in Belfast. All the while, my mother's career was developing, and it went ballistic with *The White Dragon*.

It was shortly after *The White Dragon* hit number six on the *New York Times* Bestseller List that Anne McCaffrey gave me a tremendous gift: a second chance at college. In 1970 I had enrolled in SUNY* Stony Brook, but that was the year after my parents had divorced, and I wasn't in the right frame of mind for academics. By the late '70s I was more than ready, and as Mom's success began to translate into significant financial gains, she made me an offer. I could either spend a year traveling around Europe, all expenses paid, or I could go back to college. For me it was a no-brainer, and I quickly matriculated into the University of Massachusetts, where I majored in economics.

The UMass Economics Department was unusual, and its distinctiveness was why I chose to go there. I studied traditional neoclassical theory, but I also studied its progressive critique.

---

* State University of New York.

Prepared as I now was to risk becoming "mad with the truth," I was able to shed many unhelpful myths about the true nature of the United States, imperialism, and the global economy. Mindful of what a tremendous gift my mother had given me, I became a devoted student and graduated cum laude (almost magna cum laude), was invited to submit a senior honors thesis, and earned a departmental distinction.

Despite my dedication to higher learning, I continued with my activism. At UMass I helped form a progressive student organization that was able to unseat the reactionary and somewhat racist status quo in the student assembly. In my junior year, activists on campus became outraged when UMass refused to grant tenure to a pair of African-American faculty members, chiefly, as near as we could tell, because their field was African-American studies. We revived a tactic not seen in a decade and occupied the administration building, refusing to leave until we were all arrested. Our acquittal on all charges was a pleasant surprise, but the crowning moment, and one I had to share with my mother, was when we were all invited to a Baptist Church in South Boston to be honored for our sacrifice. During this ceremony we received letters thanking us for our devotion to the struggle for equal rights. When I visited my mom for Christmas later that year in Ireland, I presented her with that letter, as there was no one else on Earth who deserved it more.

Around the same time, I became concerned about the safety of nuclear power in general and of a very specific power plant in Seabrook, New Hampshire.* I became part of the now-legendary Clamshell Alliance, which tried repeatedly to shut down the Seabrook's nuclear power station. As ever, I enjoyed

---

* My view of nuclear power is now more nuanced, considering the crisis now unfolding in the related realms of climate and energy. While I'd prefer they not be built, I'd rather a nuclear power plant over a coal-fired plant any day.

my mother's unstinting support, even as the stakes grew much higher. During the course of several actions in and around Seabrook, I was arrested twice, maced once, and savagely beaten by a pair of state troopers while I was peacefully surrendering on another occasion. One of those arrests resulted in a fortnight's incarceration. All of these arrests were the result of nonviolent civil disobedience. At this point, Mom had settled in Ireland, so I had to regale her with my adventures over the phone.

My decade-long career in software engineering started in the early '80s and gave me considerable insight into the bizarre and often insane world of corporate America. I had grown quite weary of "maximizing shareholder value," and during a visit with my mother in Ireland in 1994, it was decided that I would become her general manager, in charge of everything but her literary affairs. And so from 1995 until 2004, I lived in Ireland and did my best to manage several small businesses Anne McCaffrey owned, handle fan relations, and deal with Hollywood. My previous experience with the corporate world didn't prepare me for the vicious world of Hollywood. Lynda Obst, who produced *Sleepless in Seattle*, wrote her Hollywood memoirs under the title, *Hello, He Lied*. I came to fully appreciate her view of that industry, and it's fair to say I was out of my depth when it came to Tinseltown. Still, I loved Ireland, was largely helpful to my mother, and would probably be there still were it not for George W. Bush.

It's hard to discuss Bush without also discussing 9/11, and for me that day had personal significance as a very close friend, Anna Allison, was on the first plane to plow into the Twin Towers. I grew furious watching Cheney and Bush turn that tragedy into carte blanche for a criminal invasion of Iraq. Although never dormant, my activist self was now fully reengaged, and I got directly involved with Ireland's antiwar movement. This included participating in demonstrations outside the U.S. embassy, which had been transformed into a fortress, utterly out of place with the lovely Georgian doorways surrounding that strange spectacle. Anne McCaffrey was, of course, fully supportive of this, and were it not for the difficulty she had standing for any length of time, I'm sure she would've joined me.

In March 2003, I got to be part of a huge protest against the impending Iraq War. It was the largest gathering in Dublin since the Easter Rebellion. Yet as inspiring as that day was in Dublin and across the world, it failed to stop the "shock and awe" Bush unleashed that March. It was then that I realized that I had a duty to return to the States and, as a U.S. citizen, do everything in my power to eject Bush from the White House.

While an interesting tale could be told about my adventures leading the top canvass team in Iowa for the anti-Bush group known as America Coming Together, everyone knows how that story ended. Having worked harder than John Kerry did to give Bush the boot, I was distressed, to say the least, that grim November. And just when I thought my despair had reached bottom, my inner Bertrand Russell was confronting a rising Red Star even more alarming than four more years of George Bush, as it was then that I came to fully understand the peril we've come to call "peak oil."

I had heard a bit about peak oil even before arriving in Iowa, but during the campaign I could only nibble at an article or two and only on rare occasions. It was in that dark November that I read several books on the subject and found myself riveted by the topic, and not in a good way. Back then peak oil was a theory; now it is an acknowledged fact. It refers to the point at which global oil extraction reaches its apogee and then declines irrevocably thereafter. The reason this is such a big deal is that energy is the master resource of the world's economy, and oil remains the principal source of energy both for transportation and heating purposes, but also for food production. All fertilizer and all pesticides come from fossil fuels. More than 300,000 commonly used products, including innumerable pharmaceuticals, also come from this now-depleting resource. Even more alarming, we have good reason to believe that humanity has been able to *artificially* expand the carrying capacity for our species on this planet by about a factor of three because of our ability to exploit fossil fuels. Passing peak oil meant that energy boon would rapidly deplete, resulting in profound economic and political stresses, widespread instability, and the very serious threat of social collapse.

That November 2004, estimates for when peak oil might be reached ranged from 2007 to 2010. The International Energy Agency, which is the official body that the governments of the world rely on for the straight dope on energy, spent much of this century demonizing anyone who suggested that we were at or near peak oil. (Years later in 2010, with very little fanfare, they admitted that peak oil was real and that the world had passed it in 2006! It was a stunning about-face, but one that received remarkably little press given how significant it is.) This was, to be sure, a Red Star rising here on Earth, and only a very few people even saw it coming. As a trained economist and someone who had experienced the consequences of oil price shocks in the 1970s, it was clear to me that there would be very serious consequences. And I truly feared, and still fear to this day, for my children's future.

In 2004, when hardly anyone even knew what peak oil was, much less what a threat it posed, it was easy to feel much like Troy's Cassandra. And more than once did I recall the stories my mom told me about her father, who saw World War II coming way before most others did. The Colonel, as he was called even by his children, had a brother-in-law who was an engineer and had occasion to visit Germany in the late 1930s. He saw that they were retooling for war production, and Colonel McCaffrey took him seriously. Mom told me how her dad was the subject of much ridicule on the army base he served at when he insisted that troops under his command drill with full packs and generally prepare for the war he was certain would shortly arrive. Writing now, I find myself wondering if Mom's own father was the inspiration for F'lar. I wouldn't be at all surprised. He was a major figure in her life.

Wrapping my brain around peak oil and its implications was hugely challenging. And as you might imagine, it didn't make for pleasant cocktail chatter. The Bush administration, it turns out, knew all about it. They had the Energy Department commission a report, which came to be known as the Hirsch Report, after its lead author, Robert Hirsch. Its executive summary declared that, "The peaking of world oil production presents the U.S. and the world with an *unprecedented* risk management problem" [emphasis added]. The term "unprecedented" appeared often in the Hirsch Report, and it was a very serious warning indeed. So it should come as no shock at all that the report was repressed by the Bush administration. In fact, for a while the only place it could be found was on the Chula Vista High School website—seriously, you can't make this stuff up. I read an interview with Hirsch years later in which he confessed how tremendously frightened he was by his findings. So was I, but I soon learned that this wasn't even half of the rising "Red Star" we're now confronting.

Global warming is so much on my mind today that it's curious that I can't recall when I first came across the concept, but by early 2009 it had my full attention. I was living in Eureka, California, at the time, and some of the local activists had organized a round-trip train to Washington, DC, to be part of a big action that involved encircling and shutting down the coal-fired plant that powers the U.S. Congress. So in early March 2009, I found myself traveling from Sacramento toward our nation's capital on an Amtrak train. It proved to be a most pleasant way to traverse the country. And it delivered stunning confirmation of the seriousness of climate change on the very first day. Traveling through the Sierras, we arrived in an area covered, as far as the eye could see in every direction, with pine trees. But they were all dead; every tree that should've sported green bristles instead had dead brown ones. It was so stark that even the train conductor commented on it over the public address system. The cause was the mountain pine beetle, an insect that had never threatened these trees before but now was killing them wholesale because climate change had forced their northern migration. It was a chilling vision.

The trip was life-changing, and I called my mother, as I always did, to enthrall her with tales of my adventures shutting down Congress's coal plant that freezing March day. I did not, however, tell her about the dead trees. I didn't think there was any point in frightening her. She had given me so much for so long that I knew I could still draw strength from her without imposing the terrible burden of what I knew on her now-frail shoulders. And even now that she has passed, I find I can still draw the strength I need to fight from her lifelong support.

Today the twin perils of peak oil and global warming are even more threatening, more of a Red Star rising, than ever before. And while this bronze rider has been defeated—and painfully so, on too many occasions—I remain bolted to my wherhide saddle. My major regret is that during the last years of my mother's life, I was so busy that years went by without my visiting the Dragonlady in her Wicklow Weyr. In November of 2011, I was on my way, at last, to visit Mom and enjoy Thanksgiving with her. I had no idea that when my plane was taking off from Columbus, Ohio, my mother's life was coming to an end. The grim news greeted me upon my arrival in Dublin. I knew well before then that I would never be able to prepare myself for such a staggering loss. I think of her every day, and I speak to her often. And I hope that I will be able to do my part, as F'lar did on Pern, to raise the alarm and to take my place on the front lines in this most urgent existential struggle. I'd like to think that, thanks to Anne McCaffrey, I am equal to this challenge.

————————————

ALEC JOHNSON currently lives in East Texas with a community of activists successfully challenging the construction of the Keystone XL Pipeline in Oklahoma and Texas. In January 2013, he was arrested as part of a nonviolent civil disobedience action that disrupted the offices of TransCanada, the pipeline's builder.

Proud father of Eliza and Amelia, he draws much motivation for the global warming struggle from the confidence that he fights not only for their future, but for the future of everyone's children and future generations without a voice.

Angels come in all sizes. Mostly we don't recognize them until they're already gone from our lives. I think we all have the potential to be an angel, if only for a few seconds and only for that one person who most needs to hear our words.

Angelina "Angel" Adams writes here about how Anne McCaffrey was, in effect, her angel in a hard time.

I think you'll see when you read her words why I say it is a great honor to have her contribution to *Dragonwriter*.

Changes Without Notice

ANGELINA ADAMS

SO VERY OFTEN, the pivotal moments of our lives slip by without fanfare or notice. Such was the day I picked up my first Anne McCaffrey book. Unlike many of her fans, I had not grown up reading science fiction. Instead of curling up with a good book, I spent most of my teenage years with scripts, arias, and in rehearsals. This meant I missed joining my friends on the mass migration from horse books and classics to science fiction and fantasy. It also meant I had no idea of the treasure I was holding when I saw her name for the first time.

At twenty-four, my life was in the middle of a major shift. I was adjusting to being a new wife and mother, I had quit performing, and I was attempting to adjust to life in a new city. My cousin had come to visit, and as is often the case when traveling, he left behind a few items. Among them was a very orange book that had, of all things, a picture of someone riding a dragon on the cover. Orange had never been one of my favorite colors, and dragons weren't my thing, so I set the book aside with every intention of mailing it to my cousin.

Somehow that book kept moving around the house. It seemed every time I cleaned, it was in the way, tossed on top of a table or countertop. It felt as if I were constantly picking it up and returning it to the drawer where the other items I needed to mail were stored. One day, as I was walking the book back to where it was supposed to be, I opened the back cover and the "About the Author" caught my eye. The line "She studied voice for nine years and during that time, became intensely interested in the stage direction of opera and operetta" caught my eye. I was intrigued. I continued to read, and other words jumped out at me: children, Ireland, cats, dogs, and horses. Those were some of my most favorite things. I felt an immediate affinity for this person. She sounded like someone I would be friends with. Then I read the last line, "Of herself, Ms. McCaffrey says, 'I have green eyes, silver hair, and freckles; the rest changes without notice.'"

It was official. I was in love. Change the silver hair to auburn, and every bit of that statement resonated true for me. I was so captivated by the discovery of someone who seemed like such a kindred spirit that, despite the awful orange color, I decided to read a chapter or two. Later that night, as I put the finished copy of *Moreta: Dragonlady of Pern* on my nightstand, I couldn't wait to read the other titles that were listed in the front of the book. I had been so very wrong; dragons were totally my thing. Over the next few years, I devoured every Pern novel I could get my hands on. Once I caught up with the Dragonrider books then in print, I found some of her romances, a short story collection, and *The Rowan*. My bookshelf was showing signs of a definite personality shift.

As I was working my way through the Anne McCaffrey titles I found, I had two more children. Our family moved to a different city, and I soon found myself pregnant for the fourth time. With the stress of another pregnancy, my oldest son facing surgery, and settling the kids into a new environment, I found Anne's books a tremendous comfort. I would reread them multiple times; they felt like visiting with an old friend. The isolation and loneliness of a recent move during such emotionally trying circumstances only increased my attachment to the author whose personality was stamped so indelibly on her work.

Baby number four finally arrived. The crash team entering the delivery room was the first sign of my life completely changing course. My unanswered question of "is something wrong with my baby?" quickly switched to "what is wrong with my baby?" That question did not have a simple answer. For the first twenty-four hours after she was born, every time the doctors entered my room it was to inform me of yet another defect or complication. It was evident the doctors held little hope of her surviving the day. When I asked them if there was anything that could be donated to save another child if she died, they got very quiet. Finally one doctor spoke up and said, "She has a good liver." At barely twelve hours old, the only organ in my tiny baby girl that was functioning properly was her liver.

But she was a fighter, and she surprised us. Against all odds, she made it through the first day. I would stand in the Neonatal Intensive Care Unit, sing softly, and stroke the only part of her body I was allowed to touch: the very top of her head. When she was two days old, I was informed she needed emergency heart surgery. We were transferred to the Intensive Care Unit of the Children's Hospital, where we would remain for three months and five more surgeries. Eventually, they would figure out a diagnosis for her mysterious condition. Michelle was born with CHARGE association. While it is now classified as an actual syndrome, at the time the specialists had very little information for us beyond the basic definition and her individual manifestations of each aspect of the condition. The name was an acronym used to describe a group of defects that had begun to appear as a cluster in rare instances. The *C* stood for coloboma malformation of the eye, *H* for heart defects, *A* for atresia of the choanae, *R* for renal abnormalities, *G* for growth and developmental delays, and *E* for ear abnormalities. The specialists began to use terms such as "quality of life" to describe all the things she was likely to be without.

My husband, Michael, realized it was going to be nearly impossible to pry me away from her bedside. He asked what he could bring me from home: a change of clothes, sweater, food, or something to read? I asked him to bring me anything by Anne McCaffrey. There were several of her books on my shelf, and any one of them would have been a comforting favorite. Trying to be thoughtful, instead of bringing me a book I'd read a dozen times, he went to the bookstore and bought a couple he hadn't seen at home. I thanked him but was only slightly interested in them. My mind was on the five pounds of little girl with all the wires running in different directions and the breathing tube protruding from her mouth. I didn't have the energy needed to delve into unknown territory. However, the night after she survived the first heart surgery, which had been very touch-and-go, I reached for the books as the ICU settled down into the hush of the night shift.

The title *The Ship Who Sang* jumped out at me. Since Anne's vocal studies had been one of the things that drew me to her as an author, I liked the thought of her writing about singing. I didn't even read the blurbs on the back and had no idea what was waiting for me between the covers of that book. I turned on the nightlight, trying to avoid disturbing either of the children recovering from surgery in the neighboring glass-walled rooms. Surrounded by the beeps and hums of the machines keeping my daughter alive, I began to read.

And then I began to cry. For days, I had been trying to hold it together. I was afraid that if I let go, I would shatter and be useless. All I wanted was to be able to hold my baby girl and sing to her, but it felt as if she were being held hostage by the very tubes that were her salvation. Every day since Michelle had been born, I was constantly glancing at monitors, searching for proof she was still alive. Rather than seeing her smile or hearing her cry, I would look for changes in her oxygen saturation numbers to tell me when she was happy or upset. The isolation and despair created by this medical barrier was quietly breaking my heart. I believed no one understood how I felt.

Then I met Helva.

I was constantly visited by specialists who wanted to study or discuss Michelle's mysterious collection of birth defects. The list of possible worst-case scenarios kept growing with each discovery. With all these fears and worries bouncing around in my head, in a darkened ICU in the middle of the night, I read these words: "There was always the possibility that though the limbs were twisted, the mind was not, that though the ears would hear only dimly, the eyes see vaguely, the mind behind them was receptive and alert." The power of that statement was overwhelming.

With the tears in my eyes making it nearly impossible to focus, I kept reading those words over and over while I cried out all my fears. I had never known anyone who had the sort of severe handicaps my daughter had been born with. I had trouble wrapping my brain around the concept of who she was as a person. As a parent, I had never been of the attitude that we mold and create the adults our children grow into. I've always believed they are born as little individuals and it is our job as parents to love and support them and help them grow into these special selves. My creator daughter, tender-souled son, and genius son—*those* I knew how to interact with and encourage. But I felt lost when I looked for the baby hidden among the wires and tubes. I was terrified I wouldn't know how to be her mother, especially with specialists telling me she would never be able to fully interact with me or her environment.

But the concept of a mind that was "receptive and alert" possibly being hidden by the body that wasn't functioning had been planted. The tears dried, and I continued reading. I fell in love with Helva as I experienced her transformation from a malformed "thing" at birth to the brain of a sleek and powerful spaceship. The unique perspective her challenges had given her made it possible for her to find solutions to both physically and emotionally dangerous situations. Her intellect, tender heart, and love of music keep her the most human of the characters I have ever encountered, regardless of the machine that acted as her body. Over the years I have had the privilege of hearing many people tell me what *The Ship Who Sang* meant to them. Many talk about the adventure, the romance, or how vibrant the characters are. But for me, the lesson that was driven into my heart is how unimportant the container we live in is. Bodies, wheelchairs, titanium encasings—the external is nothing compared to the spirit within.

Because of the frequent need to put the book down and attend to Michelle's needs, it took a week or so to finish. Along with the words, I absorbed the environment in which I read them. All around me, each day the struggle for hope in the face of despair imprinted on my spirit. By the time I reached the words on the final page, "to let night with its darkness for sorrowing and sleep complete its course and bring . . . a new day," I possessed new definitions for beauty and possibilities. The image of Helva sitting on the tarmac as the notes of requiem drifted over the darkening service base was very real in my mind. I could feel the emotions as she comes to terms with all she has lost and finally manages to appreciate what she has gained in the wake of so much tragedy. In a very real way, Helva helped me connect with my daughter. The wires, tubes, and machines stopped being a barrier. I was determined to push the boundaries and defy the norm. I found nurses who would help me maneuver all the equipment so that I could hold my daughter once a day. I sat in a rocking chair, and they would carefully transition her from the warmer to my arms and drape all the wires and tubes around both of us, taping many of them to the chair to minimize the risk of removing a connection that was keeping her alive. Holding her broke all the rules. But I would sing, we could finally bond, and Michelle continued to beat the odds and mystify the doctors.

Of course, Michelle was no Helva, but she was a miracle in her own right. When we were allowed to bring her home, life became a dizzying whirlwind of therapists and doctors. I learned how to tune out and deflect statements that contained the words *won't* or *can't*. I searched for people who said things like "I don't know if this will work, but we can give it a try." By the time Michelle reached her miraculous first birthday, the doctors stopped giving me estimates of how long until we could expect her to die. Instead, they began to say things like "I don't know what you're doing, but whatever it is, keep doing it."

I was thrilled she was doing so well, but the year had been draining for me. I began to feel as if I had lost touch with myself. Because Michelle was still so medically fragile and dependent on the machines that now decorated half of our living room, I rarely left the house. My only friends were the home health nurses who came every day to attend to Michelle's needs while I got some sleep or spent time with my other children. I looked forward to the nurses arriving every day. Adult conversation was such a treasure. It was then that my husband brought home our first computer. I wasn't very sure about the new addition; my computer skills were limited to data entry and Lotus spreadsheets. I had never encountered the internet, but he suggested it might help with the cabin fever that had begun to set in after a year of isolation.

I was curious and liked the shiny, bright, newness of it, but doubted it could actually help me feel less lonely and isolated. It was just a box sitting in the den. Then he showed me how to get to the interests section of AOL and said something like "You like to read; you can search for authors in here." We clicked on the "authors" button, and a list of names appeared for us to scroll through. I was so clueless the first time I clicked on Anne's name and entered a strange new world. I had no idea how popular Anne was or that there was such a thing as fandom.

I wandered from one click to the next. There were new marvels to be found with every refreshing of the screen: tons of scrolling text discussing books and series written by Anne that I didn't even know existed. But it was the personal stories that were scattered across the message boards that really caught my attention. For the first time, I realized my experience with Anne's writing was not unique. I read dozens of stories that day, all of them describing the various ways her writing had helped someone through troubled times. All of this would have been merely a day's distraction if an instant message hadn't suddenly appeared on my screen wanting to know if I was going to be joining everyone in the dragonrider room.

I admit to being more than a tad bit alarmed when this message appeared from out of nowhere. I didn't know what a dragonrider room was, and I certainly didn't know who "everyone" was. I politely typed back that I hadn't been planning on joining them and didn't know how to get there. I closed the window and went back to reading. Another window popped up with explicit directions on how to navigate to the room. It was soon followed by several messages wanting to know if I was coming. With a sigh, I realized that whoever this was, they were going to interrupt my exploration of the Anne McCaffrey message boards until I joined them.

To say entering the chat room was a culture shock would be putting it mildly. A chorus of greetings and dragon noises sent by a barrage of Pernese-sounding screen names scrolled by faster than anyone could read. I sat stunned by the overwhelming visual noise and was about to quietly leave the room when I got a very calm message welcoming me to the gathering and explaining a few logistics. The meeting was called to order, and an actual discussion of the Pern series began. In all the years of reading the books, I'd had no one to talk to about them. Before long, simply "listening" to the discussion wasn't enough. I stumbled my way through figuring out how to join the conversation. There was a language shorthand that took me a while to figure out, but I was having a blast. Then I recognized a name from a story I had read on a message board earlier, and all of these silly anonymous screen names scrolling past suddenly became people. I began to pick out what she was saying and hear it in the context of the personal tragedy she had shared on the boards. Her reactions took on deeper meaning, and I began to see past the irritating level of silly that kept cluttering my screen to the heart of what was really going on: there were genuine bonds of friendship and trust mixed in with the juvenile remarks. And for some reason, several of my new friends decided they weren't going to let me slip away.

I was bombarded with invitations to join various clubs and with questions about my writing ability. Not sure why this was relevant, I replied that I had written lots of stories when I was a kid and did quite well with creative writing classes in school. My mailbox was suddenly overflowing with guides, rules, and writing examples. For a week, every time I turned on the computer, someone would send me a message wanting to know how I was doing and if I'd read their guide. I began to look forward to the Monday night gatherings in the dragonrider chat room. No matter the odd hour of the day or night when I would find myself awake and alone with the beeping of Michelle's monitors, there was always someone from the Pern community online to talk to. The loneliness began to fade, and I decided that if writing was the rite of passage to remain part of this community, then I would write a story.

Courtesy of Anne McCaffrey fandom, I now have a new appreciation for the phrase "gateway drug."

I joined a weyr, created a character, and wrote a story. Then I wrote another story. I joined another club. When I wasn't looking, I somehow became the leader of a club. Then I got invited to join many of my online friends at a gathering known as Dragon*Con in Atlanta.

I hadn't been away from Michelle for more than a couple of hours at a time in the first two and a half years of her life. The thought of leaving her for an entire weekend was terrifying, but my friends and family convinced me I would be better able to care for her if I remembered to also care for myself. I decided to go. Once again, having no clue what I was getting into, I entered the next level of McCaffrey fandom as a wide-eyed innocent.

I wasn't given much time to adjust. The same fandom forces that had maneuvered me into running my own club had also talked me into being on several panels. I somehow managed to survive the experience and never looked back. For the past sixteen years, I have been one of the movers and shakers of Weyrfest at Dragon*Con. I love interacting with people who truly love Anne and her work. Their personal stories inspire me as much as the friendships I have made sustain me.

I spent several years enjoying my annual romp with fandom before the next wave of unexpected life change happened. In 1999, Anne decided to return to Dragon*Con. I had heard stories from fans about how wonderful it was to meet Anne. They would sit and talk for hours about every nuance of every moment spent with the Dragonlady. The level of adoration was a bit daunting at times, but given how deeply she had impacted my own life, I understood why many of them could be moved to tears at the very sight of her. As one of the worker bees, I had more of an opportunity to interact with Anne than most of the convention attendees. I was thrilled to shake her hand and see for myself the sparkle of mischief that was always lurking in her eyes. The sheer number of people trying to get close to her, and the impressive number of people trying to keep her safe, intimidated me. So I kept to the edge of things and did my best to bring a tiny bit of order to the chaos that was Weyrfest that year. I ended up having some amazing conversations with a member of her entourage. He was intelligent, funny, and encouraging when the topic of writing came up. It was later when my new friend was on a panel that I realized Todd Johnson was Anne's son.

I would be far more embarrassed for my cluelessness, except that I am grateful I didn't know who he was when we began talking. First impressions are important, and I have always seen Todd as my friend first and Anne's son second. It was his encouragement that eventually led me to attending writer's workshops and braving the terror of sending my first manuscripts into the great unknown.

By the time Anne returned to Dragon*Con, I had become one of the directors of Weyrfest. Anne had been through a lot since the first time I'd met her, and as a result, her health was no longer as robust as it had once been. As we made preparations for her arrival, I was worried. I remembered how chaotic the press of people had been the last time she had been a guest at the convention. At the opening of Weyrfest, we tried to explain how important it was for everyone to show their love for Anne by being gentle with her. We recruited a reliable Anne Guard who would accompany her everywhere, but this wasn't to keep Anne away from her fans—it was to make it safe for her to be near them. I had underestimated the majority of the people who had gathered to see her. Once again, I was impressed by how many people genuinely loved her and took great pains to keep her safe.

This time, I spent more time with Anne than I had before. I found myself swept along to meals with her, Todd, and an ever-changing cast of fascinating characters. There was always room to squeeze another chair at the table as her friends appeared. Each meal would end up a delightful mixture of famous and fandom, with Anne reigning over her adoring court like a benevolent queen. I will never forget the way she seemed to sparkle from the inside out. Her laughter was infectious, and she had a talent for drawing stories out of people. I would sit at the far end of the table and quietly observe the subtlety of her interactions. It was easy to think she was lost in a sea of sounds as everyone around her laughed and talked at the same time. But then someone would make a remark that would catch her attention, and she would turn the full force of her charm on them. With a light touch of the hand and an encouraging smile, she would soon have them pouring out every detail of whatever anecdote she found entertaining or moving. While watching this hypnotizing dance, I came to realize why Anne's fans were so fiercely devoted to her. The love and adoration they were lavishly pouring over her wasn't just being received; it was being returned. Putting Anne and a fan together was magical. They would both get a glow of joy around them that was humbling to see.

After the convention was over, I had the opportunity to be on the receiving end of that intense charm. Anne and I were sitting in the chairs that reappear in the lobby of the hotel once

Dragon*Con is over. I was showing her pictures of my kids, and we were enjoying a nice chat. She asked me how things had been in the Weyrfest room, and I shared a few amusing stories with her. I also told her about a panel we had that year where everyone had a chance to share a "how Anne's writing touched my life" story. I briefly told her some of the things people had said that really stuck with me. She kept nodding her head and listening. Then came the touch of the hand and the smile as she said, "And what was your story?" I knew I'd walked right into her web. So I took a deep breath and told her about Michelle and Helva. She never said a word, just kept patting my hand even as both our eyes got a bit watery. When I finally finished sharing, she squeezed my hand and all she said was "Thank you." Todd had told me how special *The Ship Who Sang* was for his mom; the dedication to her father at the beginning of the book merely hints at the deep emotions, inspired by the Colonel's death, that Anne poured into the pages. I understood and returned her hand squeeze. Then she grinned and tapped a picture of my older daughter, whom she'd met at the convention, and said, "Now that one is special!" The tears were replaced with smiles as we began another round of swapping kid stories. She was a crafty one who knew how to build a bond, applying equal amounts of laughter and tears.

Over the years I would be fortunate enough to have several opportunities to interact with Anne and observe the way people opened up around her. Somewhere along the way, in my eyes she stopped being the legendary author and simply became my dear friend's mom. While getting ready for an awards banquet one year, she was treating me to a delightfully embarrassing tale of Todd while I braided her hair and helped with her makeup. I was struck by the immense contrast between the fragility of her skin and the vigorous spirit shining in her eyes. The green eyes and freckles mentioned in that long-ago author's note were very much in evidence, and in light of the force of the personality contained within—the rest truly did change without notice. It was but the shell that carried around an incredible essence that not only compelled others to respond with openhearted love, but was brave enough to love in return. I hugged her and looked at our faces reflecting back a matching set of mischievous green eyes and realized how true my first impression had been. She was indeed the sort of person I could be, and amazingly was, friends with.

A few years ago, as we began the frenzy that is part of Weyrfest planning, whenever Anne would announce she would be joining us, Todd suggested we do a staged reading of *The Ship Who Sang*. I thought this sounded like a wonderful idea and was both honored and nervous when I was given the part of Helva. Few would understand how much it meant to me to be her voice, but Todd was one of them. Unfortunately, health concerns kept Anne from being able to make the journey. Instead, we filmed the presentation to send to her as a get well wish from all of us at Weyrfest. I can close my eyes and still hear the tremble in Todd's voice as he read, before the notes of the requiem sounded, "Softly, barely audible at first, the strains of the ancient song of evening and requiem swelled to the final poignant measure until black space itself echoed back the sound of the song the ship sang." The powerful silence of a room filled to capacity with people moved to tears by the words Anne had written fifty years before was tremendous.

The impact on my life of that brief paragraph in the back of a book so many years before suddenly hit me. By reading one book, my life had taken a direction and been filled with people I never could have imagined. Those offhand words weren't just a clever disregard for the effect time has on a physical appearance; "the rest changes without notice" was life. Without my noticing what was happening, Anne managed to reach out and make profound changes in my life.

But now that I have noticed, I am forever grateful. Thank you, Anne. For every word, every smile, every tear, and every song.

Currently a resident of Austin, Texas, ANGELINA ADAMS is a mother of four and friend to many. She enjoys taking on new challenges, which has proved to be both a blessing and a curse. Since 1996, she has delighted in taking an annual break from being an upstanding member of society to devote her time and energy to the Anne McCaffrey programming track at Dragon*Con. Her daughter, Michelle, is now eighteen years old and continues to astound medical professionals with her ability to defy the odds. She is the tiniest member of her graduating class and rules the hallways with her smiles as she zooms around the school with her walker. She is a source of inspiration for all who know her.

Charlotte Moore is a force of nature. Hurricanes worship her, volcanoes erupt for her, and regular mortals either bow or get out of her way (sometimes both). That she is also an avid Anne McCaffrey fan and for many years ran the Weyrfest at Dragon*Con is only natural: after all, forces of nature do what they want, don't they?

The Twithead with the Dragon Tattoo

CHARLOTTE MOORE

ANNE MCCAFFREY TRIED to kill me once.

It was my first day of active duty as a volunteer for Weyrfest, the Anne McCaffrey programming track at Dragon*Con, and I was literally running late. Barreling through the bowels of the Hyatt Regency Atlanta, I kept my head on a swivel as I threaded my way through a glut of scowling Klingons and beaming superheroes, past cardboard robots and buxom cat-girls, around wide-eyed convention virgins with their fanny packs and camera bags and sprawling paper programs. It's important to keep one's head at a science fiction convention—in trying to look at everything, one ultimately sees very little. You certainly can't count on anyone else to see *you* (unless you're a painted Amidala in her layer cake frills or a Robocop with real hydraulic armor or a lanky six-foot-two twenty-something with a rubber penis strapped to his forehead).

Weyrfest, as it was still officially known at the time, was the only Anne McCaffrey-themed event at any convention anywhere, and in 2003 the Dragonlady herself was Dragon*Con's scheduled guest of honor. It wasn't my first convention, but it was my first year as a volunteer, and as an eager disciple of Her Lady of Dragons, I was keenly aware of my tardiness. In sprinting, I was merely trying to exercise due diligence. That, and I was hella stoked to meet Anne freaking McCaffrey.

Little did I know that I was about to.

I don't know who was more surprised when my shins crashed into the hard metal arm of a motorized scooter; I had only the impression of silver hair before my inertial dampeners smashed down.

Have you ever seen a dog lose traction on a hardwood floor? Canine physiognomy is capable of conveying a very specific, completely hilarious combination of surprise, dismay, and shame. I imagine my face looked much like that. I reflected briefly on the life I'd lived and regretted the way it would be changed by face-planting into Anne McCaffrey's crotch. *Oh well*, I thought. *I've had a good run.*

Luckily for Anne McCaffrey's crotch—less so for my tibias—I caught myself in the nick of time. She looked up at me with those green eyes of hers, and I said something apropos like, "OhmygodIamsosorryyou'reAnneMcCaffreyandI'mCharlotte I'myourjuniorstafferandit'ssonicetomeetyouandI'mahugefanan dI'mreallyreallysorry." Weyrfest's director, Anna, with her brace of chaperones—we always had a few people on Anne Guard to keep *exactly* this kind of thing from happening—grinned at me, the picture of knowing parental bemusement. I had the vivid impression of becoming a floor.

I think Anne said, "It's nice to meet you."

I fled.

Now, I know what you're thinking. "Charlotte," you're thinking, "I'm gonna be honest: it kind of actually sounds like it was *you* who tried to kill *Anne*." False.

By now it is *well* documented that when put in control of a motorized vehicle, Anne Inez McCaffrey became crazed with power. Anne Guard wasn't just meant for her safety. It was meant for *everyone else's*. One second, that mezzanine was clear.

The next, Anne, in open defiance of physics, had appeared directly in my way. I can only assume she'd worked out how to take that damn chair *between*.

The better part of my life, it often seems, has been characterized by intersections—or, if you like, near misses—with Anne McCaffrey.

Like many of Anne's fans, I was a sensitive, precocious adolescent with a voracious appetite for books. I preferred fiction as a rule, but my mother had not had much luck plying me with the dramas, mysteries, and florid classics she so loved: I snubbed *Rebecca*, ignored *Anne of Green Gables*, and demanded answers for *The Heart Is a Lonely Hunter*: Was she *trying* to bore me to death?

Jurassic Park, however, went right down the hatch. I treasured my Edgar Allen Poe anthology and took great pleasure in carting it around to my sixth grade classes, where I knew my less subtle schoolmates would have little to no appreciation for the tome. (I couldn't fathom why this endeared me to no one.) I must have read Phyllis Reynolds Naylor's Witch Saga half a dozen times. I was ten years old when L'Engle whisked me away to Camazotz. I could recite Dahl's *Matilda* in my sleep.

Yet I didn't discover science fiction as a genre until the seventh grade, when my fingers first flattened the title page of Anne's "The Smallest Dragonboy." The textbook in which it was reprinted also contained Bradbury's vitally poignant "All Summer in a Day." Together, the two stories were tailor-written for a gangly, earnest tomboy with eyes for the stars. I had never considered that dragons might be loyal, benevolent partners, but in a strange way it made perfect sense. When my teacher put us into groups to stage excerpts for our classmates, I clamored for—and easily won—the role of the hatchling dragon, and the night before the play I *slaved* over my costume (the first of many in the years to follow). Unable even to visualize "bronze," I settled for gold acrylic paint slathered over a paper snout, paper wings, and a paper tail. Inside it I felt positively alien, eager for my single joyous line: "My name is Heth!" (I think I pronounced it "Heath." Like the candy bar. Twelve-year-old girls are big into candy bars.)

Since then, a lot of people—boyfriends, mostly, but also coworkers feigning interest and curious passersby as I doodled at a sunny café table—have asked me, "Why dragons?" It's a question Anne herself was posed many times.

While they are the most enduring of the mythical creatures, with roots in every culture between here and Sumer, dragons don't really appeal to me any more or less than do unicorns or gryphons or centaurs or Elves or dark old things that live in very still water. I respect their mystique and versatility—a dragon can look like damn near anything—but ultimately, a dragon is just another creature in humankind's great mythological menagerie. It's *Anne's* dragons that are special.

Anne McCaffrey was an animal lover. So are most of her fans. So am I. And while most humans are driven by a basic biological imperative to communicate (barring Fox News pundits and people who don't use their turn signals and anyone from South Carolina), animal lovers are that much more gratified by connecting to a member of another species. We see much of ourselves in these creatures so unlike us—and many of them seem intrigued by us in turn. But while their intentions are clear, animals remain largely mute. We know that they dream, but not of what. We wonder what they would say if they could speak.

Anne's dragons exemplify the essential human longing for connection to the other. On Pern, dragons have wills, minds, and desires of their own. They fear and love and lust and hate. They are id and ego both; they are sweet children and impassioned soldiers by turns. And yet, one's dragon is a reflection of the best in one's self; they are an ever-present affirmation, a reminder to be just and to strive. Unconstrained by either space or time, a Pernese dragon is free to see the world as a place of boundless opportunity: all is achievable but that which, affronting the natural order, must not be achieved. I imagine they'd be fond of Yoda's axiom "Try not. Do, or do not! There is no try." Anne McCaffrey may have shunned organized religion, but her dragons were Buddhists, every last one.

Drawing them, reading about them, thinking about them, soothes and settles me like little else. It's not simply the idea of enduring companionship that attracts me, though of course that's a huge part of the appeal. It's the idea of dragon as peacemaker: a serene, graceful mind whose single greatest instinct is to protect and sustain. In my dreams, they smell of warm earth, of sunshine. In flight together, my dragon and I travel beyond reach, beyond yesterday. We live for now, and we are now, and now is all.

I'm not the first girl-misfit to find solace in speculative fiction, but when I was growing up there weren't a lot of other girls who shared my interest. Even now, the numbers favor readers with Y chromosomes (though, thank the maker of little green apples, this is changing). Apparently no one told Pern fandom, which is dominated by women—women of all makes and models, countless women on whose collective behalf I could never presume to speak. Maybe another of this book's more illustrious, well-qualified contributors will speculate on why women are drawn to Pern. For my part, let it suffice to say simply that women relate to Anne's work—and that this strikes me as I think about the helical shape of my connection to her and where our paths intersect at Stuart Hall School.

I can't talk about Anne McCaffrey without talking about Stuart Hall.

I had known since I was six that I wanted to attend the all-girls boarding school in southwestern Virginia, my mother's cherished alma mater. While my peers couldn't comprehend boarding school as anything but a punishment, I saw it as a godsend, a refuge from the torments of those same indifferent peers, from whom I often hid in Benden Weyr's secret passages, in Menolly's precarious seaside caves. Imagine my elation when I found Anne McCaffrey's name among the brochure's list of notables. It wasn't just a selling point. It was serendipity.

I loved Stuart Hall. It was there that I began to come out of my shell, built as a bulwark against the open scorn of my fellow adolescents. I had a role in every play. I took voice lessons and lent my ungainly mezzo-soprano to the school's small but able choir. I was one of the first students to enroll in the intensive Visual and Performing Arts program.

But I'd never been much for academics. There was too much other interesting shit going on outside the classroom—and even more, exponentially more, going on inside my head. Charlotte Moore is never where she's supposed to be, even when she is.

Pern was rocket fuel for daydreaming. I obsessively graffitied dragons on any piece of paper, any half-empty chalkboard, any virgin three-ring binder, that came within reach of my twitchy teenage fingers. Other girls were doodling horses or hearts in the margins of their carefully rendered English notes. My English notes were some halfhearted scrawls about how "The Awakening" made *me* want to walk into the ocean, followed by a dozen inept sketches of dragons dancing through the air, dragons belching fire, dragons peering into the sky. As much time as I spent practicing for my future as a liberal arts geek, I spent almost as much time doodling, procrastinating, oversleeping, neglecting home-work, and feigning sickness to get out of class—which led to nearly as many hours sitting in detention (during which time I neglected still more homework in favor of reading and drawing more Pern).

The summer following a rocky freshman year, I sent an email to Anne via the fan page hosted through Del Rey's old web-site. You may remember it—it featured the winners of an art contest, news about upcoming publications, and even a fun fea-ture where you could "go *between*" from one page to the next. It also included a contact form that, unbeknownst to me, was more or less a direct line to Anne herself.

I couldn't tell you now why or what I wrote to her. It was likely the kind of inane, nervous question you'd expect a fif-teen-year-old fangirl to write; and while I don't remember the contents of the message, I remember writing it with heat in my hands and face, with a frenzied tremor in my fingers. I don't know what I feared more: that she wouldn't answer me, or that she might.

Some time went by, and as I plunged into summer, I more or less forgot the matter. Then one afternoon I opened my inbox and there, perfectly nondescript, was a reply from Anne McCaffrey. Upon seeing it, I did what any intelligent, educated young woman would do and promptly shit myself.

That email should have been printed and framed, but instead is lost to time. Here's what I remember:

Anne glossed over whatever question I asked her. Instead, she began by (politely, always politely) informing me that she had been in touch with Stuart Hall's alumnae director, a be-nevolent, broadly smiling woman named Margaret, who had taken a liking to the scatterbrained waif tearing ass down the halls. Margaret, Anne told me, had let her know that I was not giving due attention to my studies.

Fuck, my brain suggested helpfully. *Fuck. Fuck, fuck, fuck, fuck.*

Anne went on to patiently explain that her son Todd, who was very clever and a rocket engineer, had wanted to be a pilot when he was young, so he worked very hard. I think she shared a relevant anecdote, but I confess to losing it because my brain was stuck in a positive feedback loop of *fuck, fuck, fucking, fuckety, fuck, fuck, fuck.*

She ended with the maxim that no one gets anywhere without working hard, and then leveled the most direct admonishment I had received or would ever receive again: "So STUDY, twithead!"

I began screaming. From her bedroom, I'm sure my mother thought I was being expertly murdered.

I'd experience that feeling again eight years later, when Anne would appear where I had not expected her to be, leaving me to limp off with bruised shins and pride while she, the picture of poise, continued on her way with nary a hair out of place. She had a knack for that. Formidable people usually do.

If I *had* gone to public school—if I'd been shooting up behind a mall, if I'd been touring with the Spice Girls, if I'd taken up underwater basket prostitution, if I had been literally *anywhere else*—I probably wouldn't have discovered online gaming on December 13, 1997. And I probably wouldn't have been expelled from Stuart Hall School on February 15, 2000.

I couldn't tell you now what got me wondering about whether Pern had one of those text-based "role-playing games" I'd heard so much about. But it was a Saturday, and I was bored, and I thought a Pern game might be fun. I suspect most meth heads follow a very similar line of logic. Saturday is probably tremendous for meth heads.

I wasn't sure what I was looking for or if I would like what I found, but even in those days, I was adept at bending search engines to my will (AltaVista, probably, or Magellan or Dogpile— Dogpile was my favorite). A few tentative clicks later, Pern was *real*. Really, really real. As real as anyone could make it. It was a living place populated by actual people whose stories played out in real time—and I could be part of it, with a character who looked like me (but prettier) and talked like me (but cleverer) and did all that I would do if only, only I had a fire-lizard to perch on my shoulder, twin moons to light my way, and a warm and gentle beast who knew my mind and would adore me to our last inextricable breath.

That first character's name was Catalina. I named her for Jewel Staite's rainbow-haired Saturnian girl on the tween sci-fi adventure *Space Cases* (I doubt anyone remembers it). To this day, my friends in Anne fandom insist on calling me Cat.

What began as an innocent foray into a world I loved quickly ballooned into a full-blown gaming addiction. My already pitiful work ethic took a backseat to late nights lit by the wan electric glow of my hulking CRT, and then—when my in-room computer privileges were revoked—to increasingly furtive trips to the library computer lab. I learned how to circumvent what passed for a firewall in those days, how to confound the school's monitoring software, how to keep playing even when the local host shut down for the night. The school's sole IT guy was a well-meaning middle-aged man whose ineffectual tactics my defiant teenage know-how rendered wholly impotent. And once I got my friends to play with me, entire social schedules were coordinated around Gathers, Search cycles, and fire-lizard hatchings. Except mine were the only grades in free fall.

Playing Pern certainly improved my typing skills considerably, and encouraged me to abuse synonyms like a dominatrix abuses vinyl (and bankers). There was always a friend to be made; indeed, many of the friendships I found in Pern gaming have endured to this very day. My imagination stretched to its utmost. I wrote, drew, and read constantly. But always about dragons. Never about algebra. Never about ancient world history. Even my boyfriend, already separated from me by a span of hours, had less of my attention than my computer did. The only people less thrilled than my teachers were my parents.

Though I tried hard—I did try, Anne, wherever you are, I did—my studies fell by the wayside; my second and third years at Stuart Hall were not much of an improvement over the first. But by early 2000, halfway through my junior year, I felt that perhaps I was turning a corner. I was, after all, a fundamentally good kid who desperately wanted the approval of the authorities in her life. I tried to wake up on time. I tried to focus on my studies. I tried to be good.

All that's important for you to know here is that there was a crush (shared more or less equally throughout the student body) on a teacher; that this teacher had once been engaged to another faculty member, and that their wedding was canceled months before I was due to sing in it; that this teacher was now dating another, new teacher; and that the student body, being teenage girls, were all very interested in the nature of their relationship.

I won't tell you how I guessed my teacher's email password, nor how many love letters my friend and I, conspiring over a library keyboard, read before guilt compelled us to withdraw. (Not many, and they were disappointing.) And I will leave you to infer the ripping sound my soul made when my friend, having left in some haste not long after our invasion, returned to the library to inform me, "I went to the front desk and told him what you did."

I will spare you those details. I will share only these three: that my will, hardened by the expectation of a brawl, shattered when my teacher asked me, simply, "Why?"; that my possessions were packed the next day, and I left without fanfare once night had fallen; and that my father interrupted the silence of the car ride home with some advice: "Two people can keep a secret if one of them is dead."

I didn't hear from my friends for months or years. Some of them never spoke to me again.

After that I went (willingly) to military school—where I repeated my junior year—and did very well. I completed ground school and got about forty hours of flight training under my belt, but graduated before I could solo. I received a bevy of awards and honors, including Outstanding Cadet of the Year, the United States Marine Corps Scholastic Excellence Award, and the Order of the Daedalians Award. I made National Honor Society. I became very, very good at self-discipline, though I still had a tendency to forgo homework in favor of a little harmless role-playing. A not inconsiderable swath of dorm room wall was occupied by a poster of Michael Whelan's unearthly "Weyrworld." My McCaffrey books—perfectly arranged by height, series, and chronology—still retained their place of honor on my bookshelf. But my addiction was restored to the status of an esoteric yet largely harmless hobby.

In the fall of 2000, the first year I was at military school, I convinced my dad (who did not need much convincing) to take me to the sci-fi convention my Pern pals had been gushing about for months. Though I'd never had any interest in conventions before—like most people, I assumed they were designed largely for the benefit of overzealous Trekkies and crater-pocked, grabby man-children—*this* one, Dragon*Con, had a whole track dedicated *just* to Anne McCaffrey. That was *four days* of nonstop McCaffrey programming. The mind boggled.

We arrived without incident and found our way down to the Weyrfest room, where Dad planned to leave me while he went off photographing anything that would let him. There must have been a moment when I stood alone, nervous and feeling perhaps a bit foolish in the garb my mother had so obligingly sewn me, a sleeveless red dress and gold pants like the ones Catalina wore to Gathers. But that moment would have passed when my friends—strangers only because I had never seen their faces before—snapped me up in a torrent of warmth and welcome. And I knew I was where I should be.

I've been directing Weyrfest for five years now. In the era of smartphone apps, highly graphical MMORPGs, and open-world console games, text-based online gaming—never mind *reading*—has more or less fallen by the wayside. Pern itself has not been treated well by video game studios; the TV series imploded when creator Ron Moore felt that it too was in danger of abuse. With the rights to Pern having again changed hands, there continues to be noise about a movie script—but the depths of pre-production limbo are vast and uncertain. There are many reasons why Anne McCaffrey's fans could have let their interest wane. In truth, many have.

But many, many more have not. While 2012 was its last year before merging into the Fantasy Literature track, Weyrfest was as well attended as I've seen it in years—even without an Anne McCaffrey in the world, a world made chaotic by the dual evils of distraction and cynicism. Our attendees travel to Georgia from Texas, from California, from Canada, England, and Australia year after year after year, not because

Dragon*Con is the only place they can talk about Anne's books—the internet has long since negated trivial barriers like time zones—but because that's where their friends are. Because it's like coming home.

Every once in a while I'll ask my director's second, Angelina Adams—a sweet-voiced buxom beauty with hugs that go on for miles, for eons, who I've described as "Weyrfest's mom" and whose own essay you can read in this very book—what the response to our little track has been. While I do my best to be approachable, it's a rare and bold person who would criticize an event organizer directly to her face. Yet I can't be a good director if I don't know what people are thinking.

Seeing my concern, Angel will smile, and squeeze my hands, and say, *sotto voce*, "Every year, people tell me that they come here because this is where they feel at home. They've heard that we're a safe place. Even if they've never read the books." Then she'll kiss me on the cheek and call me "gorgeous," and I'll beam and feel like we are the defenders of justice.

For all of her imagination, her prolificacy, her tenacity, Anne McCaffrey's fans are her greatest legacy. They are reflections of her fundamental goodness, her stalwartness, her belief in the power of mind over matter. So if her fans are motley and troubled and often a bit strange, they are kind. They are loyal. They strive.

On the evening of November 23, 2011, newly dragonless, I crawled into bed and wept myself hollow.

Then, when I had wrung myself out, I gathered my computer and a copy of *Get Off the Unicorn*. I set myself up in the trough of my boyfriend's substantial eighty-pound beanbag, and I opened to the book's only dog-eared page. I hit record, and I began to read: "Although Keevan lengthened his walking stride as far as his legs would stretch, he couldn't quite keep up with the other candidates. He knew he would be teased again." It seemed significant—sacred, even, in a vital, urgent way, to give voice to the first story Anne McCaffrey ever told me.

I don't know how I ended up contributing to this book. I make my living as a writer, but I write flyer headlines, product demonstrations, and company websites. As simple as those tasks should be, I've been fired from nearly every job I've ever held— "You're very talented," they always tell me, "but it feels like you're somewhere else." How could I deny it?

Yet nearly every creative effort in my adult life, every piece of work I actually *have* cared about, has been, either directly or indirectly, tied to that very first story. Anne McCaffrey didn't teach me to love writing; my mother and father did that. Anne McCaffrey didn't give me a gift for writing; my heritage, my voracity, my teachers did that. And hers are not, perhaps, my favorite books in adulthood—for there are many, many talented authors in the world, and some have resonated with me in radiant, powerful ways.

But Anne McCaffrey built refuges for dreamers. Her worlds are comfort food to aching, empty stomachs. They have been my solace and my friend. When I first applied for Clarion West, I named my story's protagonist for her; when I try again (and I will try again), I hope to find a more suitable embodiment of her spirit. And this feeble little essay, every word of which has been a struggle and an agony, is also owed to her: it is my first as a published writer.

One of the nights I was relegated to a hard wooden desk in the Stuart Hall auditorium, doing time for tardiness or mouthiness or academic delinquency, I opened the hardback edition of *The Girl Who Heard Dragons*. A compendium of short stories, its cover featured a lush scene rendered by the incomparable Michael Whelan, whose work graces the front of this book. It also contained a dozen or so black-and-white illustrations, each of which held my attention as long as or longer than the stories themselves.

Of these, the one that struck me most was that of a dragon perched on a thrust of rock, her young rider's hand outstretched in a wave—of beckoning or farewell, I have never been able to discern. Early last October, I walked into a tattoo shop to keep an appointment made at the height of summer. When I walked out again, a full-color version of that drawing was forever scarred into my flesh. That tattoo is my first, the culmination of years of earnest reverie. It is a reminder to me to take chances, to aim high, to see clearly.

I hope, someday, it will follow me to wherever Anne has gone—and that I will find her there, that glint in her eye, as she shakes her silvered head and chides, "It took you long enough, twithead."

A northern Virginia native, CHARLOTTE MOORE is a copywriter and fangirl in Raleigh, North Carolina, a marvelous little city you should probably visit. By the time you read this, she will have turned thirty but still won't own a house. She directs the Fantasy Literature track at Dragon*Con, where she collects autographs for her So Say We Wall of nerdy celebrity photos. Her blog, The Irritable Vowel, incorporates elements of copywriting and scatological humor, which aren't as dissimilar as you'd think. She may or may not be an actual redhead.

Janis Ian, like Anne McCaffrey, is someone who is best experienced. Back in the 1960s, at just fourteen, Janis had her first hit with "Society's Child." Since then, she's won two Grammy Awards, become a well-established author of science fiction, and written children's books. And she still continues to tour the world with her soft, beautiful music.

When they first met, she and Anne hit it off, and they were friends forevermore. When life was getting Mum down, Janis was one of the people I enlisted in cheering her up. If there's a hole in the universe where Anne McCaffrey once was, Janis is one of the people helping to fill it with her warmth, kindness, and spirit.

The Masterharper Is Gone

JANIS IAN

 I have a shelf of comfort books, which I read when the world closes in on me or something untoward happens.

—ANNE MCCAFFREY

I MISS HER fiercely, more than I have any right to miss her. I remind myself of this whenever I run into her at the library and am stricken with tears. She was not kin, was not connected to me by family ties, not even a distant cousin. Not even Jewish.

I have no right to miss her this much.

And once in a while, when I chide myself for my silly sentimentality, the sudden lightning that pierces my heart gives way to a duller, deeper pain. One I can live with, perhaps.

Like today, waking to a terrible cold, with headache and foggy brain I reach for solace. Put on my red flannel comfort shirt, add my favorite PJ bottoms, then a pair of fleece-lined slippers. Make my favorite tea, cover myself with an old patchwork quilt, and reach blindly for a book on my "comfort shelf."

Of course. I can't escape her. Hours later, still miserable, I finish *All the Weyrs of Pern* for the umpteenth time and scold myself for the tears that fall—first, because she is gone, and second, because I never really succeeded in telling her just how much she meant to me.

I'd never heard of her when I stumbled across *The Ship Who Sang* at my local library. I wrote to her, saying that it had moved me profoundly, wondering how a prose writer could have such a clear understanding of a musician's soul. Being one myself, I said, a musician that is. And I would like to send you a copy of my last record in gratitude.

She responded with a laugh that she had never heard of me but, oh my, her children had, and could we trade books for recordings?

And so, we began. I raced through everything she sent—such generosity, so much that it took two large boxes to ship it all. She, in turn, told me that while she appreciated the beauty of my "Jesse" and the clarity of "At Seventeen," she was writing her current novel to the beat of my one disco hit, "Fly Too High."

I laughed aloud because it made an artist's sense to me—dragons flew, and Anne flew with them, regardless of the beat.

It was the third or fourth email that she began with the salutation "Dear Petal." Petal. Me? I responded that of all the things I'd been called, no one had ever dreamed to name me "Petal." She answered briskly that obviously, they'd never seen me bloom.

From that day forward, I was her Petal, and she my Orchid.

We corresponded ferociously, both all-or-nothing no-holds-barred types, Aries to the hilt. Weekly, daily, sometimes hourly. Dropped out when one of us was "on tour," dropped back in as we could.

The time passed. Her beloved agent died. My parents passed away. She got a scathing review; I sent a few of my own. She was stuck on a chapter; I was stuck on a verse. We got unstuck, stuck again, and through it all we talked, comforting one another as only a "good hot cuppa" can.

She picked me up herself in Dublin, leaning on a cane, nervous to meet me in the flesh, until I ran into her arms and smothered her with hugs. She drove between the hedgerows with complete abandon, a total disregard for ruts or speed limits, while I clutched the seat and wondered who'd get the bigger headline if we crashed. Annie, I decided, for she was truly a two-column, bold-print kind of gal.

By then, she was always "Annie" to me, or "Annie Mac"— my larger-than-life friend who consorted daily with dragons and starlight, her own luster never dimming beside them.

Once, after she showed me the rock cliffs of the Guinness Estate and explained that Benden Hold looked just like that, she asked if I would write a theme for it. *For the movie?* I said. "Yes," she said, "A theme. Because if Menolly came to life, it would be with your voice." I say this not to brag, but to indicate the trust between us—such trust that when I got home, with no film in sight, I began sketching out some notes for "Lessa's Song." I wanted it to be haunting, the way her words haunted me. I wanted it to be sweeping, like the thrust of dragon wings. I wanted it to be everything I could bring to her, a gift for someone whose words took me out of my world and into hers.

As she said herself, "That's what writing is all about, after all, making others see what you have put down on the page and believing that it does, or could, exist and you want to go there."

I hope someday to finish that melody. I hope it's good enough for a masterharper to sing. I hope she regarded me worthy of the title. Because that's what she was for so many of us—the masterharper, singing in prose songs that reminded us of where we'd been and what we could become.

She came and stayed with us in Nashville, bringing a broken shoulder and trusting me to care for her. We visited Andre

Norton, Annie insisting I not just drive but sit with them and listen to "a bit of gossip." These two women—one writing at a time when pseudonyms were necessary for a woman to get published, the other cracking the *New York Times* Bestseller List with, of all things, a science fiction book—and by a female at that!—talked of publishers, rumors, scandals old and new, while I sat as silent as an unopened book, wishing I'd thought to bring a tape recorder.

At first, as her health declined, she bore it cheerfully. "I'm bionic now, Petal, complete with metal knees!" she declared. "Better than ever, and no pain." She kept to her writing schedule, doing what she could to help her body retain its youth. She swam every day, bragged about her granddaughter's accomplishments at school—"First prize, don'tcha know!" and commiserated over our various surgeries. *We sound like a couple of old Yiddishe mamas, comparing whose surgery was worse!* I laughed, and she laughed along with me.

Neither of us reckoned on the psychic toll. "'Old age is not for the faint of heart,'" she quoted, as her energy began to leech away.

How is it we artists always forget just how *hard* it is to write? How much *work* it is? How can we ignore the vast psychic drain that accompanies every act of creation? We both knew it from her Pern books, when going *between* enervated even the hardiest of dragon riders. But somehow, we never expected it in real life.

It's only when we lose that effervescence, through age, through illness, through sheer attrition, that we realize how necessary it is to our work—how fundamental to our beings.

"I can't write." She confessed the shameful secret to me not once, but dozens of times, as if repetition would prove it a lie. At first, playing the friend, I tried to reassure her. *Then don't! Take some time off, Annie. Restore your body, and the brain will follow. Talent doesn't just disappear, you know—it lies in wait.*

But she knew better. "I'm still not writing. I think I know how Andre Norton is feeling, too, because I suspect that she's finding it very difficult to write, as the wellspring and flexibility that did us so much service is drying up in our old age. And no false flattery. At seventy-six, I *am* old, and she's in her nineties. It takes a lot of energy to write, as much as it takes you to keep on adding flavor to your song presentation. Sorry to blah at you, but you're one of the few people who does understand the matter when an artist questions their output."

No worries talking to me about not writing . . . I sure as hell know the amount of energy it consumes. Every time you sit down to write, it's a performance. Only you don't have the luxury of props—no lights, sound, other actors to step behind when the inevitable fatigue hits. Heck, Annie, I'm feeling it more and more now, and you've got a quarter century on me. I notice it mid-show; two hours used to be a piece of cake. Now I feel myself flagging at 45 minutes, and I really look forward to that 20 minute intermission, if only so I can have some water and sit for a few minutes.

Same with writing, for me. Used to be able to sit and write for 6 hours at a stretch. Now I'm good for two if I'm lucky. Part of it's my back, but most of it is—I fear—just that I'm older. It sucks.

"Must write. There are IRS problems. You wouldn't believe. Mouths to feed, people depending on. Advances already spent and gone. Must write."

And so, she wrote, but for a while there was no joy in it. Still, I loved what she wrote, and told her so. I was proud of our friendship, not because she was so damned famous, but because she was so damned *good*. She even used my name in a book—Ladyholder Janissian—and roared with laughter when I admitted I'd been so wrapped up in the story that I hadn't even noticed.

But she knew—as artists always do—that while her ability to plot continued apace, the actual *writing* of it was becoming an endurance contest she couldn't hope to win.

"Turn more of it over to Todd," I argued. Her son had a real knack for a sentence, but it was hard for Annie to let go. Of course. What artist can?

"His words may not sing the way yours do—yet. He doesn't have your lyrical grace—yet. But he will, Annie, you've just got to let him breathe!" I said it and said it and said it, to no avail.

Then came a day when, twenty-five years younger and an ocean away, I finally lost patience and angrily berated her. "Damn it Annie, quit complaining and just *stop*! By God, you have created a *mountain* of work, an incredible legacy that will endure and be read by zillions of people long after both of us are gone—so quit whining about what you *cannot* do and start looking at what you *have* done. It's time, Anne. Take this unbearable weight off your shoulders and *stop*!"

I sent the email off and waited for her response, fearing I'd gone too far. A day. Then another. Finally, sure I'd lost a friend, I called to ask just how angry she was with me. Oh, no, not at all, she's "in the hospital." She took a fall. She'd write soon. And she did, quoting me and saying, "I knew you, of all people, would make sense."

A sweeter absolution I've never had.

We continued our friendship, bitching about our bodies, menopause, the inevitable "drying up" of everything that comes with the feminine mystique. You cannot imagine the luxury, for me, to have a compatriot a quarter of a century older. As an artist, I admired her work. But as a woman, I was relieved to have someone relentlessly honest about what was to come in my own life.

We traded constantly. I sent her Lhasa de Sela, Sara Bettens. She sent stories about her animals and the garden. One spring she changed my salutation to "Dear Crocus Petal—there are eight coming up now!"

We planned to visit Prague together in September '01, but then came 9/11, and I chickened out. To be brutally honest, I was afraid to fly. Annie gently took me to task, then went off with someone else instead.

I will regret that for the rest of my life.

She went into the hospital for the last time while I was touring the UK—just a ferry boat and an ocean of commitments away. Knowing how out of touch she'd feel, how fretful she'd be, I tried to call every day. We fell into a pattern—I'd wait until I was in the van, then phone her up and tell an off-color joke, a bawdy story, a bit of kindly gossip. Sometimes about people we knew in common, Harlan perhaps, or Scott Card, whose work she admired. Sometimes just a silly series of puns I'd found online. Whatever it was, I wanted to make her laugh, because I loved to hear her laugh.

She died while I was on vacation, just days after the tour's end. I'd brought a copy of *Dragonsinger* with me because on vacation, I always brought a few "comfort rereads." I'd fallen asleep over it, waking to an email from her daughter Gigi. "Please keep it quiet until I can reach everyone," she asked. "My older brother Alec is still in flight, and we don't want him seeing it in the paper before I can reach him."

I called with sleep still in my eyes and heard the hum of people behind Gigi's answering voice. It was fast. It was painless. It was everything Annie had wanted.

No lingering. A "good death" for her. But not for me.

It's hard to open my computer knowing there will be no "Dear Petal." It's hard, after knowing such a warm and giving shelter, to go without. Sometimes I run across a sentence that sings to me, and jot it down to show her. And sometimes, when she leaps out at me from the cover of a book, I remember she is gone, and it hits me like lightning, fast and lethal and unexpected. It stops my breath, until I remind myself that she is gone, but I am still here.

When the lightning hits, I comfort myself with this. The beauty of Anne's writing is that she makes it all seem, not just possible, but *normal*. For men to go dragonback. For women to become ships. For young, unwanted girls to become masterharpers. For brains to pair with brawns and sing opera under alien skies. And for an unlikely friendship to bloom, a pairing no one could have imagined, between a petal on Earth and an orchid in flight.

JANIS IAN is a songwriter's songwriter who began writing songs at twelve years of age and performed onstage at New York's Village Gate just one year later. Her first record, "Society's Child," was released two years after that. The seminal "At Seventeen" brought her five of her nine Grammy nominations, and songs like "Jesse" and "Some People's Lives" have been recorded by artists as diverse as Celine Dion, John Mellencamp, Mel Torme, Glen Campbell, and Bette Midler. Tina Fey even named a character "Janis Ian" in her movie *Mean Girls*!

Janis' energy does not stop at performing. Her autobiography *Society's Child*, a starred *Booklist* review and *Publisher's Weekly* pick (and now also available as an audio book), details her life and career. Her song "Stars" is also the title of an anthology featuring twenty-four major science fiction writers, all of them "tipping the hat" by writing original stories based on songs Janis wrote that affected their own lives.

Most recently, Janis' audiobook recording of *Society's Child* won her a Grammy for Best Spoken Word Album and netted her Audie Award nominations for Best Narration by Author and Distinguished Achievement in

Production. Her illustrated children's book, *The Tiny Mouse*, with illustrations by Ingrid and Dieter Schubert, will be published in September 2013.

Janis runs The Pearl Foundation, named for her mother, which has given away more than $700,000 in scholarships for returning students at various universities and colleges.

More information can be found at her website, www.janisian.com.

After two boys, Anne McCaffrey could be understood for hoping that her third child would be a girl. And what a girl! As might be expected from Anne McCaffrey's daughter, Gigi is a force to be reckoned with. Although she was distracted by Crohn's disease from adolescence onward, she has maintained her sense of humor, her love of life, and her cheerfulness.

She has also, as you will see, inherited her mother's gift with words and is one of the two people permitted to continue the legacy of the Dragonriders of Pern.

Universal Mum

GEORGEANNE KENNEDY

I FELT A lingering sense that the road had dropped away beneath my feet as I finished sorting through the last of my late mother's books and personal possessions. Throughout the process of packing, I'd looked forward to the time when I would be free to write my very own tribute to my Mum, hoping that the very act of writing would ease my grief. But I've finished cataloging and caressing books I know my mother held in her hands or crying as an ornament recalled decades-old memories. My days are free now, my hands idle, empty, and it's become increasingly difficult to sit myself down and say what's in my heart. It seems far too soon, the jagged pieces still too sharp for me to share just how deeply I miss the person who was larger than life—and such a very large part of my life.

Of course you may already know that my mother wrote amazing stories, tales that took her readers on journeys far away, where her characters were people we longed to have for our friends, whose struggles became our very own, and whose worlds appeared, at first glance, to be kinder than this giant globe we call home. But a real live, warm-blooded female person existed behind those worlds and words, a person whose experiences had shaped and framed her life, a woman who wanted more from her time on Earth than just the prescribed college, followed by marriage and kids. She grew up during the Great Depression, when the world was going to war and women were expected to follow a set path through life, fit into a prearranged mold, and above all else, be restrained and dutiful. Mum watched her father and oldest brother go to war, stood by helplessly while her younger brother suffered a horrendous illness in childhood, and was packed off to a stifling boarding school when her natural vivaciousness craved nourishment. I think my mother's innate need to stand out from the crowd, to be noticed, was at the root of her penchant for touching the lives of as many people as she could in a positive way.

I clearly recall the day, as a young woman, when my mother's greatest gift became apparent to me. I was standing on the doorstep of Mum's house, quietly watching as she comforted a physical therapist hired to help her regain her mobility after hip replacement surgery. Mum's regular window washer, Tim, joined me on the steps, and we both watched in silence as Mum offered gentle advice and a motherly hug to the young therapist. I made some silly remark to Tim about how Mum always had a ready shoulder for anyone who needed it. Without hesitation and with a dawning recognition in his voice, he said that it was because she was—and these were his words—"a universal mum." Tim's declaration couldn't have been any truer, and as soon as he'd uttered the words, while they resonated around the cosmos, we looked at one another, nodded our heads, and smiled in silent accord. One of my mother's finest qualities lay in her ability to see strength in others. She nurtured many people, men and women, boys and girls, in a way that only a mother knows how.

An old friend, now a pilot, and one of the gang to whom my mother dedicated *Get Off the Unicorn*, contacted me recently, out of the blue. He made a point of telling me that Mum's confidence in him was probably greater than his own. I got the impression that my mother's abiding faith in his abilities to achieve what he set out to do were not shared by his own parents, or by anyone else, for that matter. Mum was benevolent by nature, and she made it financially possible for him to explore a new path in life, one that proved to be not only successful, but very satisfying. Her generosity is something he'll be forever grateful for and is a quality he's tried to emulate in his own life.

When I recounted the pilot's story to a school chum of mine, she shared a recollection of her own about Mum: that when we were teenagers, she loved going over to my place—eagerly looked forward to those visits—because the house was filled with music, laughter, tolerance, and fun. I think Mum would chuckle over that—she always felt it was the young people visiting her house who kept it full of laughter and music and love. It was an atmosphere that she cultivated—cherished—and one that made any who entered into it feel immediately at ease. It wasn't just the reassurances and hugs that made my mother a universal mum. She knew how to allow young people to be themselves; she had an innate knack for accepting everyone for who they were, not who they or their parents thought they should be.

An English literature scholar, who'd first met my mother more than half a dozen years ago, here in Ireland, wrote to me at the end of last winter. The scholar was due to give a talk on James Joyce at Trinity College, in Dublin, and with a few free days in hand before her work commitments began, she wanted to pay her respects to my mother—at her grave, no less. Where Mum chose to take her final rest is on a quiet, winding, narrow road, not really close enough to any major transport links, even though it's within a few miles of the town of Greystones. Because of its somewhat remote location, I thought it was a fitting gesture to offer to meet the scholar at the train station, just as my mother had done years before, and take her to Mum's new "home."

The cemetery where Mum's buried is a wonderfully serene place, strangely lacking in the heaviness of grief, but full of light and bright, brisk air, nestled on high ground over the village of Kilcoole, and overlooking the sea beyond at Greystones. When the scholar had paid her respects—I'd removed myself a good distance and left her to do so in peace—we chatted for a while, and she told me how my mother's work had shaped her life and fueled her dreams. Our meeting was not, to say the least, a situation I'd ever found myself in before, meeting a fan for the first time over my mother's grave, but it suddenly felt familiar when she asked me a question that, once uttered, I could tell she'd been eager to know the answer to ever since we met at the train station:

"What was it like to be Anne McCaffrey's daughter?" she said.

The scholar was not the first person to ask me that question, and most likely won't be the last, and if I'd ever been any other woman's daughter, I might have a clue how to phrase a reply. But the honest-to-goodness truth was that she was just "Mum" to me. She badgered me to brush my teeth or eat my peas, disapproved of boyfriends she thought weren't good enough, entertained high aspirations for my future, grew exasperated at my lack of tact and abundance of ego, and generally behaved as every parent should—with the best interests of one's child at heart.

It's said that the maternal bond is very strong, and some would say that the bond between mother and daughter is by far the strongest. I have to admit that having only ever been Anne McCaffrey's daughter, I have a limited frame of reference, but during my adult life I've come to realize that Mum and I had a very strong bond indeed. This has become even clearer to me since she died and others have graciously recounted aspects of their relationships with their own mothers. Surprisingly, and sadly, more than a few people have told me that their experiences with their mothers were deeply flawed and unfulfilling. One woman admitted that it was a relief when her mother passed away because she no longer had to endure the burden of being a disappointment. Another woman told me that her stepmother means much more to her than her own mother. And my dear, close friend Derval, on whom Menolly was partially modeled, wept deeply alongside me when the woman whom she'd always felt was her "real" mother died peacefully in our arms. The bond between mother and daughter may be the strongest, but that connection doesn't always need to be biological. What Derval and Mum shared was just as strong.

When Mum started having children, like so many other women of her generation she took the advice of the revolutionary parenting guru of the day, the good Doctor Benjamin Spock, who encouraged parents to see their children as individuals and trust their own common sense and instincts. I guess Mum thought of kids as somewhat akin to water: we'd eventually find our own level. By the time I came along, my mother had already had a teen aged Hungarian foster son to knock the edges off the newness of motherhood, followed by her own two boys—who may have been the only kids on Earth who actively sought, and found, every bit of trouble ever devised. I think that most parents offer the least interference to their final offspring. After you've had a few kids, you tend to let nature take its course. I wasn't any less loved than my brothers (in fact, as the only girl I was highly favored, as I'm sure my brothers will avow), but I do know that my upbringing wasn't "managed," nor was I mollycoddled. I know now, although it was just "normal" for me, that my mother gave me a huge amount of freedom to find my way and do "my own thing" compared to other girls.

I admit, though with a certain degree of chagrin, that I was a burgeoning adolescent before I realized my mother was no longer the person I should run to when every little disaster and minor trauma lurched across my path. I have a clear recollection of the day I cut my knee, and even though it didn't really hurt too badly, and I could have easily tended it myself, I ran to find Mum so she could kiss the hurt better and show me how important my pain still was to her. I knew that Mum was busy writing, and as I approached her office door I squeezed out a few crocodile tears, made the usual wailing sound that had always brought her to me in the past, and entered her office, calling her name in my best whiny voice.

"Ma! I hurt myself!"

With the briefest of movements, my mother took her eyes from her work and noted that my leg was still firmly attached to my torso and the blood loss was minimal. She immediately returned her attention to her typewriter as she quietly and firmly told me, "Go away. I'm writing."

I knew then, in a rare preadolescent moment of insight, that my time as the "child" was done and that Mum would no longer entertain every little whim and worry I deemed important. So, as a whining moan began to rise in my throat, I quickly quashed it, dipped my head in apology, and silently backed out of the room, leaving my mother to far more important matters.

When I was a young woman in my twenties and living in the family home, Mum was in the unenviable position of having to "kill" a favorite character that *had* to die. She was very nearly finished writing *Moreta: Dragonlady of Pern*, but kept putting off the day when she had to write the final passage, Moreta's death scene. I knew that Mum was under pressure to complete the novel before embarking on an impending business trip, so as the days passed, each evening after I'd finished work, I'd ask Mum if she'd finally completed the book. Her answer was consistently no. After the first week passed and the scene remained unwritten, being a pragmatist, I made a flippant remark, hoping to jolt her out of her reticence. My comment went something like this: "She has to die, Mum. It's not like you can un-write what's already been written. So just go ahead and kill her!"

My exasperation was all too evident, and Mum's reaction was uncharacteristically extreme.

"Georgeanne Johnson! I didn't know you could be so heartless!"

Of course, I had to walk away at that point and leave my mother to procrastinate as all good authors must. A week passed, and one day, in between exercising horses, I was having a tea break in the kitchen at old Dragonhold when my mother sought me out, tears streaming down her face, remorse contorting her features, and her arms spread out wide.

"I did it," she wailed. "I killed Moreta!"

There comes a time in our lives when our relationship with our parent shifts onto a different path; the child becomes the nurturer as the parent becomes more like a child. As Mum's physical health began to fail and her capabilities diminished, I became increasingly frustrated by how little was left of the woman who had been my strong, decisive mother. I can only imagine how *she* felt about such changes! Aging chips away insidiously at a person's self-confidence, and as she saw little bits of "her" slipping away, Mum was fond of quoting a phrase she'd heard from my late aunt Sara: "Old age ain't for the timid."

Although quite hard of hearing, Mum was mentally sharp up to the day she died. But the frailty that had settled in her body had also chipped away at her self-confidence, diluting the essence of her. As time passed and our relationship continued that subtle transition, Mum relied on me to "fix" all things of importance in her diminishing world. It was only fitting that I give back to my mother a small portion of the love and devotion she had given to me. Caring for her was an honor and not, by any means, an arduous task; she was an easygoing and undemanding person, even in old age. I am human, though, and there were times when I wasn't happy with how our roles had evolved; changes of that sort aren't easy to embrace. In hindsight, I wish that I'd borne those moments of frustration with less impatience, greater grace, and a much finer grade of tolerance, as I'm sure my mother would have done. Those are my regrets—bumps along the road I wish I could've retraced my steps to and smoothed out.

The grief I've felt over my mother's death lays close around me, and it blankets all the other memories I have of her, making it difficult to recall happier times when life wasn't all about hearing aids, hospitals, and heart tablets. I'll be relieved when time has done its work and I can easily recall the memories that will make me smile, memories that are older but nonetheless dear.

In the early autumn of 2011, my husband, Geoff, and our son, Owen, piled into the back of our little car, leaving Mum the more comfortable front seat while I manned the wheel; we were treating ourselves to a Sunday lunch at a favorite restaurant. As we drove along the road on the half-hour journey to our destination, Mum started to hum a popular piece of music, singing the lyrics as memory allowed. I added my voice to her song, filling in the missing gaps in her memory just as she filled in the gaps in mine. Soon we were happily crooning away in the front of the car as my husband and son listened in bemused silence. Back in the 1970s, when we first moved to Ireland, Mum and I, along with my brother Todd, were fond of singing together while driving. We thought we were quite good as a singing trio, but, if the truth were told, we never had an audience to inform us otherwise. The impromptu sing-along that Mum and I were enjoying was a lovely reliving of the past but was somewhat of an unusual experience for Geoff and Owen. When Mum and I finished our little sing-along, in full operatic throttle no less, Owen exclaimed, in his quiet voice, that he belonged to the oddest family on Earth.

Amazingly, Mum's poor hearing didn't fail her on this occasion; her reply was quick and definitive.

"We aren't strange, dear, we're perfectly normal. And if there were more people like us, we wouldn't feel quite so alone."

A huge silence filled the car for a heartbeat, and then all four of us erupted into laughter. We all knew that what Mum had said was true, but her delivery was pure magic and made us laugh nonetheless.

Another little moment of joy hit me the other day while I was driving. The weather, a perpetual obsession of the Irish nation, had been dull and gray all morning long, but as the day progressed, the weather was absolutely beautiful: the temperature was mild, winds were light and gentle, and the sky was chockablock full of sunshine. It was the type of day that we all love to see, and while I drove along the road, I thought how much my mother would've loved to see that day, too. But before regret and sadness had the chance to dash my buoyant mood, a smile lit my face because some part of me instinctively knew that Mum *could* "see" it. I wouldn't call myself religious or spiritual, even though I devoutly believe in a Parking God, but perhaps at that moment I needed to believe that there's more for us than just this life, needed to feel that I still had some contact with my mother apart from genes and memories. But as I was driving that day, it was with absolute certainty that I knew Mum was appreciating the glorious weather just as much as I, even though we weren't in the same space.

I don't know where the energy that powered my brilliant,

lovely mother has gone to—whether she's out there, somewhere in the universe, existing as a wisp of a spirit, watching the stars whoosh by with long gone friends and family, or if she lives on now as a cat, or a honey bee, or a leaf on an apple tree. But I do know that she had a very worthwhile and full life and that she gave as much as she got. Above all else, I hope that she's safe out there, somewhere in the cosmos, looking forward to the journey ahead.

GEORGEANNE KENNEDY, Gigi to family and friends, lives on the edge of the Devil's Glen in Ireland with her husband, Geoff, and their teenage son, Owen. Originally trained in equine sciences, Gigi backed and broke horses until other life pursuits demanded her attention. In the mid-1990s she published three collaborative short stories with her mother. Gigi's proud to have been claimed as "favoured person" by Anne's beloved cat, Razzmatazz, who delights in daily chases—and trouncings—of the newest member of the Kennedy household, Sidney P. Q. Kennedy, a vertically challenged canine of uncertain pedigree and dubious moral principles.

Afterword

TODD MCCAFFREY

I GOT THE call at 5 P.M., LA time. My brother-in-law, Geoffrey, voice choked, gave me the news. I was numb. The waiting was over. Mum was gone. About half an hour later, I got another call from Ireland: my sister, Gigi, saying that she wanted me to get over as quickly as possible. I could use the Amex—the American Express card that Mum had provided for "emergencies" so many years before.

There wasn't enough money to bring my kid with me; I needed to go solo. I checked online, and only Virgin Atlantic had flights available. I called them, but their computer systems—based in London—already thought it was the next day and wouldn't let the reservation be made. So I had to rush to the airport, not knowing if I would get there in time to pick up one of the few remaining seats. I threw clothes—and a suit—into my handy red gym bag and was off. I called my ex and let her know what was up; Jenna was completely supportive and told me not to worry about the kid, that she'd check up.

I raced to LAX, got to the terminal, and in a hoarse voice explained my circumstances. They were very kind. I got on the plane, a flight to London Heathrow.

The flight to London, the first leg of my trip, took five hours.

Five hours by myself to recollect a lifetime of memories. To recall my mother from when I was just little, still clinging to her knee, all the way up to the point when she was an old woman, her face seamed with smile lines.

And the first thought that came to me was, "No regrets."

Mum had a good life. She was ready to go, finding the indignities of old age growing in number and the rewards shrinking. Her books had flown on the space shuttle and floated in orbit on the International Space Station! She had won every award imaginable, had fired the imaginations of millions of people, had raised an extended family to middle age and beyond, had met all her grandchildren, and more.

Mum had been feeling "puny" several days before. She'd had a mini-stroke that had required her to cancel her last trip to Dragon*Con, and I was certain that depressed her mightily. She was desperate to get her boys over because she was afraid that she would pass on before she saw them one final time. My older brother, Alec, was due over for Thanksgiving. I would come on another trip two weeks before Christmas. The flight was booked.

Gigi and I had convinced Mum to go to the hospital and get checked out. The doctors discovered that she had a blockage in the heart, and they inserted two stents. She emailed me later to say that she got to watch it on the monitor (I had a feeling she was working out how to write it in a story). In her last email to me, she pronounced herself "all repaired."

But something wasn't right, and Gigi convinced her to go back. They were just getting Mum into her wheelchair when she collapsed.

Her last words were, "I'll try." She was answering Geoff, when he'd said, "Now, Anne, we'll just lift you up into the wheelchair and then you'll be on your way. Do you think you can do that?"

"I'll try." No better epitaph could be found for her—it was practically the mantra of her entire life.

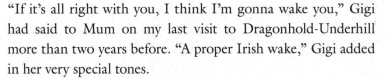

"If it's all right with you, I think I'm gonna wake you," Gigi had said to Mum on my last visit to Dragonhold-Underhill more than two years before. "A proper Irish wake," Gigi added in her very special tones.

A wake is when the coffin is open in a special room at the house and everyone comes by to pay their last respects. I thought it quite a ghastly notion.

It turns out, however, that it was perfect. We had Mum in the living room—the huge room in Dragonhold that was often the scene of her huge birthday bashes (she'd taken to having a big bash every five years). The rule of the wake, it seems, is that the children and relatives of the deceased greet each guest and ensure that they have drink—wine for some, tea for most—and food.

As usual in Dragonhold-Underhill, everyone congregated in the kitchen. People would filter through the hallway, to the dining room, and into the living room to sit beside Mum, stand with heads bowed, and pay their respects. She looked so peaceful and lifelike that I finally decided to leave a glass of wine on a table near her head just in case—in some macabre display of humor—she was "having us on." (She wasn't: the glass was still full in the morning.)

When most everyone had taken their leave and all that was left were the people who we knew were family—even though most had no blood relation with us at all—we started telling jokes. Bad ones.

"What do you call a one-legged Irishwoman?" "Eileen."

"What's the name of an Irishman covered in rabbits?" "Warren."

"What's the name of an Irishman hanging from the ceiling?" "Sean D'Olier."

"What's the name of an Irishman with a shovel?" "Doug."

"What's the name of an Irishman without a shovel?" "Doug-less."

I recounted some of Mum's favorite jokes, including "Rockefeller's Balls" and the Pope's lunch joke (it was originally Gigi's, but Mum appropriated it). Our more devout friends, who might have thought our carrying on disrespectful, were no longer present, so I—with much encouragement—made an impromptu performance of Tom Lehrer's "The Vatican Rag"—which had been an old favorite of once-Catholic Mum. On the morning of the service, alone in the silent living room, I read Mum a story that I'd written and she'd not had the chance to read: "The One Tree of Luna," which was the sequel to "Tree"—her favorite of all my stories.

As they came to take her in the hearse, Jennifer Anne Diamond—practically Mum's granddaughter—and Mum's decades-long housekeeper (the only reason Dragonhold-Underhill was ever tidy), Cyra O'Connor, decided that Mum had to have a dragon so they picked a small glass dragon, which they put in the casket with her. Gigi had already put in a quart of Baileys Irish Cream and several bars of chocolate, so Mum was in all respects ready for the final rest.

Somewhere between my reading and getting ready, I went over to Mum's computer—it being directly cabled to Ethernet—and just for curiosity's sake, looked at her horoscope. What I read so floored me that I printed it out and showed it to everyone. When Mum's literary agent, Diana Tyler, heard it, she asked me if it was a joke. It wasn't, but it was amazingly accurate.

On the day of Anne McCaffrey's funeral service and burial, her horoscope—from Holiday Mathis—read

ARIES (March 21–April 19). You will maintain your solid stance at the calm center of a swirl of activity. You'll love the show. It's like there's a parade going by just for your entertainment.

And it was.

No regrets.

Acknowledgments

FIRSTLY, I WOULD like to thank everyone at Smart Pop and BenBella Books. They have done an exceptional job bringing this work to life: their attention to detail, dedication, and love show on every page. This project was their idea from beginning to end. I'm honored that they asked me to be editor and thrilled that they wanted to produce this tribute to Anne McCaffrey. I'm certain that Mum would say, "You done me proud!"

Leah Wilson deserves special mention for her unflagging efforts in coordinating all aspects of this book, particularly in acquiring and editing. I'm glad to say that the title page properly shows this as being "Edited by Todd McCaffrey with Leah Wilson" (although I might argue that it could just as easily be the other way around).

Heather Butterfield provided us with beautiful flyers to help promote this book and went out of her way to get them to me in time for the first of many science fiction conventions. She's been instrumental in the design of the cover and the marketing, too.

Brittany Dowdle was steadfast in her copyediting, which was essential in producing this book in time and in readable format. The whole production team, from department head Leigh Camp to Monica Lowry to Jessika Rieck, displayed not just amazing professionalism but a real love of the project.

I'd like to give special thanks to Michael Whelan for providing Anne McCaffrey with her last Whelan cover.

Finally, I'd like to thank every contributor to this collection of essays. I thank you for your time, your dedication, and your love. These contributions make clear the impact Anne McCaffrey has made on the world.

Todd McCaffrey
Los Angeles, CA

About the Editor

TODD JOHNSON MCCAFFREY wrote his first science fiction story when he was twelve and has been writing on and off ever since. In 1999, he authored the nonfiction *Dragonholder: The Life and Dreams (so far) of Anne McCaffrey.*

Besides writing and collaborating on eight Pern novels with his mother, including the *New York Times* bestselling *Dragon's Fire*, Todd has written numerous short stories, contributed to many anthologies, and even written a half-hour in an animated cartoon series.

He has just released his science thriller *City of Angels* and is revising *The Steam Walker*, an alternate history steam world where Bonnie Prince Charlie captures London and restores the Stuarts to the thrones of England and Scotland.

For more information, visit his website at http://www.todd mccaffrey.org.